THE SEA SIREN OF BROADWATER BOTTOM

BOOK THREE IN THE ASTLEY CHRONICLES

COURTNEY MCCASKILL

HAZEL GROVE BOOKS

THE ASTLEYS OF HARRINGTON HALL

Edward Astley IV, Earl of Cheltenham
Georgiana Astley, Countess of Cheltenham

Edward Astley V, Viscount Fauconbridge, age 27
Harrington Astley, age 26
Anne Cranfield (née Astley), Countess of Morsley, age 24
Caroline Greville (née Astley) Viscountess Thetford, age 20
Lady Lucy Astley, age 19
Lady Isabella Astley, age 19
John Astley, deceased at age 2
Frederick Astley, age 14

loucestershire, England
March 1803

EDWARD ASTLEY HAD FAILED.

That was the thought that echoed through his head in time with his horse's hoofbeats as he cantered toward home. He didn't hold out much hope that he would make it before the storm gathering above him broke.

Perfect. He wouldn't just be a failure; he would be a failure who was soaked to the bone.

The task that had brought him to the village of Bourton-on-the-Water was a question, and the person he'd hoped might be able to answer it was his former tutor, Julian St. Cyr. Learning the answer to this particular question would go some ways toward forestalling the disaster that was bearing down upon him.

But Mr. St. Cyr hadn't had the information he sought, and now Edward had no idea what to do. He only had two weeks to figure this out, and if he couldn't...

If he couldn't, his brother, Harrington, would be the one to pay the price, exposed to their father's wrath and society's scorn. And although, in truth, this whole ridiculous situation was Harrington's fault, Edward would never allow that to occur. There was nothing he would not do for his brother. Nothing. Edward would lay down in a muddy ditch and die for Harrington without a second's hesitation.

The thought sounded strangely appealing compared to what he was about to do instead.

The path wound through a grove of cherry trees. They were in full bloom, and it was a shame about the storm, because the soft pink blossoms would've been lovely against a cloudless sky. But the sky was roiling charcoal, and there wasn't a speck of blue to be seen.

Other than… wait. Edward squinted through the trees.

There was definitely something blue deep in the grove. Blue and… copper, if his eyes weren't deceiving him. It was probably nothing, and he needed to hurry on. But the hairs on the back of his neck were suddenly standing on end, and he found himself reining his horse in. As he steered his mount through the cherry trees, a pond came into view.

That was when he saw her.

A single ray of light penetrated the gathering clouds, illuminating the girl in the rowboat like the subject of a Rembrandt. *The Naiad* would be the title of the painting, for with the cascade of red curls tumbling down her back, she truly looked like a water nymph surveying her demesne.

She glanced up at him, and the breath left Edward's body, because *dear Lord*, this was the most beautiful woman he had ever seen. In addition to her siren's mane, she had a heart-shaped face, coral-pink lips that managed to be petite and full at the same time, and the sort of delicate curves he preferred above all others.

Wait. It was difficult to think when his senses were being bombarded with so much female gorgeousness, but some-where deep in the recesses of his mind, the thought emerged that he could see a bit more of those curves than he should. He realized with a start that her dress was soaking wet, her shoulders were quivering, and those lush, full lips were a bit… blue.

He shook himself. How disgraceful to sit there gawking at the poor girl while she was freezing to death! He guided his horse to the edge of the pond to offer his assistance.

But the words died on his lips as it hit him—this wasn't just any gorgeous woman.

He knew this girl. It had been ten years since last he saw her, ten years since he had sat across the aisle from her in her father's classroom, but he was sure of it.

"Miss Elissa?" he asked in shock.

ELISSA ST. CYR had done it this time.

She was hardly a stranger to calamity; one might say it was her stock in trade. Nor was this the first time reading out of doors had been the cause of her downfall. There had been the time when she was ten and had thought she could finish the last few pages of Xenophon's *Anabasis* during the short walk to church. She had wandered straight into Mrs. Naesmith's blackberry bramble, and it had taken a quarter of an hour to disentangle herself. She could still recall the way the vicar fell silent and everyone turned to stare as she slunk into church with her dress torn and her arms covered in scratches.

There had been another incident when she was twelve. It must have been a Wednesday, because Wednesday was the day the village shop received a box of books from the big circulating library at Cheltenham to supplement the two shelves they kept behind the counter for lending. Elissa never missed a Wednesday and, besides, she had to return the book she had out, Francis Fawkes's translation of *Argonautica*. She had been reading a favorite passage one last time as she walked along.

That was when she tripped over the pig (because of course there happened to be a pig just wandering by) and fell flat on her face in the middle of the road.

She was unharmed, but the incident was unfortunate in that it was witnessed by William Ricketts, one of her father's students. More specifically, William Ricketts was the worst of her many tormentors inside the classroom. The Unfortunate Pig Incident had given him years' worth of fodder.

Then there was the Bicklebury Bog Debacle.

Elissa still did not like to think about the Bicklebury Bog Debacle. She'd had to wait for Farmer Broadwater to fetch his plough horse to pull her out, by which time a crowd had gathered to point and laugh.

That had been when she finally swore off reading and walking, but she still loved to read outdoors. There was nothing like a picturesque spot to stir the imagination. Farmer Broadwater, her rescuer all those years ago, didn't mind if she borrowed his rowboat, and when she was reading something set on the water, she liked to lie in it. The gentle bobbing gave her the feeling of being aboard a ship, right there amongst the ancient heroes.

She always kept the boat tied to the dock. She had never dreamed that anything could go wrong.

Today had been the first day of the year that had truly felt like spring, and she just had to get outside. She grabbed Plutarch's *Life of Theseus* from the library and set out after luncheon. As always, she became lost in the tale, and must have read for the better part of three hours.

She sat up when she saw the clouds rolling in. She ran a

hand over her opposite arm and was startled to find goose-flesh; she had been so caught up in the story, she only now noticed that the temperature had dropped by ten degrees.

That was when she saw what had happened.

At some point, the rowboat had come untied from the dock and had drifted into the center of the pond. A quick search revealed that there wasn't an oar in the boat, but no matter—the pond was small enough. Surely she could use her hand to paddle back to shore.

It was when she failed to make any progress that she noticed the rope had become entangled in one of the under-water trees that had been left in place when they flooded the basin. Try as she might, Elissa was unable to work the rope free. And although she picked at it until her fingers bled, she couldn't loosen the knot.

By this time, the weather was really starting to turn, and she shouted as loudly as she could for Farmer Broadwater, whose house was just over the knoll. This was to no avail, and that was when she began to grow fearful. A storm was coming, a bad one, and she was about to be stuck on the water with absolutely no protection.

The only option she could come up with was to wade to shore. Although she couldn't swim, the pond was small, and most of it wasn't very deep. Perhaps she could touch bottom.

Trembling, she lowered herself into the water, and was quickly disabused of that hope. The outside of the boat was slimy with moss, and she immediately lost her grip. Her chest seized with panic as her head went under, but she managed to grab a tree limb with a flailing arm and pull her head back out of the water. It was a struggle to get back into the slippery boat, especially after her hair became snarled in the tree, and she tried and failed so many times it began to feel like she would never make it out of the frigid water. By the time she finally collapsed into the bottom of the boat, her hair had unraveled from its pins, and her whole body was shaking with fatigue and terror.

That had been perhaps an hour ago, an hour in which the temperature had continued to plummet. The thin, blue muslin gown that had seemed perfect for a sunny spring afternoon was grossly inadequate for the current conditions. She couldn't stop trembling and her thoughts were growing muddled, leading her to worry that this was more than a mere chill.

She had mumbled every prayer she could dredge from her frozen brain. Elissa had always prided herself on being self-reliant. She may have her head stuck in the clouds, but she had never been the type to sit around and wait for someone to come to her rescue. Life had taught her there was no such thing as a prince on a white horse.

But if ever she had needed someone to be her hero, it was right now.

And then she heard it—the cadence of hoofbeats on the nearby path. She tried to cry out, but her frozen throat could only manage a sad, little croak.

The hoofbeats slowed, and she could see something moving through the trees.

It proved to be a man.

A man on a white horse.

And—oh, God, surely this could not be happening…

Although Elissa knew she needed help and had, in fact, just spent the better part of two hours praying fervently for someone, anyone, to happen along, she could not believe her terrible luck.

Because if there was anyone on the face of this earth she did not want to witness her in this, the most humiliating moment of her remarkably humiliating life, it was *Edward Astley.*

CHAPTER 2

It had been ten years since last she saw him. He had been seventeen, as she recalled (*as she recalled*—as if she did not recall it all perfectly!) At an age when most boys had been spotty-faced and awkward, Edward Astley was already breathtakingly handsome, showing every indication that he would become this outstanding specimen of the male species, whom, according to the newspapers, the tittering ladies of London had dubbed "Prince Charming."

Certainly, he deserved it. He looked much the same as she remembered, save for being taller, squarer-jawed, and broader-shouldered. He looked the part of the ideal country lord. He was riding a gorgeous, white Irish Hunter and was impeccably turned out in buff breeches and glossy top boots, with a cream waistcoat and flawlessly white linen. His coat was the color considered most suitable for the country, a pale brown shade called drab. On anyone else, it would have looked, well, *drab*, but on Edward Astley, the dull color only served to make his thick, glossy, dark-brown hair look richer. And as for his eyes...

They called them the Astley eyes. She'd heard that his

mother had them, as did four of his six siblings. They were huge, and as blue as… Elissa didn't even know how to finish that sentence, because she had never seen anything as blue as Edward Astley's eyes. Even from fifteen yards away, she could make out their color.

Those eyes were currently staring at her in shock. Oh, but this was mortifying!

Get hold of yourself, Elissa. It wasn't that bad. He didn't seem to recognize her.

Gracious, after all these years, he probably didn't even remember her!

"Miss Elissa?"

Er—so much for that hope. She cleared her rusty throat. "Lord Fauconbridge," she replied, using his title (because as the eldest son of the Earl of Cheltenham, he was known by the courtesy title Viscount Fauconbridge). She sifted through her brain for the appropriate manner in which to converse with a viscount whilst floating on a pond in a translucent dress. "How—er—lovely to see you again."

"Yes, what an unexpected plea—" A sharp rumble from the sky cut him off. "Forgive me, Miss Elissa, but are you perhaps in need of some assistance?"

"Indeed I am." She gestured to the front of the boat. "The rope has become entangled in this tree, and I cannot free it. I fear I am stuck. I—I cannot swim, you see."

He swung down off his horse. "I see," he said, draping the reins over a branch.

"If you would be so kind, Farmer Broadwater's house is just over that rise," she said, gesturing. "He can fetch the neighbor's boat."

"Ah," he said, brightening, "there is another boat. Where is it? I am sure that, given the circumstances, its owner would not object to my commandeering it."

Elissa flushed. "I wouldn't want you to go to such trouble."

"It is no trouble at all."

She swallowed. "It is a mile, maybe a mile and a half, down the road."

"A mile and a half—" He broke off, looking affronted, and began peeling off his coat.

"Wha—what are you doing?"

"You cannot wait that long," he said firmly. He hung his coat from another branch and began tugging at one of his boots.

Oh, dear God, he meant to come in after her! "Please, my lord," she sputtered, "I would never expect for you to—"

"You should," he said, grunting as the boot slid free. "Only a blackguard would leave you there with a storm coming."

He had never seemed to understand that she wasn't the kind of girl who received such solicitude. "I'm not worth the trouble," she said ruefully.

He looked startled that she would even suggest such a thing. "Of course you are."

She sighed. This was why Edward Astley would always be her *beau idéal*. Not because he was devastatingly handsome (which he was), or because he was rich, or because he was heir to an earldom. Not even because he was so intelligent, although she had always found that even more appealing than his good looks. After leaving her father's tutelage, he had gone on to win just about every award the University of Cambridge gave out, including its most prestigious, Senior Wrangler, which was given to the best student in mathematics. He had also been named second Classical Medalist, having completed the near-impossible feat of being a top student in both mathematics and classics.

But more than any of those things, the reason Edward

Astley had always made Elissa a bit weak about the knees was because he had always been so kind to her.

By the time Elissa had been old enough to join her father's classroom, Edward had been at Eton. But during school breaks, he would ride over twice a week to take some additional lessons. The days when he was there had been completely different. Her father's other students seemed to be universally of the opinion that it was unnatural for a girl to study Greek and Latin. Mostly, they would ignore her, but there were a few, led by William Ricketts, who seemed affronted by her mere existence, and were constantly making remarks just skirting the inappropriate, trying to get a rise out of her.

But Edward would not brook any boorish behavior in her presence. As soon as William Ricketts started in on her, he would clear his throat, say, "Come, Ricketts," and nod toward Elissa with a genial smile. He always assumed the best about everyone, assumed that Ricketts was a good sort who had momentarily forgotten that a lady was present (Elissa could have disabused him of that notion).

It hadn't been anything extraordinary, just little things like the way he would smile and say, 'Good morning, Miss Elissa,' when she walked into the classroom. He often made an interested observation after she read her translation aloud (an event that was usually followed by the sound of crickets, at best). Once she had broken the nib of her pen, and he had immediately handed her his spare.

She knew very well that he didn't *like* her, at least, not in the same way she liked him, nor did she expect him to. But he had treated her like his fellow student at a point in her life when everyone else had treated her like an oddity. It was a small thing, but one that meant a tremendous amount to her.

From the bank of the pond, he cleared his throat,

recalling her to the situation at hand. "And it is obvious that you are rather cold."

Oh dear—he had caught her woolgathering. "I cannot deny it," she said, hugging her arms around her chest.

He divested himself of his second boot and waded into the pond. Once he was waist-deep, he leaned forward and began slicing through the water with smooth, precise strokes.

He made three attempts to disentangle the rope, twice diving under the water and not resurfacing for what seemed like too long. After the last attempt he ran a hand through his hair, pushing it back from his forehead (gracious, she had never seen a man with such thick hair in her life!) "You're right," he said. "It is well and truly tangled. I fear there's nothing for it. We'll have to swim. Please do not worry. I am confident in my ability to convey you safely to shore."

She had no concerns on that front; she had seen how efficiently he'd cut through the water. The only question was the mechanics of how this was to be accomplished. "Thank you, my lord," she said, her voice trembling with sincerity. "Um, how should I, er—"

"Let's see. I can pull down on the side of the boat. Can you—"

"Yes, let me just—"

Her dress snagged on the lip of the boat as she slid into the water. She felt a rush of cold air all the way up to her thighs as her skirts were pulled up. Oh, dear—well, she was into the water so quickly, he probably hadn't seen any higher than her knees. At least, that was what she was going to tell herself. She was gripping the side of the boat with both hands, in the water up to her collarbone, when he wrapped a warm, firm arm around her waist, pulling her body flush against his.

Even in the icy chill of the pond, he was warm beneath

his thin linen shirt, and she instinctively curled into him, a groan of pleasure escaping from her throat. She had never been this close to a man. Never. Her breasts pressed into the firm planes of his chest, her stomach lay flush with his, and their legs tangled intimately beneath the water. His head was so near to hers she could feel his breath on her lips when he murmured, "All right?"

"All right," she confirmed, her voice a squeak, and he was leaning back to push away from the boat when she remembered. "Oh—wait—I almost forgot my book!"

"Your... book?" he asked, his brow creasing.

She reached over the side of the rowboat, feeling around. "You know how my father is about his library. I'll never hear the end of it if I leave one of his books out in a rainstorm. Here it is," she said, pulling it from the boat.

His face broke into a broad grin as he took in the title. "You read Plutarch in a rowboat?"

"I—er—yes." She cleared her throat. "Of course, much of it is set on the ship of Theseus, and the rocking of the rowboat makes you feel like you're on the water, and... and..."

She trailed off, ducking her head. Had she thought being caught in the middle of a pond in a sodden dress was embarrassing? It appeared she had stumbled upon something even worse.

But a soft smile stole across Edward's face, a real smile, without even a trace of mockery. "That strikes me as the ideal place to read it."

The sky gave another rumble, and he glanced heavenwards, serious again. "I'll need a hand to swim. Can you hold the book up out of the water? Perhaps we can manage it if you wrap your other arm around my neck."

The only advantage of being half frozen was that it prevented her cheeks from bursting into flames as she hooked her arm up around his shoulders. Now her entire body was pressed against his, and a shudder rippled through her.

"We must get you out of this cold water," he said, misinterpreting the reason for her trembling. He shifted so he was floating on his back, pulling her on top of him, wrapping one arm around her back and resting his hand gently on her waist. "Is that all right?"

Was that all right? She was lying on top of *Edward Astley* with naught but a few layers of wet muslin to separate them. She might feel mortified now, but she had a feeling this would go down as the best moment of her whole entire life.

She nodded her assent, and he let go of the boat. He floated along on his back, making slow, smooth strokes with his free arm, propelling them steadily toward the shore.

Mere seconds later, he put his feet down. "Here we are." He grasped her about the waist again and helped her rise to standing.

"And we even managed to keep Plutarch dry. More or less," she laughed, holding the book between two fingers in an effort to keep it from being soaked by her wet hands.

He grinned. "Excellent." He released her waist and offered his arm. "Now, let's get you back home before—"

She started to sway as soon as he withdrew his hands. She hadn't realized she was quite so cold, but it was clear her legs wouldn't hold her. He snatched her up about the waist, pulling her body flush against his.

Plutarch was not so fortunate. The book slipped from her tenuous grasp and plunged into the pond.

"Oh, no!" she cried. "Father is going to *kill* me."

"I'm terribly sorry," he said, somehow managing to hold her upright while bending down to fish the book out of the water. "That was my fault."

"It absolutely was not." She gave a bleak chuckle. "Disaster is my signature. It has a way of following me wherever I go."

"Are you all right now?" he asked.

"I think so," she said, taking a step forward. "I just—"

Her knees promptly buckled. Edward was on her in an instant, living up to his nickname as he scooped her up in his arms and carried her to shore.

He seated her on a log and immediately draped his coat around her shoulders.

"Oh!" Elissa raised her hands in protest. "But... will you not be cold, my lord?"

"I insist," he said as he pulled the flaps closed around her. "You've been soaked through in this chill air for too long already." He scooped up his boots and found a spot farther down the log upon which to sit.

As soon as he turned to his boots, Elissa buried her nose in the collar of his coat. *Bergamot.* It was the same shaving tonic he had started to use when he'd been around sixteen years old. She could remember catching a hint of that musky citrus scent as she rounded the corner toward the classroom, and the thrill of anticipation that would go through her, because she would know before she even saw him that he was in attendance that day.

All semblance of rational thought fled as Edward scooped her up again and carried her to his horse. He lifted her up onto the saddle easily, then adjusted the stirrup so she could insert her foot. She was seated sideways, even though it was not a sidesaddle.

"I won't go faster than a walk," he said. "Do you think you can manage?"

"Of course," she replied, grabbing the pommel for purchase.

She really thought she could, but after only a few steps, she began to sway, and came close to tumbling off.

He immediately drew his gelding to a halt. "Miss Elissa?" he asked, his expression sincere.

She felt mortified. "I'm so terribly sorry. I—I guess I'm colder than I realized."

"It's no trouble." He studied her for a beat. "I apologize—this is not going to be entirely proper. But I can't think how else to get you home before this storm breaks."

He led his horse slowly back to the log, keeping a hand hovering near her leg in case she started to sway. He climbed up behind her, then lifted her up and settled her on his lap. He wrapped one arm securely about her waist, holding her firmly against him, and took the reins in the other.

"Is this all right?" he asked tentatively.

All right? Of course Edward Astley sweeping her up in his arms and carrying her away on his white charger was not "all right."

It was her every schoolgirl fantasy come true, is what it was.

But she could hardly tell him that, so what she said was, "It's all right."

"Come," he said, "let's get you home."

CHAPTER 3

*E*dward had never imagined a context in which he might think to himself, *Thank God I'm wearing these soaking wet, ice-cold trousers.*

But considering he had the delectable Elissa St. Cyr in his lap, those trousers were the only thing preventing him from dishonoring himself.

The first thing he had done after getting her out of the pond was to wrap her in his coat. He had done this out of genuine concern for her health, but it also had the positive effect of covering her siren's body, deliciously displayed in that whisper-thin, clinging dress.

Not that he wasn't still picturing what she looked like beneath his coat, to say nothing of the moment she slipped into the pond and her dress had been pulled up to her thighs. Images of delicate ankles, finely turned calves, and petal-soft skin were going to be seared on his brain for all eternity. But the coat helped.

A minuscule amount.

God, when he had told her she looked "rather cold," he

had somehow managed to look her square in the eye instead of staring longingly at her nipples.

He hadn't been that proud of himself in quite some time.

His horse picked his way through the grove of cherry trees to the path, and Edward pointed him back toward Bourton-on-the-Water. He studied the sky. "I think we can make it before the storm breaks."

"Thank you," she said, peering up at him shyly. There was a rather large clump of pondweed tangled in her hair. Several clumps, truth be told. He wondered whether he should mention it and decided against it. He suspected this was the type of thing a lady might find embarrassing.

Even slightly blue and covered in pondweed, she managed to look alluring. She'd wrapped her arms around his neck for balance, giving him an unimpeded view of her eyes. They were pale green with just a hint of blue. Her eyelashes were a shade darker than her hair, and the contrast with those sea glass green eyes was mesmerizing...

She cleared her throat, and he realized he had been staring. "May I ask what brought you out this way?" she said.

"I paid a visit to your father," he said, grateful for the distraction of some conversation. "There was something I needed to ask him."

"Oh? What was that?"

"I'm sure you've heard about the recent edition of Longinus's *On the Sublime*, the one by the anonymous translator that has caused such a sensation."

"Of course."

"The publisher is sponsoring a contest, pitting their mystery translator against all comers. It is to be held at Oxford three weeks hence."

This was about as much information as Edward had about the contest. The organizers were keeping the exact format a secret, as they wanted to determine the contestants' extemporaneous abilities, rather than what they could compose a month in advance. But Edward was a Cambridge man and had spent four years vying for various Browne Medals and Member's Prizes. He knew how these things generally went. You were allowed a lexicon and a dictionary. You would be given a Greek work to translate into English, or an English poem to translate into Latin. Or perhaps the judges would select a theme, and the contestants would compose an original work on that theme. It could be in Latin or Greek, and in either poetry or prose. Or you would be asked to compose a Latin ode in the style of Horace, or a Greek epigram in imitation of those in the *Anthologia*. The exact format wouldn't be revealed until the morning of the contest, but it was usually something along those lines.

"I heard about the contest as well," Elissa said, biting her lip as she peered up at him. "Will you, uh, will you be entering?"

"I will," Edward confirmed.

Given a choice between eating a bucketful of broken glass and entering this contest, he would have pulled out a spoon and tucked in. He hadn't touched a volume of Greek verse since taking his degree from Cambridge five years ago. His university experience had been grueling in the extreme. It was fine for his friends to spend four years carousing, but, having shown promise in the classics from an early age, Edward's family had high expectations for his university career.

And so he had spent most evenings shut in his room, translating Latin and Greek until he nodded off at his desk. And… it wasn't that he had nothing to show for his efforts. He had a half-dozen Browne Medals and Member's Prizes shoved in the back of his desk drawer. But there was only one accolade that really mattered: the Chancellor's Classical

Medal. He could still recall the day he had learned of the award's existence. He'd been six years old and had memorized the opening of the *Aeneid* in Latin. His tutor, Mr. Brownlee, had brought him before his father, and after Edward had recited the lines, Mr. Brownlee had excitedly informed the earl that he had never seen so much talent at such an early age, and that Edward "might win the Chancellor's Classical Medal someday."

Edward's father had nodded proudly. "That would really be something." Six-year-old Edward had never heard of the Chancellor's Classical Medal before, but from that moment, he'd been determined to win it. And the more he studied, the more it became a refrain. He'd heard some version of how he was a legitimate candidate for the Chancellor's Classical medal from every one of his teachers and tutors.

But he hadn't won the Chancellor's Classical Medal. After damn near killing himself, Edward had lost the only award he really cared about to the son of a baker from Lancashire named Robert Slocombe.

The fact that he had unexpectedly been named Senior Wrangler, the title given to the top student in mathematics and universally considered to be the higher honor, had done nothing to quiet the voices in his head with their endless refrain: *failure, failure, failure.*

So, entering this contest... This was not something he did. Not anymore. The thought of attempting a Latin or Greek translation literally made his throat seize, his pulse fly, his—

"And what was it," Elissa asked, recalling him to the conversation, "that you wanted to discuss with my father?"

How embarrassing to have been caught not attending to the conversation. "I heard a rumor suggesting the translator might be local to Gloucestershire."

"You heard *what*?" Her voice rose half an octave in pitch

on the last word. "How—how surprising. What was the rumor?"

"The sister of one of our maids works at the Plough Inn in Cheltenham. One day last week, the mail coachman came in with a parcel that had been dropped in the mud. It was addressed to the Prince of Wales. He asked her to re-wrap it before the mud soaked through. When she peeled off the soiled paper, she found the new translation inside, with a note from the author saying he had been honored to receive the prince's request for an autographed copy."

"Oh, my gracious! Could she, uh, could she make out the signature?"

"She didn't even see it. The note was folded so that only the first few lines were visible, and she could hardly go snooping through the prince's correspondence with the coachman looking on. But if the package came through Cheltenham, then the author must be from around these parts. That was what I wanted to discuss with your father. I thought it might be one of his former students."

"Oh. I see. And did he have any guesses regarding the identity of the translator?"

Edward applied the gentlest pressure to the reins, slowing his horse a touch. Given the way Elissa was clinging to his neck, she must be feeling unstable. "He did not."

"Not even an inkling?" she asked.

"No, he said he hadn't the slightest clue."

"Oh." She looked down for a beat, then swallowed before peering up at him again. "May I ask your opinion regarding the translation?"

"It is excellent," he said at once. "If you are yet to read it, I cannot recommend it highly enough."

"Really?"

"Oh, yes. One reads so many translations that are without

feeling. You could argue that the words are right, but they somehow fail to capture the spirit of the work. This was the exact opposite. Whoever did this has a true understanding of Longinus. And more than that…"

He paused, trying to find the right words. "It's difficult to describe, but it was written with such enthusiasm, such genuine love of the work, it was contagious. It reminded me of everything I used to love"—catching his slip, he cleared his throat— "that is to say, everything I love about classical verse."

That was the problem, all right. Whoever had performed this translation was *brilliant*. He was more than just a competent technician; the man was a poet in his own right. Hell, this mystery translator had even managed to capture a hint of the original Greek meter, an almost-impossible task given that Greek lacked the stress-accents that gave English its cadence.

Edward had never mastered the trick of that. But no matter how rusty and out of practice he might be, he was going to have to find a way to beat this man, whoever he was, because his little brother had drunken himself into a stupor and wagered Augustus Avery fifteen thousand pounds that Edward was going to win that bloody contest.

There was no getting out of it; it was in the betting book at White's and everything: *Mr. Harrington Astley bets Mr. Augustus Avery fifteen thousand pounds that his brother's poem will be the one read aloud by the Vice-Chancellor of Oxford University at the upcoming contest on the first of April.*

The money wasn't even the worst of it, although it was extremely bad (fifteen thousand pounds—what had Harrington been *thinking*?) The worst of it was the misery in Harrington's eyes when he begged Edward to enter. "Father won't just cut me off if he finds out," Harrington had said.

"You were there when he threatened to ship me off to India if I set another toe out of line. He already thinks I'm such a wastrel. A waste of good linen, that's me."

Edward had objected immediately. Honestly, how Harrington could fail to understand that he was everyone's favorite was beyond him. Harrington had the quickest wit of any man Edward knew, and an effervescent personality. Everyone's mood improved the instant Harrington walked into a room.

Edward may have been the clever brother, but Harrington was the loveable one.

He could still recall the precise moment he had come to understand that.

It had been a hell of a lesson to learn at the age of eight.

But Harrington was convinced their father thought he was worthless, and none of Edward's arguments had swayed him.

Although Edward suspected Harrington was right about his father packing him off to India if he made another mistake. Edward had been there when the earl made that threat, and his impression was that their father meant every word.

It was imperative that Harrington not go to India. Although a career with the East India Company was considered to be an acceptable option for a younger son, it would not have been Edward's choice for his brother. Harrington had a good friend, Peter Ferguson, whose mother was from the Bengali region and whose father was Scottish. Ferguson had grown up in India and was now a frequent guest at Astley House. Edward had come to know him well. Over the years, Ferguson had related enough tales of incompetency and even malfeasance on the part of the East India Company that Edward could not help but think that the local inhabitants would be better off without the British Empire's "guid-ance," such as it was.

But, in addition to the dubious nature of the mission he would be performing, Harrington suffered from attacks of asthma, and the adjustment from England's dreary dampness to India's tropical climate was challenging even for those in a robust state of health. Edward had done some research and had been alarmed to discover that more than half of all Englishmen who sailed to India perished within five years.

Edward had a terrible foreboding that if Harrington was forced to go to India, he would never see his brother again. And that meant that the earl must not find out about Harrington's imprudent wager.

And the only way Edward could prevent that was to win the bloody contest.

He sighed. No matter how much he loathed the prospect of resuming his career as a classicist, there was one thing that was even worse, and that was letting his little brother down. If there was any chance that he could save Harrington from their father's wrath, Edward was going to do his damnedest.

From her perch on his lap, Elissa cleared her throat and dabbed at her cheek with the sleeve of his coat. She had the biggest smile on her face. What had they been discussing? Oh yes, the translation. "It sounds wonderful," she said.

"It is." He laughed bitterly. "But listen to me—lavishing praise upon my enemy."

Her eyes flew to his. "Your—your enemy?"

"Of course," he said, guiding his horse to the left as they came to a fork. "I have to beat this mystery translator in the contest, after all."

She gave a nervous chuckle. "But surely that makes this person your competitor. Not your enemy."

"My enemy," he insisted. "I mean to win this contest. Had

it been the mystery translator I came across floating in that pond, I would've been sorely tempted to leave him there."

She flinched. "I'm only jesting," he hastened to say, but her sudden movement was enough to upset the lump of pondweed on her head.

The first thing that happened was for a slimy tendril of pondweed to snake its way down the side of her head. Elissa frowned and began patting her hair uncertainly.

Her searching hand startled a huge, black water beetle, which must have been lurking inside the clump of pondweed this whole time. It scurried straight across her forehead.

"Yeep!" she screamed, clawing at her face. "What is it? Get it off me!"

Edward pulled his gelding, who had begun dancing nervously, to a halt. "Bucephalus, stand!" he commanded.

Elissa screamed as the beetle scampered down her nose. Edward tried to grab it, but it escaped into her hair, causing her to arch her back in horror. She clocked him in the nose with her elbow as she raked her fingers through her hair.

"Everything's all right," he grunted, struggling to find it amongst her thick curls while avoiding her flailing arms. "It's just a... water beetle."

The beetle suddenly emerged from her hair, tearing across her cheek. Elissa screeched and swatted desperately at her face, finally launching it into a nearby bush.

She was breathing hard, as if she'd just fought off a wild boar rather than a tiny beetle. "There was a bug. A giant bug."

"Indeed, that was the largest specimen I've ever seen."

She cut her eyes to him sharply, and he came to understand that this had not been the correct thing to say. "But it's gone now," he added.

"It was *in my hair,*" she said, squeezing her eyes shut with horror.

"Strictly speaking, it wasn't in your hair. It came out of that lump of pondweed on top of your head."

Her eyes whipped up to his. "What lump of pondweed?"

"Er—" In retrospect, perhaps it would have been better not to mention the pondweed. "Would you like for me to, uh—"

She cleared her throat, staring off into a copse of trees. "If you would be so kind. I should hate to find out if the largest water beetle you have ever seen has any brothers or sisters."

She shuddered as he tossed a huge clump to the ground. "Thank heavens that's over," she said fervently.

"There's just a bit more over here," he said, sifting behind her ear.

"There is, is there?"

"And back here," he grunted, struggling to dislodge a particularly stubborn tendril.

"Take all the time you need," she muttered.

Four clumps later, he declared victory. "I believe that is all of it."

"Thank you," she said in a clipped voice, not meeting his eye.

Edward nudged Bucephalus forward and cast about for a topic that might restore her composure. "Your father mentioned that you have continued your studies."

"I have," she said, staring at the ground.

"May I ask what you've been working on?"

She gave a bleak laugh. "Why, just this afternoon, I have conceived an idea for an original ode."

"Ah, what is to be the subject?"

She muttered something quickly in Greek, almost under her breath.

Almost. But not quite.

"*What?*" Edward cried, reining Bucephalus to a halt.

Elissa froze, then slowly swung her gaze up to meet his.

Her eyes were wide, her mouth ajar, her face a portrait of dawning horror. "*Oh, dear,*" she whispered.

Oh, dear, indeed.

Because unless he was very much mistaken, her forthcoming ode was to be entitled *Prince Charming and the Sea Hag of Broadwater Bottom.*

CHAPTER 4

hy had she said that out loud?

Elissa partly blamed the cold, which had numbed her brain every bit as much as her arms and legs. Then there was the sudden and disorientating turn her afternoon had taken.

One minute, she had been riding along in the arms of Prince Charming himself, when, of all possible topics, he began speaking about *On the Sublime*.

Edward was right about one thing—the mystery translator was from the area, and far closer than he realized.

She was, in fact, sitting on his lap.

She had been a bit terrified to ask what he thought of her work. There was no one whose talent she admired more than Edward Astley's. No one. His translation of *Prometheus Unbound*, the one he had completed in his final year at Cambridge, was exquisite in every particular. Her copy was dog-eared, she had read it so many times, and she probably had more of it memorized than not. She was startled to realize there was no one whose good opinion mattered to her more, not even her father's.

She had given up trying to earn her father's good opinion years ago.

But then he had begun praising her, and it had felt so *validating*. To be sure, the critical acclaim, the fact that her book was in its third printing just two months after publication, and the request from the Prince of Wales for a signed copy had all been wonderful.

But she rather had the feeling that if all the world had loved it save for Edward Astley, those other accolades would have tasted not of wine, but of vinegar.

She had been on the cusp of telling him it was her. The only person who knew, other than the publishers she had queried, was her sister Cassandra. And she knew that telling her deepest, darkest secret to a man whom she had not seen in ten years, a man she scarcely knew, would be foolhardy.

But this afternoon had a whiff of fate about it, and she had felt the words rising to her lips, against her better judgment.

That was when he had said it—*my enemy. That* had startled her into silence.

And then it turned out that the largest water beetle Edward Astley had ever seen had been *living in her hair*, to say nothing of the fact that she had been riding along all this time, thinking this the most romantic moment of her life, while, unbeknownst to her, she had seven pounds of pondweed on top of her head.

This turn of events would have been disorienting for any girl, and so her momentary lapse was perhaps understandable.

No less humiliating, however.

She peered up into his face, which was frozen with shock. God, but this was awkward. Should she say something? Were they going to sit here forever on his horse, just—

Abruptly, the corners of his eyes crinkled, while those of

his mouth turned up, and the next thing Elissa knew, Edward had thrown his head back and was laughing uncontrollably.

This was apparently an unusual turn of events, because his horse cocked his ears back and skittered to the side. Elissa had released her grip on Edward's neck while they were sitting still, and was forced to grab him again to maintain her balance. He responded by wrapping an arm around her waist, pulling her against him. His chest shook with uncontainable mirth, and her face wound up buried in his neck.

After a minute, Edward managed to compose himself enough to say, "Steady, Bucephalus." His horse calmed immediately, and he loosened his grip on her. She looked up to find him grinning broadly.

Dimples was the only thought Elissa's frozen brain was capable of forming. Edward Astley was handsome enough without trying, with his thick dark hair and otherworldly blue eyes. But to have him smiling at her, at close range, with those dimples?

It was literally stunning.

He should be made to wear a placard around his neck: *Staring directly into the dimples poses a great risk to a woman's sanity.*

Elissa shook herself. "Stop laughing at me!"

"I'm not laughing at you, I'm—" He promptly disproved this statement by dissolving into another gale of laughter.

"Laughing at me," Elissa muttered.

"If you could have seen your face," he said, struggling to regain control of himself.

"Humph."

"I suppose I am laughing at you, but not for the reasons you think. I'm laughing at your wit. And your adorably horrified expression."

Adorably? What on earth was *that* supposed to mean?

She felt a few scattered raindrops on her face. He stuck out a hand, noticing them as well. He nudged Bucephalus forward. "I look forward to reading your ode, Miss Elissa, although I regret to inform you that your title will not do."

"Is that so?"

"It is. Firstly, the word you want is not *harpyia*. Clearly the term you are looking for is *seirēn*."

"Remind me of the passage in which Homer described the bugs living in the sirens' hair."

He ignored her. "And then there's this business about Prince Charming—"

"Prince Charming is apropos. We do get the papers out here, even if they're a week late. I know very well it is your nickname."

"An entirely unfounded nickname, I assure you."

"You just rescued a damsel in distress. You even ride a white horse!" Some strange and entirely improper impulse had her poking him in the ribs as she said this.

He gave a ticklish flinch but was smiling at her. "There's no such thing as a white horse. Horses that appear white are considered to be grey."

"A white horse," she insisted, "whom you have named *Bucephalus*." Bucephalus being, of course, the famed steed of no less a prince than Alexander the Great.

Edward groaned, giving her a look that was equal parts grin and glower. "*I* did not name him Bucephalus. He was a gift from my brother-in-law, Lord Thetford, who runs a breeding establishment. He thought it a lark to see me riding around on a white horse named Bucephalus—"

"Because you are Prince Charming, and everyone knows it. *Quod erat demonstrandum*."

"I do not concede," he said, flashing his dimples at her again.

She clutched her heart and recited, "'The oracle decreed

that he should be lord of the world, whom Bucephalus would suffer to sit upon his back.'"

His smile was soft and held a touch of wonder. "I am trying to give you a stern look, as it is positively unsporting of you to tease me. But I find I cannot glower at anyone who quotes Quintus Curtius Rufus from memory."

Emboldened, Elissa pressed the back of her hand to her forehead. "'O, Alexander, seek out a kingdom suitable to the greatness of thy heart, for Macedonia is too small for thee!'"

"Now that is a bridge too far. You leave me with no choice but to retaliate with Homer. 'First you will come to the Sirens who enchant all who come near them.'"

Elissa dropped her arm and gaped at him. "Enchant! Which did you find the more enchanting, the pondweed, or the beetle?"

They had reached her house. Edward reined in Bucephalus but made no move to dismount. He was smiling at her, and if she did not know it was all a disorder of her frozen brain, she would have said he was doing so tenderly. "Mostly the part where you made me laugh harder than I've laughed in a very long time. Elissa—"

Elissa? Had he just called her *Elissa?*

There was a bang as the front door burst open. "Elissa! Oh, thank heavens!"

She turned to see her sister Cassandra running across the garden. "I've been worried sick," Cassandra said in a rush. "I checked all your favorite haunts—the meadow, the willow tree, the bend in the river. I was just on my way to Broadwater Bottom."

"That's where I was," Elissa said. "The boat drifted away from the dock and the rope got tangled in a tree. I was very fortunate that Lord Fauconbridge came to my rescue."

"Thank you, my lord," Cassandra said, pressing a hand to her heart.

Elissa made to climb down, but Edward squeezed her waist. "Let me help you," he whispered. He lifted her just enough to slide back, setting her gently on the saddle, then he swung down. Elissa expected him to lower her to the ground, but instead he slid her straight into his arms.

Their sole groom (who also served as footman, gardener, and butler, as it were, as they only had one manservant and two maids-of-all-work) rushed over to take charge of Bucephalus. Edward began striding toward the front door with Elissa in his arms, speaking with Cassandra as she trotted alongside him. "She has taken a terrible chill. You'll note the bluish cast of her lips, and she was unable to stand a short time ago. It is urgent that we get her warmed up."

Cassandra nodded in agreement. "We'll take her up to my room—it's the smallest and easiest to heat. Amelia," she called to one of their maids, "stoke the fire in my room, please. We'll need hot water and—"

"There you are." Elissa cringed into Edward's shoulder at the sound of her mother's voice. "How on earth did you become so bedraggled?"

Elissa swallowed. Had she thought Edward discovering her at the pond was humiliating? It appeared that the real humiliation had yet to begin.

"I had a bit of a mishap on Farmer Broadwater's pond," she began.

Her mother cut her off with a snort. "It's always 'a bit of a mishap' with you. I see that this time you have inconvenienced Lord Fauconbridge. I cannot apologize enough for my daughter, my lord."

"There is nothing to apologize for," Edward said, setting Elissa gently upon a bench in the entryway.

"Oh, look at your beautiful boots!" her mother cried. "And you're soaked to the skin."

"I am fine—" Edward began.

"Amelia," her mother said, stopping the maid as she came back down the stairs, "heat some water. Lord Fauconbridge will require a hot bath."

"Thank you, but that will not be necessary. It is your daughter who—"

"Lord Fauconbridge?" Her father had wandered into the foyer to see what the fuss was about. "What brings you back here?"

"I happened upon Miss Elissa at the pond," Edward said, gesturing to Elissa on the bench.

Her father did not seem to have noticed that both she and Edward were drenched in pond water, that her hair had tumbled from its knot, or that she was wearing Edward's coat.

He did, however, notice the sodden volume in her lap.

"Is that my copy of *Theseus*? What have you done to it?" he demanded.

"It was an accident—" she began.

"Careless girl!" he said, snatching up the book. "I don't know why I even let you use my library."

"I am sorry, Father. I will replace it."

"Replace it! With what, I should like to know?"

Of course, he didn't know that Elissa was the author of the literary world's latest sensation, nor that just yesterday she had received another bank draft from her publisher, this one for one hundred and twenty-five pounds.

But this was not the moment to tell him.

So what she said was, "I've some pin money saved up—"

"We can discuss that later," her mother said, gesturing to Edward. "Look at poor Lord Fauconbridge, drawn into her mess. Amelia," she called toward the kitchens, "where is the water for his lordship's bath?"

"Truly, I am fine," Edward said. "I am most concerned about your daughter, however—"

"She got herself into this mess," her mother said. "She'll just have to wait."

"Please, Mama," Cassandra said, taking her mother's arm. "Look at her lips. They're blue! We've got to get Elissa warmed up."

"Indeed," Edward said. "I fear she is not yet capable of walking up the stairs, but if you will direct me toward your room, Miss Cassandra—"

"She is Mrs. Gorten now," her mother interjected. "The only one of the four girls we managed to marry off, and she came right back to us a widow."

"Mrs. Gorten, my apologies," Edward said smoothly. "If you would be so kind as to—"

"And is it any wonder we haven't been able to marry this one off?" Warming to one of her favorite themes, her mother did not seem to notice that she had interrupted a future earl, and several times at that. Elissa ducked her head as her mother began ticking points off on her fingers. "She can't sew. She can barely dance. She wouldn't know the current fashion if it came up to her in the street and trod upon her foot. Not that it matters, when she goes around looking like a drowned rat and smelling like pond scum."

Elissa squeezed her eyes shut as her mother droned on. And to think, she didn't even know about the water beetle!

Truth be told, her mother had the right of it. Elissa knew full well she would never marry, but not for the reasons her mother cited. Although none of those things were points in her favor, the sin that was truly unpardonable was that she was so bookish.

She might be able to find a man who would overlook the fact that she was a clumsy dancer. But no man could abide a woman who was more clever than him.

And so Elissa had abandoned dreams of romance and marriage years ago. But she didn't need to marry to secure her future, and that of her mother and sisters. She had another plan.

Her translation work.

It seemed her mother had not yet finished. "And if she's not boring a man to tears by droning on about some Greek poet who's been dead for two thousand years, then she's staring off into space, ignoring him."

"Mother," Cassandra said sharply, but her mother did not seem to hear.

With each passing moment, each additional humiliation, Elissa felt herself shrinking smaller and smaller upon the bench. The worst thing was knowing that her mother was correct. She did lack the feminine graces and had a rare talent for catastrophe to boot.

But did her mother really have to catalogue her failings before the one man whose good opinion she valued?

She chanced a glance up at Edward. He wasn't frowning, precisely, but he had squared off his jaw. Twice he tried to interject, but her mother allowed him no opening.

Finally his eyes took on a flinty look, and he spoke over her mother. "Mrs. St. Cyr, I beg your pardon." Elissa's eyes widened, because this was a voice she had never heard Edward use before. It was impeccably polite, as he always was.

It was also a tone that brooked no argument. A tone that very much said *I am the future Earl of Cheltenham, you are going to do as I say, and you are going to do so right now.*

"There seems to be some confusion. Miss Elissa has experienced an unfortunate mishap through absolutely no fault of her own. She has been wet and cold for far too long, and I fear she is chilled to the bone. She requires a hot bath and a warm fire. Immediately."

"But my lord," her mother interrupted, "what about you?"

The look Edward gave her mother had just a hint of

sharpness to it, though his tone remained cordial. "I am perfectly well and I require nothing. Thank you, Mrs. St. Cyr. Now, I will carry Miss Elissa up the stairs. Mrs. Gorten, would you be so kind as to direct me?"

"Right this way, my lord," Cassandra said as Edward scooped Elissa up.

Cassandra led them to her own room and drew the chair from her writing desk close to the blazing fire. Edward set her gently upon it. The maids had already set a copper tub close to the hearth. Although Elissa remained well-covered in his coat, she felt her cheeks flush at the implication—that in a few minutes, she would be naked in that tub before the fire.

Edward seemed to share her sense of awkwardness. "I will take my leave so you can, er—" He cleared his throat. "Be well, Miss Elissa."

She caught his hand as he started to turn. "Thank you, my lord. For *everything*." She could hear her own voice shaking with sincerity.

There was a gentleness to his voice as he answered. "You are most welcome."

And then he was gone.

Cassandra was already clucking over her, peeling off her wet clothes layer by layer. "Oh Elissa, are you sure you're well?"

"I'll be all right," Elissa reassured her sister.

And she would be, physically, at least.

But on the inside, she suspected she would never be quite the same.

CHAPTER 5

*E*dward would have ridden home immediately were it not for the lightning. He didn't mind a bit of rain.

What he very much minded was imposing upon the St. Cyrs. This was his least-favorite part of being a future earl: the way people insisted upon making a fuss.

From his vantage point in the library, he could hear Mr. and Mrs. St. Cyr whispering. It had been determined that Edward must borrow some dry clothes, which he supposed was practical. At present, he could not sit down and was actively dripping upon the floor. But the St. Cyrs were now urgently discussing which of Mr. St. Cyr's garments were the least offensive, as well as which bedroom would make the most presentable dressing room.

He sighed. He knew exactly what would happen while he was changing. Mrs. St. Cyr would rush to the kitchen and order the sort of meal usually reserved for Christmas and Easter. He cringed to think of them going to such expense on his behalf. Had it been up to him, he would not impose upon their supper, but would spend an hour or two poking around the library, then ride home as soon as the rain let up.

He had always loved Julian St. Cyr's library. The library at his family estate, Harrington Hall, was designed by Robert Adam in elegant shades of bronze and mint green. All the books were bound in an identical shade of golden-brown calfskin, dusted daily, and alphabetized within an inch of their life.

The St. Cyr library, on the other hand, had stacks of books everywhere, precariously leaning against the wall, each other, and a bust of Socrates complete with a spider dangling from the philosopher's right ear. The surface of the desk wasn't visible due to multiple layers of books, most of them still open to whatever page had interested Mr. St. Cyr at the time. The pair of leather wing chairs before the fireplace looked no less inviting for being patched in a few places. Scattered amongst the shelves he saw a broken astrolabe, the capital of an ancient ionic column, and a human skull.

The overall effect was such that if the wizard Merlin had strolled around the corner with his nose buried in a book, he wouldn't have looked at all out of place. Yes, Edward would very much prefer to pass a couple of hours in here, digging through the shelves for buried treasures.

But if there was one thing he had learned in the course of his twenty-seven years, it was that what one wanted counted for absolutely nothing, at least when one was a future earl. What one was expected to do trumped it every single time.

It took five minutes for the St. Cyrs to formulate a suitable plan. He was led to a tiny bedroom upstairs, next door to the one in which Elissa was having her bath.

He glanced about the room, surmising that it must belong to one of the four St. Cyr daughters, as someone had draped an elaborate trellis of tiny white faux flowers around the window. A plush old chair was positioned beneath the archway—the perfect reading nook. How he wished he could show his little sister, Isabella. She would love something like this for her room. He peered at the thin vines, thinking that he had never seen such delicate silk flowers before, only to discover that both vines and blossoms had been painstakingly cut from paper.

He shook himself and began exchanging his wet clothes for the dry ones he found draped over the back of the chair, which included his own mostly dry coat. As he was buttoning one of the shirt cuffs, something caught his eye on the little shelf over the writing table. It was *Roberti Stephani Thesaurus Linguae Latinae*, a book he recognized immediately, having used it daily from age seven to twenty-two.

He knew exactly what the presence of *Roberti Stephani Thesaurus Linguae Latinae* meant.

He was in Elissa's bedroom.

He strolled over to her desk to see what else she kept readily at hand. Its tiny shelf had room for only a handful of volumes, but there was the Samuel Clarke translation of the *Iliad* (an undisputed classic), Lemprière's *Bibliotheca Classica* (essential for any scholar), and Parkhurst's *Greek and English Lexicon* (exactly what he would have chosen as well, and far superior, in his opinion, to the lexicons of Caryl or Schrevelius.)

He blanched as his eyes fell upon the final book on the little shelf, the one Elissa had chosen to keep in her bedroom, where she had so little space.

It was his own translation of *Prometheus Unbound*.

He knew he shouldn't snoop, but he found himself pulling it from the shelf and flipping through the pages. It looked well-thumbed, with the occasional bent corner, and… was that a tea stain? He could just picture her making her adorable *oh dear* face as she blotted at the pages, an image that caused the corners of his mouth to curl up.

Edward shuddered as he read a few lines of his work. A

part of him had been excited when his tutor assigned him to translate Aeschylus's lost masterpiece. It had been the talk of the academic world—after being lost for centuries, a Bavarian monk had noticed a moldering folio tucked inside of another book. It proved to be the only surviving copy of *Prometheus Unbound.* It picked up where its precursor, *Prometheus Bound,* left off: with the eponymous Titan chained to a rock for all of eternity, an eagle eating his liver each day, a punishment from Zeus for having dared to give mankind the gift of fire.

The problem was that the manuscript was literally crumbling and therefore incomplete; in particular, the triumphant final scenes in which Prometheus won back his freedom had only a few passages extant. His tutor had come up with what he felt was a brilliant solution: Edward would compose original verse to fill in what was missing.

Now, Edward could translate, and he could write an elegant Greek ode. These tasks were expected of any man who called himself a classicist. But he felt deeply presumptuous putting words in the mouth of the great Aeschylus.

Almost as bad, *Prometheus Unbound* was the rare Greek tragedy that had a happy ending. The tone was triumphant. Uplifting. Jubilant, even. And although Edward secretly enjoyed reading such high-spirited works, composing one was entirely out of the question. His own writing was elegant, but sedate. Restrained. *Masculine.*

But in order to match the extant passages and be true to Aeschylus's intent, he had been forced to write in increasingly lofty tones that had been entirely unlike himself. And for a man who was so, so careful to guard his innermost feelings, to never show the world anything but the perfect future earl it required him to be... His tutor might as well have asked him to take off his clothing and run naked across Trinity Bridge. That was how exposed he felt.

Edward *hated* what he had written, but at least his tutor would be the only person to ever read it.

Or so he had thought.

In fact, when he went to present his translation, he found that Thomas Postlethwaite, the Master of Trinity College, had also turned up.

He felt queasy, but read out what he had written, both the Greek verse and his English translation.

When he finished, both men remained silent. Then Dr. Postlethwaite stood and asked if he might take the manuscript with him. All Edward wanted was to hurry back to his rooms and throw the cursed thing straight into the fire, but he could hardly refuse his head of house.

The next thing he knew, all the fellows of Trinity College had read his detested work, then it was all the fellows of every college, and then half the undergraduates as well. And everyone, absolutely everyone, was pestering him about when he was going to publish it.

Edward flipped a page, and noticed that Elissa had marked a passage toward the back with a slip of paper. He shuddered when he saw it was the triumphant ending, which was his own original verse. This was the section he hated the most. Even now, he couldn't stand the sight of it. He shut the book a bit more sharply than he had intended and slid it back into place on the shelf.

Some papers on her desk caught his eye. He realized with a start that she was working on a translation of the Roman poet Catullus:

LET US LIVE, *my Lesbia, and love,*
And value at one farthing the talk of crabbed old men.
Suns may set and rise again. For us, when the short light has set,

Remains to be slept the sleep of one unbroken night.
Give me a thousand kisses, then a hundred,
Then another thousand...

IT WAS OBVIOUSLY a work in progress. Not only was it incomplete, but many times a word was scratched out, or even a whole line, its preferred replacement scrawled in the margin.

But even in this rough form, Elissa's talent all but burst off the page. Anyone could perform a literal translation of the words, but she had captured Catullus's voice, his unique ability to be ardent and irreverent at the same time.

He thought of the ride home, and how nimbly she had deployed classical quotations in order to tease him. Talking to her had made him feel exhilarated in a way he hadn't felt in years. She had always been clever, but he was starting to suspect she might be *brilliant*. How he wished he could talk to her, just for an hour.

Although... an hour would never be long enough. An afternoon? A week? A month?

A lifetime?

Gad, he needed to stop his thoughts from running away with him. But then there was the fact that she was translating *Catullus*. Although this particular work was a conventional love poem, many of Catullus's works were salacious in the extreme. Had she read those? What had she thought of them? Had the same becoming blush she'd worn this afternoon stained her cheeks as she read the more lascivious passages?

His hand itched to leaf through the pile of papers on her desk to see if he could discern the answers to his burning questions. Instead, he curled his fingers into a fist. He needed to stop snooping. He spun away from her desk, but this turned out to be even worse, because now he was facing her *bed*. He knew he shouldn't, but he found himself crossing the room. He gently lifted her pillow and brought it to his nose, and the scent of honeysuckle washed over him.

Suddenly all he could picture was Elissa lying on this bed, wearing a chemise even more transparent than the sodden dress he'd seen her in that afternoon. Images began to flash across his mind—the rosy outlines of her peaked nipples. Her gorgeous legs as she had slipped into the pond. The way her body had fit against his as he swam them to shore. Her delicious curves just inches from his longing hands as he settled her on his lap. The sweet weight of her arms around his neck—trusting and timid in equal measures. And now he was picturing her naked on this bed, her red hair a riot of curls beneath her, and then he was imagining himself naked on the bed with her, his hands cupping her delicate breasts, their mouths tangling together, her legs parting for him as his body covered hers...

That was when he heard it—the faint but unmistakable sound of a splash from the room next door.

The room in which Elissa was bathing.

Now all he could picture was Elissa groaning with pleasure as she leaned back, naked, in that tub of warm water set before a roaring fire. And the knowledge that she really was naked on the other side of that wall...

Suddenly he could take no more. He loosened the falls of his borrowed trousers as he crossed the room, seizing a handkerchief. He shoved the trousers down just enough to pull his cock out as he sank into Elissa's chair. As he began stroking himself, he again caught the scent of honeysuckle.

He knew this was wrong. Not only because abusing himself in a young lady's bedroom (in her favorite reading chair, for Christ's sake!) was the height of disgraceful behavior. But because Elissa St. Cyr was wrong for him in every possible way.

Which was not to say that he agreed with Elissa's mother that no man would want her. Elissa St. Cyr was *delightful*. Were he the second son, with a little more latitude, he'd have asked for permission to court her already.

But he wasn't the second son. He was the heir to an earldom, and his family expected him to marry the daughter of a peer. Someone with impeccable bloodlines and a large dowry. Someone who had been born to the life he was expected to live, and whose connections would enhance his family's influence. Someone who would make the perfect hostess, who would never set a toe out of line.

He absolutely could not marry the penniless daughter of his tutor, a girl who went around with pond weed in her hair. A girl who had never attended a proper ball in her life, much less planned one. A girl who could not so much as read a book without instigating an elaborate series of catastrophes.

It did not matter one whit that she might be the only woman in the British Isles with whom he could have a meaningful conversation about the things that really interested him. It didn't matter how beautiful she was, nor did it matter that she could not have looked more like his feminine ideal if some ancient god had sculpted her from clay and brought her to life especially for him, from her red hair to her delicate-yet-tantalizing curves to the delightful, open-book expressions she was prone to making. It didn't even matter that she had made him laugh so hard he cried, that she had made him feel happier than he had felt in—

God. He couldn't even remember the last time he'd felt that happy.

But none of that mattered, because he absolutely could not marry her, and Edward Astley was not the sort of man who would dishonor a virginal young woman by taking her as his mistress. He would never have her, and that was final.

No, he thought, as he imagined the way she would look at him with those sea glass green eyes in the moment the pleasure was upon her, Elissa St. Cyr was not for him. He quickened his desperate strokes and bit down his cry as he came into the handkerchief, his entire body shaking and the chair screeching against the floor as he had the most powerful climax he had experienced in ages.

Definitely not for him, he thought as he threw the handkerchief into the fire.

CHAPTER 6

Three hours later, Cassandra declared Elissa's hair sufficiently dry that she was allowed to leave the confines of her sister's sweltering room.

By then, the rain had let up, and Edward had long since departed. She sighed. She would probably never see him again.

That wasn't quite true—she was guaranteed to see him one more time: at the forthcoming contest at Oxford, in which she would face her challengers.

She glanced around her room, which she knew full well he had used to change out of his wet clothes. She had heard him speaking to her father through the wall while she'd been in her bath. The thought of him here, in her most intimate space, was delightful and mortifying in equal measures. Gracious, what must he have thought of her fairy bower? She had cut those flowers by hand when she was thirteen. They might seem silly for a woman grown, but she still loved them. Had he noticed her copy of his book just above her desk? She felt a bit embarrassed, but also disappointed that she hadn't thought to have him sign it for her.

Had he sat upon her bed? Most probably not, but he must have sat in her chair, for at one point, she'd heard it screech against the floor. She crossed the room and sank into its familiar plush embrace. Was it her imagination, or could she detect just a hint of bergamot?

She stared at the fire and tried to picture him standing there. Not just standing there but peeling off his wet clothes. Because Edward Astley hadn't just *been* in her room.

He had been *naked* in her room.

A faint moan escaped from Elissa's lips. She paused, listening carefully to make sure everything was quiet. She didn't usually do this until late at night when she was lying in her bed and felt sure that the entire house was asleep.

But the truth was, she had been craving it ever since the moment he had pulled her flush against his chest in the pond. She had been craving it all afternoon, and she didn't think she could wait another second.

She padded silently to the door and turned the key in the lock as quietly as she could.

She then tiptoed over to her bed, hiking her skirts up as she lay on her back and spread her legs. She reached into the little drawer of her bedside table and withdrew a tiny stoneware pot. It contained a cream scented with honeysuckle that she used for her hands.

At least, that was one of the things she used it for.

She took a dollop on her index finger, using her other hand to spread the folds between her legs. She had been longing for this so much, she was already throbbing, so rather than starting with her breasts, her fingers went straight to the little rosebud between her legs, making light, slick circles. Oh, that felt so sweet! She was so close already! She thought about her body pressed against Edward's in the pond. She pictured his eyes, tender and sincere, in the moment he scooped her into his arms to stop her from falling. She thought about how *Edward Astley* had wrapped his arms around her and carried her away on his white charger.

She thought about him just a few short hours ago, standing naked in this very room. She had never seen a naked man before, so her image was indistinct. But so much Greek verse was erotic, you sometimes stumbled across passages that stirred the imagination.

Which happened to be how she had figured out how to do this.

Oh, she was so aroused, her hand between her legs felt *so good*. She paused and began circling the other way, biting down a cry as new nerves sparked to life. Suddenly an image sprang into her mind of Edward lying on top of her, smiling, his dimples on full display, his blue eyes crinkled not only with laughter, but with affection.

Just like that, she was right there, right on the edge, and the pleasure was overwhelming. It felt *so good*, it felt... oh... oh... *oh...*

She bit her lip to keep from crying out, but her legs were shaking so hard as she peaked, she heard the bedframe thump twice against the wall. She struggled to control their shaking as she gentled her hand, drawing out the final few pulses of pleasure before collapsing boneless on the bedspread.

She listened alertly but heard no sounds from the surrounding rooms. It appeared she had gone undiscovered.

She sighed. She had the feeling that Edward Astley would be fueling her midnight fantasies for quite some time to come. Even more than he already had.

But she needed to remember one thing: it was nothing more than a fantasy.

Elissa knew full well he would never be interested in the likes of her. The references he had made that afternoon—to her being a siren, to her horrified expression being "adorable,"—those were just gallantries. He was the consummate gentleman and had been trying to make her feel better. It spoke well of him, but was not indicative of any true regard.

Edward Astley was probably going to marry the daughter of a duke. A girl with blue blood and a huge dowry, who could throw together a dinner party in an afternoon, who never set a toe out of line. The type of girl who would never trip over a pig. Not a girl who read Plutarch in a boat, had giant water beetles nesting in her hair, and courted disaster wherever she went. It wasn't even worth dreaming about. She would make a remarkably terrible countess. Edward would never choose the likes of her.

Honestly, what he felt for her right now was likely nothing but pity. But just wait until after the contest…

The contest was the idea of her publisher, Mr. Findley. He had been pressing Elissa to reveal her identity to the world, because the news that the mysterious translator was a woman was bound to cause a sensation, and sensations sold books.

But Elissa knew from a lifetime of experience that the world would see a female classicist not as a sensation, but as a curiosity, the literary equivalent of Snowdrop the two-headed cow. To be sure, *everyone* went to gawk at Snowdrop at the fair.

But no one bought season tickets to see Snowdrop. They paid the fare precisely once, peered over the fence, muttered, "I'll be demmed," and forgot all about Snowdrop by supper.

Elissa could not afford to become a curiosity, a mere flash in the pan. She needed to establish a successful career as a translator. She was the youngest of four sisters, and her father's health was failing. He was seventeen years her mother's senior, and the heart palpitations he had suffered for years had recently grown worse. Why, he had even collapsed twice in the last two months! What little there was of her father's estate was entailed and would one day be inherited by his detested younger brother, who had given them no reason to hope he would support his brother's widow and daughters.

As the last girl, the one who had dashed all of her father's hopes by failing to be a boy, Elissa had always felt a personal responsibility to provide for her mother and sisters once their father was gone.

So when Mr. Findley wrote suggesting she unveil herself as the anonymous translator, Elissa had forcefully declined.

A flurry of letters ensued. Mr. Findley could not imagine that the world would hold being a woman against Elissa. But Mr. Findley was a rare sort. His mother, whom he described as the most intelligent person he had ever known, had run the editorial side of his family's press for years, and Elissa was convinced this was the reason he had been unperturbed upon learning that the *E.* in *E. St. Cyr* stood for Elissa. She wrote back explaining that the seven other publishers who had suddenly noticed a myriad of flaws in what they had previously described as a *brilliant* manuscript were, in her experience, more typical.

Mr. Findley had countered that, if seven of his rivals were aware of Elissa's identity, the secret was bound to come out sooner or later, and it would be better to make the announcement on her own terms.

He had a point there, and the compromise they had settled upon was the contest. It appealed to Mr. Findley's sense of the theatrical; indeed, it was already drawing significant press. And he had agreed that they would only reveal Elissa's identity if she won.

There would always be some who would read her work in a different light upon learning that she was a woman. But if she could win, the contest also had the potential to serve as a credential. Elissa would never earn a university degree, much less any of the medals and honors Edward Astley had won. Oxford and Cambridge didn't even allow women to enroll.

But if she could beat the same men who had won those medals, then no one could dismiss her as a mere curiosity.

That was why Elissa had to win this contest. She *had to*. She couldn't settle for one successful book; she needed a successful career. Her ability to feed and shelter her mother and sisters was dependent upon it.

And that was the other reason she needed to stop dreaming about Edward Astley. He was entering the contest, too. If life had taught her one thing, it was that men could not *stand* to be bested by a woman. And Elissa was going to have to whip him like a French chef making a meringue.

After she defeated him, any fond feelings he might harbor for her would be gone. Forever.

Yes, the sooner she accustomed herself to the idea that Edward Astley would come to feel nothing for her but scorn, the better.

No matter how much she might wish otherwise.

THE FOLLOWING MORNING, a groom arrived from the Earl of Cheltenham's seat, Harrington Hall. In the back of his cart was one of the Earl's famous Gloucestershire Old Spot pigs, accompanied by a note from Lord Fauconbridge begging Mr. St. Cyr to accept it in thanks for the gracious hospitality he had received the previous evening.

The receipt of three hundred pounds of pork and bacon went a way toward quieting her mother, who had been grumbling nonstop about their having been forced to serve the Sunday roast two days early (which, of course, was all Elissa's fault).

Elissa had expected a gesture of this sort, given Edward's impeccable manners.

What surprised her was the delivery that arrived just before supper.

Amelia came and fetched Elissa, as her father was out. At the bottom of the stairs, she found a footman in the mint green and bronze Cheltenham livery bearing a paper-wrapped parcel.

"If you wouldn't mind, miss," he said, handing the package to her, "take a look and make sure I got the right one. I gave them his lordship's note at the shop, but I can't read those letters."

Elissa unwrapped the package to discover a brand-new copy of Plutarch's *Life of Theseus*. Like the copy she had ruined by dropping it into the pond, this one was in the original Greek.

She felt tears forming. "It's the right one," she said, swatting at her cheek as one escaped. She gave the groom a crooked smile. "Which shop in Cheltenham stocks Plutarch in the original Greek?"

He laughed. "None, miss. His lordship sent me to Oxford for it first thing this morning."

She sighed. Of course he had.

While Amelia took the footman back to the kitchen for some refreshment, Elissa dashed off a note to Edward, thanking him sincerely for his kindness. She found a slip of paper tucked between the pages of the book. It was only the instructions for the groom with the title and a list of bookshops to check. But it was written in his precise, confident hand.

She took the note upstairs and tucked it inside her copy of *Prometheus Unbound.* She knew she was being foolish.

But it was all she would ever have of him.

CHAPTER 7

Three days later, Edward was about to head down to breakfast when he found himself pulling Elissa's letter from his desk drawer and reading it for what must have been the hundredth time. It was a half-page note thanking him for the volume of Plutarch, remarkable perhaps in its sincerity, but otherwise unexceptional.

So why could he not stop reading it?

Edward thrust it back into the drawer, which he closed a bit more sharply than he had intended. This would not do.

He made a decision.

As he strode down the hallway toward the central rotunda that connected the four wings of the house, Edward reflected that the problem was not Elissa St. Cyr.

The problem was with him.

Specifically, that he was a virgin.

Edward held himself to a certain standard, one that did not entail cornering the housemaids or soliciting prostitutes. The fact that these were the usual methods by which young men divested themselves of their virginity had made things…

complicated. Still, he hadn't planned on being entirely without experience at the age of seven and twenty.

It turned out that having a reputation for unimpeachable honor in a world of rakes and cads did not always work to one's advantage. People assumed he was the type of man who would come up to scratch rather than besmirch a young lady's honor, regardless of the circumstances. And so, the scheming families of the *ton* began laying their traps.

He'd had his first kiss at eighteen. He had thought nothing of it when his dance partner complained of the over-heated ballroom and asked to take a turn on the balcony. He had been surprised, but not entirely displeased, when she had thrown her arms around his neck and kissed him.

But the thrill had ended when her parents emerged from the shadows, demanding satisfaction for his having 'ruined' their daughter. As if that had not been bad enough, quickly following them onto the scene was his own mother, who had seen him leave the ballroom, anticipated the ruse, and watched the whole thing from the balcony doors. The countess routed the schemers, but Edward was left with the stinging humiliation of his *mother* having witnessed his first kiss.

He was careful after that. He studiously avoided balconies, gardens, and any dark corners where a young lady might be lying in wait. But the young ladies of London were resourceful. He had been ambushed (there was really no other word to describe it) another half-dozen times. On one memorable occasion, Miss Araminta Grenwood, the daughter of one of his mother's friends, actually leaped from behind a potted palm in a deserted corridor while he was in search of a chamber pot. How Miss Grenwood, who was as mean-spirited as she was haughty, had formed the impression that he would, under any circumstances, consider an alliance with her, he could not imagine. He had done his best to disabuse her of this delusion in a manner that was polite but firm.

That was when he began avoiding London. He was willing to take precautions, but asking his brother to accompany him to the necessary was a bridge too far.

And so, looking back on it, his distracted state probably had little to do with Elissa St. Cyr. Having any reasonably attractive woman in his lap would have elicited the same reaction, no doubt. The only cure he needed was a woman—any woman—in his bed, and he could have that.

All he had to do was marry.

As appealing as the idea of having a wife in his bed was (and for a twenty-seven-year-old virgin, the idea was very appealing indeed), it filled Edward with a certain amount of terror. A man who was a virgin on his wedding night wasn't unheard of, but it was unusual.

As someone who prided himself on competency, the thought of his wedding night made him break out in a cold sweat. It would've been one thing to be a young man of eighteen, learning the finer points of making love from an experienced widow. But he was far past the age when he could be excused for fumbling his way through. And his bride was likely to be a virgin, too, and even more ignorant than he was.

The idea of admitting that he didn't know what he was doing was unthinkable; the thought of trying and failing to please his bride, even worse. His only hope lay in his understanding that most men were indifferent lovers. He would have to pray that his future mother-in-law would set her daughter's expectations nice and low. With any luck, his bride wouldn't know what she was missing.

He entered the breakfast room. As one of seven siblings, meals at Harrington Hall tended to be crowded affairs. But today he found his mother seated alone at the table.

Perfect.

She smiled when he entered. "Good morning, Edward."

"Good morning, Mother."

He filled a plate and took the seat opposite her. He cleared his throat as he began to slice his ham. "I was wondering if I could ask a favor of you."

His mother looked up from pouring her tea. "Of course, darling. Anything."

"It's regarding the house party you're hosting next week. Could I add a few additional guests?"

"I don't see why not," she said, dropping a lump of sugar into her cup. "Whom did you have in mind?"

He strove to sound nonchalant. "I was hoping you could invite some young ladies. I have decided it is time for me to marry."

She looked up from stirring her tea, smiling like the cat that had got into the cream. "And which fortunate young woman has prompted this decision?"

Edward resumed slicing his ham. "No one," he lied.

When he chanced a glance at his mother, she had arched a skeptical eyebrow. "No one? You expect me to believe that?"

"I am approaching the age of thirty. It's high time I produced an heir." Seeing his mother's quizzical look, he sighed and laid down his fork. "With Anne's date drawing near, everyone has been commenting on how her child could use some cousins to play with." Anne was his little sister and had recently married the heir to their neighboring estate, Michael Cranfield, the current Earl Morsley and future Marquess of Redditch.

"Those remarks are in jest, darling. There is no need for you to rush into anything."

"I know that. But, as I said, I have decided it's time."

His mother looked perplexed. "But if you don't have a young lady in mind, then whom would you have me invite?"

"I trust your judgment. If you will invite a handful of suitable girls, I will choose one of them and be done with it."

His mother sighed as she laid her spoon upon the saucer. "This is an important decision, Edward. Whomever you choose, you will have to live with this woman for the rest of your life. I am happy to invite some potential candidates. But if it turns out that you do not feel an affinity for any of them, I would hate for you to rush to the altar out of some misplaced notion that the time has come."

"I do wish to marry. I..." Edward trailed off. He could hardly tell his mother that he had been in a state of perpetual sexual frustration ever since he held Elissa St. Cyr in his lap, that he was sick and tired of being a virgin, or that the thought of having a woman in his bed each and every night seemed like some impossible paradise.

Although, judging by her knowing gaze, she was probably surmising as much.

He snatched up his fork and knife and resumed slicing his ham. "I wish to marry, and I would very much like to do so in the coming weeks."

"Of course, darling. I will invite a few young ladies. But you must guide me a bit. Was there anyone you met in London with whom you felt you might suit?"

"There was not. Just invite whomever you think."

"Not a young lady from London, then. Perhaps..." Edward didn't much care for the way his mother was studying him. "Perhaps it is a local girl who has inspired this train of thought?"

"No. There isn't any local girl." His voice came out in more of a rush than he liked. He tried to distract himself by spearing a piece of ham, but the fork slipped in his clammy hands, clanging against the plate.

"I know it is an awkward thing to discuss with your mother. But if there is someone you admire—"

"There is not." When he glanced up, his mother's face was a portrait of skepticism. "I know what is expected of me, Mother. I have always known. And I will do my duty. What I want is for you to choose the young ladies. If you do the choosing, then I will know that they are acceptable to you and Father—"

"Oh, Edward." Now the countess's eyes were sorrowful. "You have always been the most dutiful son. But your happiness is a consideration, too. An important consideration. If there is someone who has caught your eye—"

"There is not."

"—we would consider her, even if she does not have a *Lady* in front of her name."

Edward bit back a bitter laugh. His mother was probably imagining he was pining for one of Baron Staverton's six daughters, who lived on the far side of town, or one of the Beauclerk girls, who were granddaughters to a duke, even if their father lacked a title. A step down from the heir to an earldom, to be sure, but solid members of the local landed gentry.

If she realized that the woman he couldn't stop thinking about was the daughter of his *tutor*, there would be no more talk of Edward's happiness being a consideration.

His mother's gaze turned shrewd. "Honestly, Edward, I've suspected something was going on. The past three days you've been nothing like your usual self. I wish you would just tell me—"

"There is no one." The chair clattered behind him as he surged to his feet. "I beg your pardon, Mother, but I have suddenly recalled some urgent business." He was out the door in a flash, leaving his uneaten ham behind.

～

THAT AFTERNOON, Edward paid a visit to his neighbor, the Marquess of Redditch. Lord Redditch had been a widower for fifteen years and had never remarried. When his only son, Morsley, had moved to Canada four years ago, Edward had fallen into the habit of spending Tuesday afternoons with the marquess. He had suspected Lord Redditch could use a little company.

Now that Morsley was back from Canada and married to Edward's sister, Anne, he didn't worry so much about the marquess being lonely. But Edward kept up his weekly visits. He genuinely liked Lord Redditch, and even though the marquess was more a contemporary of Edward's father, Edward considered him to be one of his closest friends.

It was also nice to have an excuse to see Anne every week (not that this was a rare occasion—the Redditch estate, Ravenswell, was only two miles from Harrington Hall, so Anne came to visit regularly). Today, Harrington had come along.

They were all drinking coffee in the library when Lord Redditch said, "Fauconbridge, I was wondering if I might ask you a favor."

"Of course," Edward said at once.

The marquess strolled over to his desk and pulled out what looked to be an invitation. "There's to be an assembly two nights hence in Bourton-on-the-Water. I always put in an appearance, as most of those in attendance are my tenants. Unfortunately, some business has come up that I cannot avoid. I have to go to Gloucester to see an applicant for the living."

The longtime rector of the parish church, John Chenoweth, had died the previous October following a fall from his horse. His daughter, Cecilia, was now living at Harrington Hall, as her mother had died when she was two, and she was now alone in the world. Ceci was close friends with Edward's sister Caroline, and Edward thought of her as practically his own sister. Although his mother had made it clear to Ceci that she was welcome to stay indefinitely, Edward could tell she worried she was imposing.

Lord Redditch had the parish living within his gift, and he had been searching for a new rector for months. "Have you found someone suitable, then?" Edward asked.

The marquess snorted. "I highly doubt it, based on his letter. He sounds as dissolute as the rest of them. But his uncle is the Bishop of Worcester, so I can hardly refuse him a hearing. I would normally send Michael to the assembly," the marquess said, nodding to his son, "but he hates to leave your sister even for an evening."

Anne was heavily pregnant, with the baby expected in the next few weeks. "I suggested we go together," she said.

Morsley, who was sitting beside his wife upon the sofa, took what Edward would term a deep and calming breath. He looked to be on the verge of some sort of thrombosis, truth be told, and Edward wasn't without sympathy, given that Morsley's own mother had died in childbirth when he had been a boy of nine.

"If you wish to go, we will go," Morsley finally managed, doing a creditable job of holding his voice steady. He turned to Edward, looking him square in the eyes. "But I thought one of my brothers-in-law might be *so good* as to spare your sister a long carriage ride over a bad road and represent the family on our behalf."

Morsley accompanied this statement with what was not so much a speaking look as a shouting look.

"I thought it a capital idea," Lord Redditch said. "After all, you're family now."

Edward froze. Normally, he would do anything to help his friends and neighbors, to say nothing of his own sister.

But this assembly was in Bourton-on-the-Water, which

meant that Elissa St. Cyr was bound to be in attendance. And if there was one person on the face of this earth whom he needed to avoid, it was Elissa St. Cyr.

He cleared his throat, preparing to make an excuse and suggest Harrington attend instead.

But somehow the words that came tumbling out of his mouth were, "Of course—yes—I should be glad to."

Edward frowned. Where had *that* come from?

Morsley exhaled with relief. "I knew I could count on you, Fauconbridge." He turned to Anne. "Is that all right, darling?"

"It is." Anne laughed. "Truth be told, I wasn't much looking forward to the carriage ride."

Morsley took his wife's hand. "Only think of how vexing I would be, asking if you were well every time we hit a bump."

Anne beamed at her husband, looking not the slightest bit vexed. "You are exceptionally vexing, it's true."

Edward caught Harrington studying him. "Bourton-on-the-Water, you say? Why don't I come along and keep you company?"

"Excellent," the marquess said. "This has worked out better than I could have hoped. Instead of me, they'll get two handsome bachelors. They'll hope I have a conflict every year. I daresay they will schedule it themselves."

They all laughed, and the conversation moved on, but Edward spent the rest of the visit with a strange mixture of excitement and dread mingling in his stomach.

CHAPTER 8

Two nights later, Elissa went with her family to the New Inn, where the tables and benches that usually adorned the main room had been neatly stacked away so there would be sufficient room to hold the village's spring assembly. She took up her customary position: standing in the corner with Cassandra.

Elissa would have preferred to stay home, especially with the contest just two weeks away. She needed every spare minute right now for study and preparation. But her mother always insisted she go, saying, "You never know who might be there."

Well, Elissa had attended a great many local assemblies over the years, and Prince Charming had never been in attendance.

Suddenly the room fell silent. She glanced at Cassandra to see if she knew what was going on, but her sister looked as confused as she was. She joined those around her in craning her neck, trying to see what the commotion was about.

Just as quickly as the room had fallen silent, it filled with whispers. Cassandra gasped and grabbed Elissa's forearm.

"What is it?" Elissa asked.

"It's the *Astley brothers*," Cassandra whispered, her expression full of glee. "Elissa, he's here."

~

As soon as Edward and Harrington entered the assembly room, the crowd fell silent, then burst as one into whispers.

Edward sighed. He didn't enjoy being stared at, but he was used to it.

Beside him, Harrington seemed unperturbed. "So," he said conversationally, "which one is she?"

Edward gave his brother a strange look. "Which one is who?"

"Oh, come off it."

"I don't know what you're talking about."

Harrington was scanning the crowd. "I'm talking about the fact that ever since you went to Bourton-on-the-Water, you've been staring forlornly out of windows, heaving heartfelt sighs into your soup, and scarcely attending to the world around you. All of which points to a woman. So, which one is she?"

Edward drew himself up to his full six feet, two inches, which was conveniently one inch taller than his brother. "You're imagining things."

"Aha—the redhead in the corner, unless I'm very much mistaken."

Edward was torn between gaping at Harrington and whipping his head around. As he could do neither in public, he scanned the room, striving to keep his features disinterested. Surely enough, the redhead in the corner proved to be Elissa. "Could you be referring to Miss Elissa St. Cyr?"

"So you know her! I knew it was her. You've never been able to resist a redhead."

Now Edward knew he was gaping at his brother. How did Harrington know that? He'd certainly never said as much.

"Miss St. Cyr," Harrington mused. "That'd make her the daughter of your tutor."

"Correct."

"The very tutor you went to see last week."

"Indeed," Edward said, striving for a look of dispassion. "I actually asked after Miss Elissa when I called, having not seen her in ten years. But she was out."

It actually happened to be true.

Although he might be omitting a few pertinent events that had occurred later on.

Harrington frowned. "Then you're not interested in her?"

"Miss St. Cyr is a very nice girl from what I can recall, and I would never say anything against a lady. But..." Edward shrugged helplessly.

"Oh." Harrington's shoulders slumped, and he didn't trouble to hide his disappointment. He turned back to Elissa, considering. "Well, in that case, you can introduce me. I'd quite like to dance the first set with her."

Without thinking, Edward seized his brother around the wrist. "Don't you *dare*," he growled.

"I knew it! I knew it was her! She's exactly what you like—"

"Will you shut up?" Edward muttered. "Someone's approaching."

It proved to be the local magistrate, Mr. Hyatt. Edward explained that they were attending on Lord Redditch's behalf, and Mr. Hyatt presented his daughters. Edward made the minimum amount of conversation required, then moved precisely two feet closer to Elissa, at which point another gentleman appeared and presented his daughters.

This pattern repeated itself four times. Edward had

scarcely made any progress toward Elissa. At this rate he would never reach her before the dancing began. But good manners demanded that he exchange a few pleasantries, so what was he to do?

It happened that his brother didn't give a fig about good manners. Harrington grabbed Edward by the arm and began towing him through the crowd. "Beg pardon, my good sir… excuse me, coming through… need to get my brother to a chair, his rheumatism's acting up again."

"What?" Edward hissed. "I don't have *rheumatism.*"

"Who cares? It's working," Harrington muttered. "Pardon us, make way—oh, now what do we have here?"

They had reached the corner where Elissa stood with her sister. A small circle formed around them, as absolutely everyone openly stared.

Edward cleared his throat. "Good evening, Miss Elissa." She looked slightly terrified to be the center of attention. She wore a forest green dress in a practical woolen fabric with long, fitted sleeves. It was completely unadorned, without even a bit of ribbon—the mark of a girl who spent every penny of her pin money on books. Its waistline was a good three inches lower than what the ladies were wearing in London, but all Edward could think was *God*, she looked beautiful in it.

Harrington elbowed him in the ribs.

"And Mrs. Gorten," Edward said, shaking himself from his stupor. "May I introduce my brother, Mr. Harrington Astley?"

Curtseys were bobbed and introductions were made. Elissa seemed to be at a loss, so it was Mrs. Gorten who spoke. "We did not realize we would have the pleasure of your company this evening, my lord."

"Indeed," Edward replied, "Lord Redditch asked us to attend on his behalf. He had a last-minute engagement that could not be avoided."

Harrington leaned toward Cassandra conspiratorially. "You should have seen how quickly he said yes."

Edward gave his brother an incredulous look before turning back to Elissa. He cleared his throat. "Miss Elissa, might I have the pleasure of a dance?"

"You may," Cassandra said, reaching behind Elissa, seizing her by her upper arms, and shoving her forward. "She's available for this one."

Up until this point, Elissa had looked petrified at finding herself the center of attention. But as her sister thrust her forward, she met Edward's eye with an expression he recognized as, *why must my own sibling humiliate me in this way?*

A sympathetic grin sneaked across Edward's face. He nodded subtly to Harrington and strove for an expression that said, *you think* you *have it bad?*

She gave a silent giggle, and he felt a tightness in his chest he hadn't realized was there relax.

He offered his arm. "Shall we?"

She placed her hand gingerly upon it and gave him a tiny smile. "We shall."

She glanced back at Harrington and Cassandra as they crossed the room. Edward did the same and saw that they had their heads bent together, discussing something with great animation.

"Ugh," Elissa groaned. "Just look at them. How I hate to leave them alone together. Goodness knows what they must be plotting."

"Indeed," Edward said, "yet we have no choice, as supervising them requires us to remain in their company, which is even more intolerable."

She laughed out loud at that, and he felt better than he had in days.

He found them a little space along the wall. "How have

you been?" he asked, turning to face her. "Are you fully recovered from your chill?"

"I am," Elissa said. "All thanks to you. I only needed to get warmed up a bit."

"I am glad to hear it."

"I'm the one who's glad—glad you're here tonight, that is." A becoming flush rose to her cheeks as she peered up at him.

He felt his chest expand. "Are you?"

"I am." She bit her lip. "There's something I wanted to tell you—"

"Beg pardon, my lord." Whatever Elissa had been about to say was interrupted by a squat man with thinning hair and a jolly look about him. "Hugh Warner, at your service. I'm serving as master of ceremonies tonight. Would you two honor us by leading us in a country dance?"

Edward forced a smile to his lips. It happened that he would rather not. The couple who led off a country dance would have to select a dance figure, which they would perform for the entire room to see. They would then work their way down the line, performing the steps with each and every additional couple, and then dance them a few dozen more times for good measure.

Were it up to him, he would lead Elissa straight to the bottom of the set where they would have a good ten minutes to talk while they waited for the lead couple to make their way to them. That should afford him sufficient time to discover what she wanted to tell him that had her blushing so prettily.

He sighed. As usual, what he wanted was immaterial. He was the ranking man in the room, and he was not about to insult Mr. Warner by refusing.

He glanced down. "Miss Elissa?" he murmured. Unless he was misreading her expression, she too would very much rather not lead off the dance, but she gave a small nod, so

Edward turned back to Mr. Warner. "What an honor. We should be delighted."

A hush fell over the room as he led Elissa to the top of the set. The speaking looks and delighted laughs she had gifted him with moments ago were now gone, replaced by a ducked head and a tight smile that bespoke her discomfiture.

How he hated to do this to her, hated for her to be stared at and gossiped about, even for one evening. He, at least, was used to it.

They took up their places. Strictly speaking, it was for the lady in the top couple to choose the dance figure, but Elissa looked petrified. Everyone was staring at her, waiting for her to say something.

Edward gave her what he hoped was a reassuring smile. "Cross over two, lead up one?" he suggested, naming a common dance figure.

"Oh, erm, yes," Elissa replied.

The music started, and the dance began.

ELISSA COULD NOT BELIEVE she was doing this.

She had never led off a dance, not once in her life. Not even when her family gathered at Aunt Frederica's house in Chipping Campden for Christmas, and they would roll up the carpets so the cousins could dance after supper.

The reason Elissa had never been chosen to set the figures was because she was widely acknowledged to be an indifferent dancer. Her sisters had tried to teach her the steps, but she could only bring herself to turn the same circles so many times before the urge to return to her book became impossible to suppress. And what little time she had found to submit to their instruction, she usually spent with her mind somewhere else.

Yet here she was, with just about everyone she knew watching her stumble through the figures.

Edward danced elegantly, which was unsurprising, as there was nothing he was not good at. He had selected the perfect figure—simple enough that any competent dancer could pick it up, yet not so basic as to imply that the present company was lacking in skill. And Elissa was managing it.

Some of the time.

Edward took her hand as they promenaded back up the center aisle, before crossing each other and passing to the outside of the next couple in line. Cross again, make a tight circle around the next couple… not too bad for the girl who had once tripped over a pig. At least on that front she was safe—there were no pigs present tonight.

As they met in the center, Edward smiled at her encouragingly, his eyes as bright as stained glass next to his midnight blue coat, and she tripped over her own foot.

Elissa sighed. As humiliating as this was, it was worth it. She hadn't even considered saying no, not even when Mr. Warner requested that they lead the dance. For the rest of her life, she would cherish this memory of the time she danced with *Edward Astley*.

Besides, they must be almost done by now. Why, they had already performed the figure seventeen times!

Elissa peered down the set and saw that they were not even halfway down the queue of couples.

She sighed. At least she would be getting some practice.

EDWARD FELT INTENSELY guilty for putting Elissa through this. She was clearly nervous, as anyone would be, after being thrust so unexpectedly into the center of attention. But she was doing remarkably well, gaining confidence with each repetition of the steps.

He knew he should leave her alone. Being near him brought her nothing but pain and scrutiny. And he knew nothing could come of it. And yet...

He couldn't seem to leave her alone. He was just... drawn to her, as if she were the moon and he were the tides.

Tonight would probably be the last time he would ever see her. Surely it was not so terrible to beg a dance or two from the girl he truly fancied?

Toward the bottom of the set, he encountered Harrington, who was dancing with Cassandra. As he circled his brother, Harrington muttered, "Haven't seen her in ten years, have you? You filthy liar."

Edward did not so much as glance at his brother.

But he did make a point to tread upon his foot.

WHEN THE DANCE ENDED, Edward made a valiant attempt to lead Elissa to the refreshment table.

But, in a strange and entirely unprecedented turn of events, Elissa found herself surrounded by young men vying for her hand in the next set.

She glanced to her left and saw that Edward had been similarly set-upon by young ladies. Which was not the least bit surprising.

But it was unfortunate in that it prevented them from speaking. And Elissa knew she needed to tell him... something.

The thought of telling him her secret, that she was the anonymous translator of *On the Sublime*, made her stomach churn with terror. She had so much to lose if he were to expose her before the contest.

But what she had assumed had been an isolated encounter at Farmer Broadwater's pond had turned into something more. First, he had replaced the book she had destroyed. And now he was here tonight.

Both of these gestures likely meant nothing. The first was a sign of his impeccable manners; the second, a mark of his consideration toward his neighbor, Lord Redditch. To be sure, he had asked her to dance the first set, but as he was not from the immediate area, she was likely the only woman he knew in the room.

Still, with each accumulating gallantry, her original plan to say nothing began to feel graceless. She could picture the shock on his face crystalizing into hurt when he walked through the door on the morning of the contest and saw her unexpectedly in the room. The image made her feel ashamed.

She knew she needed to say *something*.

Now she just needed to figure out what.

She blinked as she came out of her trance. They had obviously taken too long to find new partners, because Mr. Warner had appeared, genially announcing that the second dance was about to begin.

"I've asked Miss Elissa to dance," declared Arnold Hyatt, the magistrate's son, who had never shown her the slightest interest before.

Edward cast her a glance that looked almost mournful. He surrendered her to the younger Mr. Hyatt. "Miss Smith," he said, extending his hand to one of the girls in the scrum surrounding him, "may I have the honor?"

Unsurprisingly, Miss Smith was delighted. As Arnold Hyatt led her away, Elissa could only hope she would get another chance to speak with him before the night was over.

❧

Two hours later, Edward forced himself to unclench his fists. *Again.*

The problem was, Elissa was so very easy to spot, her red hair standing out like a mermaid in a school of brown trout. He was constantly spying her talking to someone else, strolling with someone else, or dancing with someone else.

When he wanted her to be talking to *him*.

On six occasions he danced a single turn with her as he and his partner made their way down the row. It was pathetic that he had counted, but there it was.

Each time he had smiled at her, unable to think of something pithy to say in the five seconds he got of her company.

And now the dance was all but over, and she was on the far side of the room where he had no hope of reaching her.

He smothered a sigh as he prepared to ask one of the girls fluttering around him for the last dance. It didn't really matter which one.

That was when he noticed that Elissa's sister Cassandra had joined their ranks. If he couldn't dance with Elissa, perhaps he could at least speak about her. "Mrs. Gorten," he said, bowing, "might you be available for the final set?"

"I am, thank you, my lord," she said. "Might we visit the refreshment table before the dance begins? How I would love a glass of punch."

"Of course," he said, offering his arm. "Please excuse us, ladies."

They wove their way through the crowd. "I would ask what you were discussing with my brother," he said, "but I suspect I would rather not know."

She laughed. "It's not as bad as you fear. I spent at least half the time peppering him with questions about your sister, Lady Morsley. I am her greatest admirer, you see."

Edward smiled. There was some rather ferocious competition for the title of Anne's greatest admirer. Anne had founded her own charity, the Ladies' Society for the Relief of the Destitute, which supported hundreds of women and children upon whom most of society had turned their backs. She'd cemented her status as a champion of the wretched last year when she broke up a criminal ring that had been selling underaged boys into a life of misery as chimney sweeps, kicking in the door and shooting the ringleader herself.

"So, half of your discussion was about Anne. Dare I to ask what you and my brother discussed the rest of the time?"

"Mostly it consisted of a full rendition of your heroics in rescuing my sister."

He groaned. "There will be no living with him now."

"I rather suspect there never was."

"You suppose correctly. Speaking of siblings, I have yet to greet your older sisters. They will think me shockingly discourteous."

Cassandra gave him a wry smile. "I beg you not to trouble yourself on that account. Helen and Daphne have lived with our aunt in Chipping Campden these past two years, and are not here toni—oh, dear," she said, stopping short.

"What is it?" Edward asked, concerned.

"Nothing serious, but I seem to have torn my hem." Cassandra abruptly changed direction and began towing him through the crowd. "A thousand apologies, Lord Fauconbridge, but I will have to see to this right away, and—ah, good evening, Elissa."

It was unbecoming, the speed with which Edward's head whipped around. There she was, the girl he'd been longing for all night, standing close enough for him to touch.

Ahem. Not that he would ever do something so grossly inappropriate, of course.

"Elissa, thank goodness you're here," Cassandra said. "I was to dance the last set with Lord Fauconbridge, but I've just torn my hem."

"Really?" Elissa leaned forward. "It looks fine from here."

"*As I was saying*," Cassandra said, whipping her skirts back and glaring at her sister, "I must see to this right away." She turned to Edward. "You don't mind if I leave you in the company of my sister, do you, my lord?"

Edward knew he was grinning, which was terribly gauche. He also knew there was not the slightest chance he could stop. "Not at all, Mrs. Gorten."

"Excellent," she said, already weaving her way through the crowd.

Edward turned to Elissa. "May I have this dance?"

"I should be delighted," she replied, smiling shyly up at him.

"So," he said, offering his arm, "you said earlier that there was something you wanted to tell me?"

"Yes." She swallowed. "You see—"

She was cut off by the sounds of the musicians tuning up. And right on cue, there was Mr. Warner, smiling as he crossed the room to invite Edward to take his place at the top of the set. *Again.*

Edward groaned. To be sure, he was in a rare state of frustration, to not even be able to exchange three sentences with her.

But even he was shocked by his next words.

"Miss Elissa, I apologize. I know I asked you for a dance, but… is there a balcony or a garden about which we might instead take a turn?"

"There is not," she said.

He sighed. He had spent the past nine years avoiding balconies and moonlit gardens as if they were malarial swamps, and the one time he actually wanted a tête-à-tête with a pretty girl, there wasn't one.

"But," Elissa continued, blushing ferociously, "they always set torches out along the river. There are a few benches, and it's nice for a stroll if you, um, if you wanted to."

"That sounds lovely," he said. He offered his arm, then led her across the room, through the doors, and out into the night.

CHAPTER 9

Outside, the river was streaked with gold from the torches lining its banks. Edward saw that they were far from the only ones with the idea to escape the confines of the assembly room and take a little air. There were several dozen groups, both couples and small clusters, scattered along both sides of the river.

They strolled down the river a way, looking for an unoccupied bench. Edward admired the torchlit scene. The river wound its way right through the center of town, the banks on both sides lined with trees—oak, maple, and weeping willow. Set a few feet farther back were pretty cottages of golden Cotswold stone, each of which seemed to be trying to outdo its neighbors with its front flower garden.

But the crown jewel of Bourton-on-the-Water was its bridges—four of them, low and arching, made of that same golden Cotswold stone, that gave the town the charming feel of a miniature Venice.

"I've always loved Bourton-on-the-Water," Edward said. "It has to be the prettiest town in all of England."

"I've hardly known anything else," Elissa said.

"There's not much out there that's better than this. Have you never been to London, then?"

"No, but I made it as far as Oxford once."

Edward nudged her with his elbow. "What did you think of the bookshops?"

She made a sound of pleasure so sensual that he felt it in his groin. "It is fortunate that Oxford is a full day's journey away. Otherwise, I would've bankrupted my family twelve times over."

"That good?"

"Oh, yes." They had come to one of the footbridges. "Let's cross here," Elissa suggested.

The crowds had thinned, and the sounds of the dance were fading into the background. Now he could hear the gentle babble of the shallow river as it meandered through town and the hooting of an owl from the next tree over.

They found a deserted bench. Across the river, they had a lovely view of a willow tree, its pale branches trailing all the way down to the water's surface. Edward settled Elissa upon the bench, then peeled off his coat and draped it around her shoulders.

"Oh! You don't have to—that is, I wouldn't want you to be cold."

He answered her with a steady look as he sat down beside her, a look that said *surely you do not believe I would ever allow a lady to be cold?*

She abandoned her protests, sensing their futility. "Thank you."

"You are most welcome." They watched the river in silence for a moment, then he said, "I want to apologize for earlier."

She glanced up at him, her brow crinkled. "Apologize? Whatever for?"

"I could tell you would rather not have led off the dancing."

She laughed. "As you saw, I'm not much of a dancer. But truly, there's no need to apologize."

"It is kind of you to say so. I fear that being around me is often a burden."

She studied him in the moonlight, and he forced himself not to squirm. "I cannot imagine that anyone who knows you would agree."

He cleared his throat. That had come out a bit more baldly than he had intended. "So, what's this announcement you've been teasing me with all night?"

"Two things, actually. Firstly, speaking of the bookshops of Oxford, I wanted to thank you. It was exceptionally kind of you to replace the copy of Plutarch I ruined."

"It was my pleasure," he said, meaning it. He realized he wanted to make Elissa St. Cyr happy, to make her life easier and better. If something as simple as a book would make her look at him the way she was right now, her green eyes filled with an intoxicating combination of sincerity, gratitude, and awe…

He would buy her a thousand volumes of Plutarch.

"It meant so much to me. Thank you." She fell silent, staring at her clasped hands.

The suspense was killing him. "You said there were two things," he said, nudging her with his elbow. She jolted beside him on the bench, then laughed, bringing a hand to her heart.

"Miss Elissa?" he asked. He had been jesting when he used the word "announcement," but now he was dying to know what it was she had to say.

"I should just come out and say it," she said, swallowing. "It is in regard to the contest being held at Oxford. The one you're entering."

He froze. "What about it?"

She peered up at him uncertainly. "I received an invitation to enter it, too."

He blinked at her, scarcely comprehending.

This was… this was *awful.*

"That's… that's wonderful," he sputtered, his shoulder giving an involuntary twitch.

Awful, his brain repeated.

It wasn't that he minded Elissa entering the contest. He certainly didn't think she should be barred from doing so just because she was a woman.

And yet… an image suddenly sprang to mind of Robert Slocombe, the man who had beaten him out as Senior Classical Medalist, and he felt the familiar darkness rising within him.

Two finalists were named for the last stage of the competition, so everyone had known the winner would be either him or Slocombe. They had been assigned a topic upon which to declaim, on opposing sides, in Latin. So when the time came for the announcement, every eye in the Senate House had been darting back and forth between the two of them. When the vice-chancellor announced Slocombe as the winner, Edward had made sure he was clapping. His smile had felt brittle, but he'd made sure it was plastered across his face. He'd caught Slocombe's eye and inclined his head in a manner he hoped appeared gracious. He had even made a point of finding him after the ceremony to shake his hand and offer his congratulations, even though all he'd wanted to do was go back to his room, shut the door, and not get out of bed for a week.

And why not shake Slocombe's hand? He didn't hate Robert Slocombe, not really.

The one he hated was himself.

To come in second… that simply was not who he was. Not who his family required him to be. It wasn't as if he was

Harrington, who was so funny, so good-hearted that everyone loved him exactly as he was. No one cared that Harrington hadn't opened a single book in his four years at Oxford. He made everyone around him happy just by being himself.

But it had been made clear to Edward from an early age that he was not like that. He was expected to be the best, to be a credit to his family.

And he had failed.

But no one could accuse him of having been a poor sport. He had put on a good enough front to pass in front of Robert Slocombe.

But he knew he couldn't fool Elissa. Those sea-glass-green eyes already saw far more than he wanted her to. And even if he could never have her, even if he would probably never see her again after the contest, he wanted Elissa to think well of him. Which meant he did not want her to be sitting right next to him as he grappled with his innermost demons. The last thing he wanted was for her to discover that he was the kind of monster who couldn't even be happy for good-hearted Robert Slocombe (or whoever won the bloody contest).

He glanced down, and sure enough, Elissa was studying him carefully. She gave a bleak chuckle. "You don't look as if you think it's wonderful."

See? Already she discerns too much. He wiped all traces of expression away, but her face remained a portrait of skepticism. He sighed. "I'll be honest. I don't much relish the idea of competing against you."

She laughed. "I don't relish the idea either. I've read your *Prometheus Unbound* and it's brilliant." She closed her eyes, a look of rapture settling across her features. "The final section, the one you composed, is probably the most beautiful Greek verse I've ever read." She shook her head. "I love

Aeschylus, but I must say, his lines suffer greatly in comparison to yours."

He strove to make his tone light so she would not see how deeply uncomfortable he was. "Why Miss St. Cyr, I would not have thought to hear such blasphemy from you."

She laughed. "I pray you won't mention it to my father. But I will confess something. Your translation is what I reach for whenever I'm feeling low." She pressed a hand to her heart as she quoted, "'Day after day, I lay on this rock, bleeding, forgotten, in chains, and yet, I am still here. The king of the gods himself has not managed to destroy me. I have that one thought to cling to, and it is enough.'" She made an appreciative sound. "It lifts me up when nothing else will." She smiled up at him, and he watched her gaze sharpen. "Wait—are you *blushing?*"

"Probably," he said, noticing that his shoulders were hunched. He forced himself to straighten. "Could we discuss something else?"

"Of course, although I confess I am surprised. Most men like nothing better than to have praise lavished upon them."

"Only when such praise is deserved."

She tilted her head to the side, studying him. "I assure you it is."

"I assure you it is not."

She bit her lip. "Do you truly not understand how excellent it is? I am far from the only one who thinks so. Surely you read the reviews."

He stared off into the darkness. "I think it is common enough for authors to see nothing but the flaws in their own work."

"I cannot think of a single one," she said softly. They lapsed into silence. After a moment, Elissa cleared her throat. "The point is, you're going to be tough to beat."

"You're the one who will be tough to beat. You're obviously brilliant."

She gave a startled laugh. "Much as I hate to argue with a man who just called me brilliant, I'm not sure how you came to that conclusion. You haven't read any of my verse since I was fourteen years old." She glanced up at him, and the guilt must have shown on his face, because she froze. "What is it?"

"I'm sorry. I shouldn't have done it," he said in a rush, "but the other day, it was your room your parents brought me to. To change out of my wet clothes. And I… I could not help but notice the project you had out upon your desk. The translation of Catullus," he clarified.

"Oh!" A becoming flush stained her cheeks, and she seemed at a loss for words, which was no wonder considering he had just introduced the most inappropriate topic of conversation imaginable: *when I was naked in your room*.

His palms felt clammy inside his gloves. "I only glanced at the top sheet. But I should not have read even that much, and I apologize."

"No, it's all right. I daresay I would have read it, too. I'm only a bit embarrassed because it was still very rough."

"It was excellent," he hastened to reassure her. "You captured Catullus's voice, and that is the hardest thing."

"Th-thank you." She still looked flustered, but also pleased.

He cast about for a change of subject. "May I ask how you came to the attention of the contest's organizers?"

She blanched. He had known her only a short time, but he felt certain that in that moment, the emotion Elissa St. Cyr was feeling was *panic*.

"Um," she said after a moment. "Well, you know those poetry contests they used to run in the local Oxford papers?"

"Of course." He chuckled. "I even entered a few of them when I was sixteen."

"I used to enter them, too."

"Ah." That explained it, then. "Did you ever win?"

"Once. That was what brought me to Oxford—to claim my prize. One entire guinea."

He smiled at the thought of a young Elissa and how excited she must have been. "At least you're in practice. I haven't done any meaningful study since leaving Cambridge."

Elissa looked up, surprised. "Have you not? I felt certain you would be a lifelong scholar."

Edward repressed the urge to squirm or look away. "No, I have the running of my family's estate. It quite occupies my time."

This was not precisely true. Edward did handle the estate business, and it did occupy his time. But he could have left it to his father. Then there was the fact that he could probably generate ninety percent of the estate's current profits (which had doubled on his watch) while putting in half as much time.

But even though he wasn't quite so busy as he pretended to be, the idea of working on a translation was paralyzing. After his experience with *Prometheus Unbound*, and then losing to Robert Slocombe, he found he had difficulty starting anything. Flaws were inevitable. His efforts would never be good enough and he knew it, which made it impossible to convince himself to begin. It was so much easier to fill his days with the mundane.

Beside him, Elissa was shaking her head. "That is truly a shame. A great loss for us all." She glanced up at him. "What have you been doing to prepare for the contest?"

He sighed. "Not much. I should probably shut myself in the library for the next week and do nothing but study."

She gave him a wry look. "And instead, here you are, consorting with the enemy."

"You're not my enemy," he said quickly, willing it to be true.

"That's not what you said the other day."

"Nonsense," he said, striving to inject some levity into his voice. "My only enemy is the mysterious translator of *On the Sublime*."

"Right." She tilted her head back to gaze at the canopy of leaves above them. "Of course."

There was a hum of excitement down the river. It seemed the dance had concluded.

"Come," he said, rising to his feet and offering his arm. "Your family will be missing you."

Elissa returned his coat just before they re-crossed the river. As they strolled along in silence, Edward told himself this was for the best. His future could not include Elissa St. Cyr, so it was better that he resume thinking about her with the proper reserve. If the news that she would be competing against him was a bit like a bucket of cold water dumped over his head, well, he probably needed that bucket of cold water (dumped three feet lower, truth be told).

And so he returned her to her parents, wished them all a cordial good night, and went in search of Harrington, whom he found lounging on a bench, being fawned over by a flock of twenty-some-odd young women.

Harrington mocked him for the duration of the carriage ride home, but that was all right.

He would see Elissa St. Cyr precisely one more time—at the upcoming contest. By then, he would be betrothed to another. He would be safe from her.

CHAPTER 10

$\mathscr{E}$lissa received the first letter the following day:

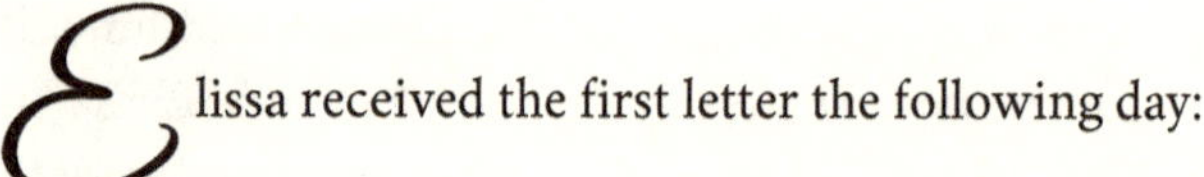

MISS ST. CYR,

I pray you will forgive the imposition of my writing to you without an introduction, but I am hosting a house party next week, and it would please me greatly if you and your sister Cassandra would consent to attend.

I will send our carriage to collect you at one o'clock on Monday.
Yours,
Georgiana Cheltenham

ELISSA BLANCHED. She could not imagine why Edward's mother was inviting her, of all people, to a house party.

But she absolutely could not attend.

Ever since Edward had rescued her from the pond, she had been steeling herself for his eventual disdain. She had expected it would come after she defeated him in the contest.

But judging by his stilted response when she told him of her intention to enter, it had arrived earlier than expected.

She sighed. She had tossed and turned half the night, scrutinizing his reactions, from the brief flash of paralysis that had washed over his face when she'd told him to the cordial-but-distant way he had taken his leave. To be sure, he had not said anything untoward, but his abrupt change in manner surely indicated his disapproval of a woman supposing she was good enough to compete against the men.

Didn't it?

As she pulled out a sheet of paper to respond to the countess, she reminded herself for the thousandth time that it did not matter. Edward Astley had no place in her future.

The sooner she got that through her thick skull, the better.

MAY IT PLEASE YOUR LADYSHIP,

I lack sufficient words to express how honored I was to receive your kind invitation. I fear, however, that I would be entirely out of place at such an elegant gathering. I must confess that I do not own even one dress that you would deem presentable. I pray you will forgive me for therefore having to beg off, and that you will accept instead my most sincere thanks for thinking to include me.

Your humble servant,

Elissa St. Cyr

A REPLY CAME the very next day in a cheerful, looping hand.

DEAR MISS ELISSA,

My name is Lucy, and I am Edward and Harrington's little sister. Mama showed me your letter, and we were distressed to think that you might decline to join us for a reason that is so easily overcome! My brother Harrington has informed me that we are of a size, and there is nothing I should like better than to share all of my gowns with you. Please believe me when I say that I have plenty, and you will never again need to worry about such a thing. Here I would normally tell you about my sister Caro, who is constantly commissioning new dresses for us all whether we need them or not, but I will spare you the details as you will be meeting her for yourself in just a few short days.

We all cannot wait to meet you!

Yours affectionately,

Lucy Astley

DEAR LADY LUCY,

I was touched beyond measure to receive your generous offer. I must confess, however, that my reluctance stems from more than my humble wardrobe. I am but a simple country tutor's daughter and would be sorely out of place at such an elegant gathering. I tremble to think how many faux pas I would commit on the first day alone. I pray you will show this to your mother and beg her pardon on my behalf. Thank you so much for your kindness, which I shall never forget.

Yours sincerely,

Elissa St. Cyr

THE FOLLOWING day brought a response from yet another hand, this one all sharp angles and... Elissa touched the paper tentatively. Where did one obtain purple ink?

MISS ELISSA,

I am Isabella, Lucy's twin. At first, I took great offense when my mother asked me to write to you. I am sure you will agree that it is galling to admit that your parent has the right of something, but on this isolated and almost unprecedented occasion, I find I cannot contradict my mother.

I therefore wish to inform you that your concerns about lacking the polish to attend our house party are unfounded, because, in Mama's memorable turn of phrase, "she could not possibly be less refined than you, Isabella." I fear it is true. I am, how you say, a hoyden. I have none of the feminine graces. None. I do not sew. I do not pour tea. I do not make polite conversation. I answer only to my inner muse, which means I say precisely what I think at all times, in all situations. When I was six years old, I told the King of England himself that I thought his waistcoat ugly. Fortunately, he laughed, rather than having me beheaded. But I digress.

My point is, you need not concern yourself that anybody will remark upon whatever minor foibles you might commit, because they will be far too busy gossiping about me.

I therefore look forward to meeting you three days hence.

Yours,

Isabella Astley

Dear Lady Isabella,

I pray you will forgive me, as I suspect you might not consider the word "charming" a compliment, but that is what I found your letter. As to your assertion that nobody would remark upon my missteps, I fear you underestimate my innate talent for disaster. I once tripped over a pig. And I beg you not to force me to confess to the Bicklebury Bog Debacle.

Alas, I would be entirely out of place at your mother's house party. But please accept my thanks for your exceptional kindness.

Yours sincerely,

Elissa St. Cyr

. . .

THE FOLLOWING DAY, the elegant hand from the first letter had returned.

MISS ELISSA,

How I have enjoyed reading your feeble attempts to get out of attending my house party, after I have specifically requested your presence. I have found them ever so diverting. I would not have thought there was a corner of England, much less of Gloucestershire, where my reputation did not precede me, but as you do not appear to know with whom you are dealing, I regret to inform you that I am the most manipulative woman in all of England, and I always get my way.

Checkmate.

Yours,

Georgiana Cheltenham

PS- YOU NEED NOT WORRY yourself on account of the pigs. Although my husband is renowned for his herd of Gloucestershire Old Spots, we keep them fenced.

PPS- You will want to hide this letter and get out the first one I sent you before your sister comes bursting through the door.

ELISSA FROWNED AS SHE COMPLIED. What on earth did that—

The door to her room slammed against the wall as Cassandra came flying in, a letter clutched in her hand. "Oh, Elissa," she cried, "you will never believe the good news! I have received a letter from *Lady Anne Astley*—that is to say, she is Lady Morsley now, of course, as she has married the marquess's son. She says her mother, the Countess of Cheltenham, is hosting a house party in just a few days' time. And we are to be invited!" Cassandra pressed the letter to her chest. "Lady Morsley lives just two miles away from the house and will be in attendance daily. Her brother, Harrington, told her about my admiration of her charitable society, and she condescended to write and say how much she is looking forward to meeting me. *Me!*" Cassandra pulled out a handkerchief and dabbed at her eyes. "Oh, Elissa—it is too wonderful. I will get to meet my heroine!"

Elissa stared at Lady Cheltenham's letter in wonder. She felt no annoyance at having been bested, only awe at the countess's display of tactical superiority.

It seemed that war was about to resume with France. Elissa wondered if anyone had considered deploying Lady Cheltenham to the Continent.

Cassandra looked at Elissa hopefully. "Did you receive an invitation from the countess?"

"I did," she said, passing it to her sister.

"Oh, my gracious—she is sending the Cheltenham carriage for us! We only have two days to prepare. We will need to start packing immediately."

Cassandra proceeded to flutter about the room, planning, while Elissa pulled out a sheet of paper to compose her surrender.

CHAPTER 11

On the day the house party was to begin, Edward was in the front parlor trying to convince himself to open the copy of Euripides' *Hippolytus,* one of several volumes he had brought from the library so he could finally get some studying done when his father appeared in the doorway.

He sprang up from the Chippendale writing desk. "Good morning, Father."

The earl nodded as he entered the room. He was tall and broad-shouldered, his waist trim even in his fifties, and had the same dark hair as Edward. Other than the blue eyes Edward had inherited from his mother, he was almost a mirror image of his father.

The earl gestured for Edward to resume his seat but did not sit himself. "I'm surprised to find you in here. I went looking for you in the library."

"I wanted to be near the front of the house so I could greet our guests as they arrive."

The earl squinted at the stack of books on the desk.

"Although it looks as if you have brought the library with you."

"That contest taking place at Oxford is only one week away. I was hoping to do a little studying. I did go over the numbers from last month earlier this morning. I wouldn't want you to think I'm neglecting—"

"I know you would never neglect the estate. And next week at Oxford, I'm sure you'll trounce the lot of them. You always make the family proud. Unlike your brother." The earl raked a hand through his hair. "You're not the one causing a scandal with some opera dancer."

"Truly, Father, that wasn't Harrington's fault. The girl was unattached. That Markham fellow has a reputation for being a hothead and could not handle his disappointment when she chose Harrington."

The earl snorted. "Yes, well, I never have to worry about *you* getting challenged to a duel over some bit of fluff."

Edward swallowed. "I hope I do not create the impression that I am contradicting you, sir. But I do believe that Harrington did everything within his powers to restore the peace."

His father clapped him on the shoulder. "It speaks well of you that you would defend your brother. But Harrington had to be brought in line. Twenty-six years old, no prospects, and splashing the family name across the scandal sheets." The earl shook his head. "But the threat of sending him to India seems to have made an impression."

Edward dropped his gaze to the ledgers. He hadn't necessarily disagreed with his father that Harrington needed a push. Not because of the recent incident, but because it was high time his brother embarked upon a career. There were a number of possibilities—the army, civil service, the church (all right, perhaps the church wasn't the *ideal* option).

Harrington could be very persuasive, and Edward fancied he might do well in politics.

But it was difficult for a man to establish himself in any of these careers. All of them required either funds, connections, or both. And after the scandal, their father had made his threat that if Harrington set a toe out of line one more time, the only career he would support would be with the East India Company.

Edward shook himself. It would not come to that. He would not allow it. He would find some way to win that contest. The alternative was too horrible even to contemplate.

His father nodded crisply. "Yes, I daresay the threat of India has done it, and we won't be seeing any more misbehavior from Harrington. But I'm not here to talk about your brother and his opera dancers. Your mother informs me that you are contemplating a more respectable alliance."

"You have been informed correctly, sir."

"Is there a particular young lady you have in mind?"

"There is not. I asked Mother to choose the candidates. I trust her judgment."

His father squeezed his shoulder. "That's the way. I daresay your mother will find you the perfect girl. Then we'll have you well-settled, in addition to Anne and Caro." The earl barked out a laugh as he strolled across the room toward the door. "I despair of finding a man willing to take on Izzie. And pity the poor girl who finds herself shackled to Harrington. But yours is the marriage that matters most. You're the one who will continue the family line." The earl paused in the doorway. "I'm sure you'll make me proud once again by picking the perfect countess."

"Thank you, sir." Edward felt slightly queasy as he watched his father's retreating form. He opened the volume of Euripides and tried to concentrate on the words, but his thoughts kept straying. He was curious about which young ladies his mother had invited. He hoped she had found someone he might like. A girl who was intelligent. Intelligent and well-read. Someone who made him smile.

Would it be too much to ask that she have red hair?

Edward groaned. This line of thought was useless. The perfect countess, that was who he needed, who he would be required to choose. The sooner he put Elissa St. Cyr out of his mind, the better.

"My lord," the butler said, appearing in the doorway, "your first guests have arrived."

Edward rose and straightened his coat. "Thank you, Harding."

One carriage had pulled up beneath the columned portico, and he could see another coming up the drive. A footman rushed to open the door of the first carriage, and Edward smiled as he saw his close friend, Marcus Latimer, the Marquess of Graverley, emerge.

"Graverley," Edward said, jogging down the steps to shake his friend's hand. "Welcome. It was good of you to come."

"It was, wasn't it?" Graverley said. Edward snorted, but they were both grinning. Graverley was the only son of the Duke of Trevissick and due to inherit an outlandish fortune of silver and copper mines. He was widely considered to be the most eligible bachelor in all of England and was not lacking in self-regard.

The second carriage drew to a halt, but before the footman could lay his hand upon the door handle, it swung open and out climbed Archibald Nettlethorpe-Ogilvy.

Edward strode over, extending his hand. "Mr. Nettlethorpe-Ogilvy, welcome."

Mr. Nettlethorpe-Ogilvy's grandfather was an obscenely wealthy blacksmith-turned-iron-magnate. His only grandchild was rumored to have inherited the engineering acumen that had unfortunately skipped his father's generation. He clasped Edward's hand, his grip a hair firmer than was comfortable. "Fauconbridge, thank you for having me."

"It is our pleasure." Edward gestured toward the marquess, who had wandered over. As the three of them served together on the board of Anne's society, introductions were not necessary, so Edward said, "You know Graverley, of course."

"Good afternoon, Graverley," Mr. Nettlethorpe-Ogilvy said, then strolled around to the back of his carriage. Edward watched in astonishment as he began unstrapping his own luggage.

"Stop that," Graverley snapped. "A gentleman does not carry his own trunk. Leave it for the footmen."

"Hmm?" Mr. Nettlethorpe-Ogilvy looked up. "Oh, I just wanted to see to my bassoon. It's fragile."

Graverley pinched the bridge of his nose. "Tell me you didn't really bring a bassoon. And what in seven hells are you wearing?" He gestured toward Mr. Nettlethorpe-Ogilvy's jacket with a flick of his wrist. "I sent you to my tailor. You have proper clothing now. I've seen it. And yet you show up here, wearing that hideous sack."

Mr. Nettlethorpe-Ogilvy frowned. "I brought my old things. Are we not supposed to dress less formally in the country?"

Graverley made a sound of frustration and stalked up the front steps.

"Ignore him," Edward whispered, leading Mr. Nettlethorpe-Ogilvy inside.

They repaired to the parlor in which Edward had been working. Harding poured a round of drinks.

Graverley took his brandy to a tall, wing-back chair in the corner, but Mr. Nettlethorpe-Ogilvy remained standing, draining his glass of port in one go. "Thank you. If you'll excuse me, I'd like to take this to the music room," he said, patting his bassoon case.

"Of course," Edward said, setting his own glass down. "Let me summon someone to show you—"

"Why don't I show him?" said a feminine voice from the door behind him. Edward turned to see Cecilia Chenoweth, his sister Caroline's good friend and the daughter of their recently deceased rector, standing framed in the doorway in a dove-grey half-mourning dress.

"Miss Chenoweth," Mr. Nettlethorpe-Ogilvy said warmly as Ceci entered. He bowed over her hand. Ceci was also on the board of Anne's charity, so they knew each other. "I imagine you could find it with your eyes closed."

Ceci smiled. "I probably could." Ceci was an amazing talent on the pianoforte and did indeed practice for several hours each day. She turned to Edward. "I was just wondering if Caro had arrived."

"Not yet, but when she does, you will be the first to know."

"Excellent." She accepted Mr. Nettlethorpe-Ogilvy's arm. "Did you bring any sheet music? I don't think the Astleys have much of anything for bassoon, but if you have the scores, perhaps I could accompany—"

As they turned toward the door, she noticed Lord Graverley seated in the corner. The words died on her lips, and she staggered to a halt. "My lord, I—" She cleared her throat, then dropped a hasty curtsey. "I'm so sorry, I—I didn't realize you were..." She trailed off, her eyes fixed on the carpet.

Graverley arched a single eyebrow and spoke in a voice as dark as a Haut-Brion vin de Bordeaux. "Miss Chenoweth."

She stood frozen in the center of the room, cheeks aflame, until Mr. Nettlethorpe-Ogilvy laid his hand atop hers. "Shall we?" he asked softly.

"Y-yes." She curtseyed again. "Please excuse us, Lord Graverley, Lord Fauconbridge."

Once they'd left the room, Graverley asked, "Is she usually like that?"

Edward took the chair facing Graverley's. "If you mean chatty and cheerful, then yes." He gave his friend a pointed look. "She would have been less startled had you alerted her to your presence by standing when a lady entered the room."

"I didn't know she could speak. I hated to interrupt her."

"She's usually quite gregarious."

"She never says a word at board meetings."

"That's because you're terrifying."

"Me?" Graverley smirked. "I am the merest pussycat."

Edward rolled his eyes.

Graverley took a sip from his glass then set it aside. "That girl is a tragedy."

"It's terrible, yes. To lose her mother so young, and now her father, too."

"That's not what I meant." At Edward's curious look, Graverley held up a hand. "Don't get me wrong, I know all about dead mothers." Graverley's own mother had died when he was ten, and Edward was surprised to hear him mention it. Even though Graverley was his closest friend, Edward didn't know how she had died. Whenever someone mentioned it, Graverley would pointedly change the subject.

"What I mean," Graverley continued, "is that it's a tragedy to have all of that *lusciousness*"—he traced a curve in the air—"wasted on a mousy little rector's daughter too timid to string three words together."

That didn't describe Ceci's personality at all, but Edward wasn't about to say as much. He gave his friend a sharp look. "I see that now would be a good time to mention that I have known Miss Chenoweth since she was two years old, and I consider her to be practically my own sister."

Graverley wrinkled his nose. "You never let me have any fun. Next you'll tell me that not only may I not debauch Miss Chenoweth, but there will be a horde of respectable young ladies swarming me all week."

Edward laughed blackly. "I'm afraid you have it exactly. They're meant to be swarming me, but they're likely to latch onto you as well."

"Is your mother after you to wed, then?"

Edward wiped a drop of condensation from the side of his glass. "I asked her to invite them. I've decided it's time for me to marry." He glanced up and found his friend scowling. "Oh, come off it, Graverley. Don't look at me like that."

"I will look at you precisely how I wish. Especially when you're making a mistake of this magnitude."

"I'm going to have to marry someone. As will you, one of these days."

"True. And I would not object, were there a woman in whom you held the slightest interest."

Edward snorted. There was a woman who interested him, all right.

He just couldn't have her.

"There are only so many 'acceptable' options, and I've already met them all. I may as well just go ahead and pick one."

Graverley leaned forward. "There are new girls coming out every year. Including my sister, Diana. I think the two of you would suit."

Edward paused, considering. He had never met Lady Diana. He was given to understand that after Graverley's mother died, she had been sent to an obscure corner of Yorkshire to be brought up by a great aunt.

As the daughter of a duke, she was bound to meet his parents' criteria. "How old is she again?"

"Eighteen."

Edward shook his head. "Too young. Were she a few years older, I would consider it. But I mean to marry this year. In the coming weeks, if I can manage it."

Graverley gave him a baleful look. "You do realize you're dashing my plans to marry you off to Diana."

"Since when have you been planning this?"

Graverley sighed. "Since about three minutes after I met you. No, it's true," he said, seeing Edward's skeptical expression. "You're the only man on the face of this earth who's good enough for *my* little sister."

Edward leaned back in his chair. "Careful. That sounded almost like a compliment."

"Indeed." Graverley stood. "I dole one out once every decade or so."

Edward snorted, then signaled a footman to show Graverley to his rooms. "We have you in the best room in the house."

"Tell me something I don't know," Graverley called over his shoulder as he disappeared down the hall.

CHAPTER 12

*E*dward spent the next two hours busily employed.

First, it was Graverley, who came storming back into the parlor fifteen minutes after having departed. He slapped both hands on the desk in front of Edward. "I can hear the bassoon," he said through gritted teeth.

Indeed, it did sound as if Mr. Nettlethorpe-Ogilvy and Miss Chenoweth had settled in to play a few duets. "Your room sits directly over the music room," Edward confirmed.

"Then I will be needing a new room."

"But that is the best room in the—"

"I do not care," Graverley snapped. "If my ears are subject to that ghastly croaking sound, then it is demonstrably *not* the best room in the house."

Edward shrugged. "Harding," he called to the butler, who promptly appeared in the doorway. "Move Lord Graverley to the Etruscan room, will you?"

Harding bowed. "At once, my lord."

This gave Edward something new to worry about between greeting guests, as moving Graverley to another room necessitated reshuffling the room assignments. He asked Harding to fetch his mother, as this was more her realm, but was informed that she was occupied. He did his best, but feared his mother, the perfect hostess, would find his choices lacking.

It was midafternoon and almost all of the guests had arrived when Harding appeared in the doorway. "Another carriage, my lord."

"Thank you," Edward replied, standing and straightening his coat. Outside, he was surprised to see the Astley carriage pulling up. Funny, he thought as he jogged down the short flight of steps leading to the drive, he hadn't recalled that any guests were making use of the family carriage.

The door opened and out popped the bonneted head of Elissa St. Cyr. Edward completely missed the last two steps and went careening headlong into the drive, barely managing to keep his feet.

He felt his shoulder give a violent twitch. How could he have been so careless? How *humiliating*.

But it didn't seem that Elissa had witnessed his stumble. With her head tipped back and her mouth hanging open, she appeared fully occupied in gaping at the columned portico.

Edward straightened his coat, then approached. "Miss Elissa," he said, reaching out to hand her down, "welcome to Harrington Hall."

Her head whipped around, her green eyes wide as saucers. "Edward! Oh, my gracious, I didn't..." Her mouth closed with a pop, and color rose to her cheeks. "That is to say, Lord Fauconbridge—"

Edward was only a trifle less disoriented, and found that the words, "You can call me Edward," were what came blurting out of his mouth.

May, he silently corrected himself. You *may* call me Edward. Good God, she would think he hadn't the slightest command of the English language.

But Elissa did not appear to have noticed, for she was still babbling. "I'm so sorry, you caught me off guard, I cannot believe I said that out…" She trailed off, performing a slow spin as she took in the flawlessly manicured sweep of the lawn, the Palladian bridge spanning the man-made stream that had been mapped out by Capability Brown himself, the northwest wing made of golden Cotswold sandstone that glowed in the afternoon light, and the portico with its six Corinthian columns of gleaming white marble. "This is your *house?*" she sputtered.

Edward could not suppress a smile. "Not yet. Why do you ask?"

"Because it is the most exquisite sight I have ever beheld. If it's not too much trouble, I would like to sit just here," she said, indicating the top step of the portico, "for the next week, gazing out over the lawn. I think I would find myself perfectly content."

"I believe we can do better than that," Edward said. "Wait until you see the Greek folly."

Elissa's face lit up. She turned to her sister, who had emerged from the carriage. "Cassandra, they have a Greek folly!"

Edward reached up to hand her sister down. "Mrs. Gorten, welcome."

"Thank you so much for inviting us, my lord," Cassandra replied smoothly, striding up the steps before he could offer his arm, leaving him to pair with Elissa.

The carriage pulled off toward the stables and two footmen started up the steps, one carrying a small trunk, the other only a leather satchel. "Is this all of your luggage?" Edward asked, offering his arm.

"Yes," Elissa replied, laughing. "The trunk is Cassandra's. I only brought the satchel. It's mostly books. I scarcely brought any clothing—" She broke off, cringing, then turned to him with a familiar expression of mortification.

Edward was trying very hard not to laugh. "Please, tell me more."

"Your sister, Lady Lucy!" she squeaked. "You see, when your mother first invited me, I begged her to excuse me as I have nothing appropriate to wear. Lady Lucy replied with the kindest letter, offering to share her gowns with me."

"That's our Lucy," Edward confirmed.

"I then attempted to decline on the grounds that I am completely lacking in anything resembling social polish. Oddly, your mother was not deterred." She shook her head. "I told her about the time I tripped over the pig and everything!"

"You tripped over a pig?"

Elissa went perfectly still, then peered up at him, biting her lower lip. "I would appreciate it if you would forget I said that."

Edward grinned as he led her up the steps. "Not a chance."

She wrinkled her nose at him. "In any case, your mother is strangely persistent and downright underhanded, if you will excuse my saying so."

"I cannot object, as it is demonstrably true."

"She is absolutely impossible to refuse. At first, I couldn't imagine why she even wanted us here, but I finally figured it out. It was really very kind of her. Apparently, your brother told her how much Cassandra admires your sister, Lady Morsley, and that is the reason she..." Elissa trailed off as they came into the circular rotunda at the center of the house. "Oh, my *gracious*..."

Her head tipped back again as she took in the sky-lit space. The alabaster columns ringing the room soared fifty feet to the ceiling above, gleaming white against walls of

Wedgewood blue. The ceiling was elaborately decorated with vines and medallions, the white plasterwork clean against the saturated blue background, culminating in a large, painted roundel at the apex of the dome.

Their footsteps echoed on the marble floor as Elissa wandered unconsciously through the room, her mouth open and her eyes darting everywhere as she took it all in. Her head was tilted back to the ceiling, and she would have collided with a recumbent statue of Hector succumbing to his wounds had Edward not steered her around it. She was so entranced, she didn't give the slightest sign of having noticed what he was doing.

She gasped as she noticed the painted roundel in the center of the ceiling. "It's Cupid and Psyche!" she exclaimed, a smile lighting her face as her eyes found his. "'She sees those radiant locks, ambrosia-scented, the milk-white neck, the damask cheek over which wander those glorious curls, whose brilliancy makes the very lamplight tremble.'"

"Apuleius's *Metamorphoses*," Edward said at once. "I've never read that translation. Whose is it?"

"Oh, it's—it's mine," she said, looking down, abruptly self-conscious.

Why was he not surprised? "It is excellent. I have always despaired of those lines. It is impossible to do them justice. It confounds the mind that they were written by Apuleius, of all people. For almost all of *Metamorphoses* he alternates between the crass, the gruesome, and the farcical, and then without warning he writes—"

"—the most incandescently beautiful sentences in all of Latin prose," Elissa said, finishing his thought.

"Yes!" he said, gazing at her with a touch of wonder as he led her across the room. He gestured to the walls. "If you look at the bas-reliefs, they tell the rest of the story. Here is Psyche, awakening in the enchanted grove. And here is

Cupid, sent by his mother, Venus, to curse her for possessing such beauty as to rival a goddess, instead falling in love at first sight…"

Edward broke off, as the lines between myth and reality began to blur. He glanced down at the girl he had stumbled upon in an enchanted grove. Her cheeks were scarlet, and she did not meet his eye as she gestured to another panel and said, "And here is Psyche, willing to descend into hell itself to win a future with her beloved."

Edward found he had seized her hand. "Elissa—"

A cough echoed through the vastness of the hall. Edward jerked upright as he recalled that they were not alone.

To be specific, they were being watched by Elissa's sister, Harding, and two footmen, both of whom were openly gaping. No doubt they had heard every word in the cavernous hall.

Harding cleared his throat. "My lord, to which rooms shall we convey Mrs. Gorten and Miss St. Cyr's things?"

Edward suddenly knew precisely where Elissa St. Cyr belonged. "Take Mrs. Gorten's things to the primrose bedroom. And Miss Elissa will be just down the hall, in the jade green room."

One of the footmen's mouths actually fell open, as Edward assigned Elissa to the most elegant room in the house, originally intended for the likes of Lord Graverley. Harding's eyes were all but twinkling. "At once, my lord," he said with a bow.

CHAPTER 13

*I*t was not proper for him to accompany Elissa to her bedroom, even with her sister there to chaperone. Edward knew that.

But he found himself doing it, anyway. He was not about to miss her reaction. So here he was, leading the way up the stairs with Elissa on one arm and Cassandra on the other.

"The house has four wings that connect to this central rotunda. It forms the shape of the letter 'H,' for 'Harrington Hall,'" Edward explained. "You will have the southwest wing to yourselves. Most of the rooms are closed for repainting. We had hoped to complete it in advance of the house party, but it's been so miserably wet of late. You will be just here, Mrs. Gorten," he said, gesturing to a cheerful room of primrose yellow.

"How lovely," she said, peering in.

"And you," he said, glancing down at Elissa, not wanting to miss a second of her reaction, "will be here, in the jade green room."

She didn't disappoint him. As Elissa crossed the threshold, she gasped out loud, one hand flying to her heart, the other coming up to cover her mouth. The room was ornate, to be sure, from the gold gilt doorframes to the delicate Chippendale furniture in cream and gold. But its crown jewel was the wallpaper. Imported from China, it was a pale jade green silk, hand-painted with white flowers, delicate vines, and dozens of brightly colored birds.

The wallpaper reminded Edward of the hand-cut flowers Elissa had used to adorn her reading nook. He'd had a feeling she would like it.

She wandered across the room and up the two steps that led to the bay window overlooking the back lawn. Set off from the rest of the room by two columns, it had just space enough for a cream silk chaise longue framed in gold.

Across the room, Cassandra was feigning an intense fascination with a large porcelain urn. Meanwhile, Elissa stood staring out the window as if in a trance. A full minute passed, and she said nothing. Edward cleared his throat as he came around the chaise to stand beside her. "The wallpaper was imported from China," he offered. He waited a few beats, then added, "The birds and flowers were painted by hand." She gave no indication of having heard. He gestured to the view out the window. "I mentioned the Greek folly earlier. You can see it just there, upon the hill."

Still she remained silent. "This is the queen's favorite room," he added after a moment. "She always stays here when the royal family comes to Cheltenham to take the waters."

This seemed to shake Elissa from her stupor. She turned to face him, and he saw that her face registered… despair?

"I cannot stay here," she said, her voice quavering.

"Why ever not? Don't…" He swallowed down the bitter taste of failure that was rising up in his throat. "Don't you like it?" he added softly.

"Like it!" she exclaimed. "I never even imagined anything could exist that is so utterly exquisite."

He felt his shoulders relax a fraction. "Then what is it?"

"I don't belong here. I mean—" She wrung her hands. "You've seen my house. It looks nothing like this. I am not from this world. And besides," she said, making a sweeping gesture with her hand, "how on earth did I come to be assigned to the queen's favorite room?"

"In truth, Graverley was to be in here," Edward admitted.

Elissa's face was blank. "Graverley?"

"You know, the Marquess of Graverley." She gave no sign of recognition. "Heir to the Duke of Trevissick?" Her face registered nothing. "Have you truly not heard of him?"

"Should I have?" she asked, her brow creasing. "Is he local to the area?"

"Er—no, he is not."

Elissa shrugged. "Well, whoever he is, if he is the heir to a dukedom, then he is a far more suitable occupant for this room than I."

And suddenly Edward understood what made Elissa St. Cyr special: she had no idea who the most eligible bachelor in all of England was. She could not be bothered to care, because, unlike the rest of the world, she did not spend her time obsessing over the latest fashion, the largest fortune, or the loftiest title. No, she spent her free moments reading Plutarch in a rowboat, because that was what actually made her happy.

Edward had spent all afternoon greeting guests who took great pains to appear unimpressed by his family's stately home, who were careful to display a fashionable ennui even as they calculated the value of every candlestick down to the last farthing.

And then in walked Elissa, unable to conceal her delight.

Edward never showed his true feelings to anyone. He

knew what reactions society expected, and he responded accordingly. The mere thought of showing his true emotions seemed bizarre. Foreign. *Terrifying.*

And yet… when was the last time he had felt the unbridled joy Elissa had radiated when she stepped into the rotunda?

Elissa continued, "And what will this Lord Gravy think—"

Edward tried and failed to stifle a laugh. "It is Lord *Graverley.* Although I will give you any forfeit you like if you will call him 'Lord Gravy' to his face."

She wrinkled her nose at him, but she was smiling. "Lord Graverley," she amended. "What will he think when he arrives to find the best bedroom already occupied?"

"He arrived hours ago and promptly asked for a different room."

Her jaw dropped. "He found *this* room unsatisfactory?"

"On account of the bassoon," Edward added.

She frowned, then slowly turned, searching the room in confusion. "The—the bassoon?"

"Yes. We're directly above the music room, you see."

Just then, a delicate melody drifted up through the floor. "Oh, that is beautiful!" Elissa exclaimed. "When I thought this room could not get any lovelier, it even has music."

"That is Miss Chenoweth," Edward hastened to explain. "She is a rare talent on the pianoforte."

Elissa's eyes were closed in apparent rapture. "I have never heard her equal."

"But, you see, Mr. Nettlethorpe-Ogilvy plays the—"

He was interrupted by a squawking sound reminiscent of a donkey's bray, and loud even through the floor that separated them, as Mr. Nettlethorpe-Ogilvy made his entrance. Elissa jumped, and when she opened her eyes, she wore one of her familiar open-book expressions, an adorable combination of befuddlement and alarm.

"—the bassoon," Edward finished awkwardly.

Elissa's face held the horrified expression for five excruciating seconds, before the corners of her eyes crinkled and her lips curled up.

The next thing Edward knew, they were both laughing uncontrollably.

He felt rather than saw her grab his arm for balance. Just when he thought they were getting themselves under control, he made the mistake of looking at her, which caused them both to dissolve into a fresh fit of laughter.

After another minute, he offered Elissa his handkerchief, which she accepted to dab at her eyes. "And so you see," he said, "the room is not nearly as fine as you had imagined."

She swatted at his arm. "The room remains exquisite, and the bassoon does not detract from it in the least. Mr. Nettlethorpe-Ogilvy is not bad at all once you, er, know what to expect." Her face fell a fraction. "Although I will not be around to hear him. I really should go."

Deep down, Edward knew this was for the best. As much as he didn't want her to leave, in the end, he could not have Elissa St. Cyr in his life. What good would it do him to have her here for a week? He was already far too attached to her. And with the contest looming next week… he didn't know precisely what was going to happen, or how he was going to react. But he had a nagging feeling that he was going to ruin her good opinion of him.

But instead of offering to summon the carriage, he found himself taking both of her hands in his. And then he did something even more startling.

He said what he really felt.

"I like the thought of you in this room. Of it being used by someone who will properly appreciate it. I like the thought of you sitting here"—he nodded toward the chaise longue—"whiling away the afternoon with a stack of books. I want to take you to see the Greek folly. To show you the library—"

Her eyes snapped into focus. "The library?"

"The library," he said quickly. "Did I not mention the library?"

She bit her lip. "Is it very grand?"

"That depends. Do you consider six thousand volumes to be grand?"

"*Six thousand!*"

"Not all of them relate to the classics, of course."

"Oh." Her face fell a trifle.

He grinned wickedly. "Only around two thousand."

She gasped. "Two thousand!" She gazed longingly toward the door.

He sensed that he had her. "Perhaps I could just show you?"

"I—I should probably just go…"

He gave her a stern look. "You're not really going to leave without even having seen the library, are you?"

She looked torn. "I shouldn't."

He shook his head. "And here I thought you a true scholar."

She narrowed her eyes. "It is positively unsporting of you to manipulate me in such a shameless fashion."

"It is," he agreed. He paused before adding, "Is it working?"

She let out a frustrated laugh. "You know full well it is."

He offered his arm. "You cannot be surprised by my underhanded techniques. I am my mother's son, after all."

She huffed at him, but her lips were twisted into a reluctant smile.

Edward turned to her sister. "Mrs. Gorten, might I impose upon you again? We're on our way to the library."

CHAPTER 14

wo hours later, Elissa made her way back to her bedroom accompanied by three footmen (three strong men being the number required to carry all of the books that had caught her eye).

As soon as they'd arrived at the library, Cassandra plucked the first novel she saw off the shelf and retreated to a chair in the corner, leaving Edward to give Elissa a tour.

It had been the two most delightful hours of Elissa's life. Not just the books (although the Astley's library was like something out of her daydreams) but looking at the books with Edward. She had never had such a conversation before. She would exclaim over a volume of Euripides, and somehow, he would unerringly quote her favorite passage. They would then fall into arguing over who had done the better translation, Gascoigne or Ascham, until another title caught her eye, at which point the process would repeat itself.

He stacked every book she admired on the desk until it was covered. She felt mortified when she noticed how many she had chosen and said she would just pick two or three to take up to her room. He ignored her, instructed a footman to find a spare bookcase and put it in her room, and continued to pile them high. He seemed delighted by her response to the library, and it was a rare moment his dimples were not on full display. Elissa's own face hurt from smiling so much.

But now it was time to dress for dinner, and so they reluctantly parted ways.

Elissa entered her room to discover a glossy, three-shelf rosewood bookcase standing along the wall near the reading window. "Thank you so much," she said to the footmen as they set down their loads. "If you'll set them on the chaise, I'll arrange everything on the shelves." Truth be told, she was looking forward to going through the books again.

"There were a few more downstairs, miss," one of the footmen said. "I'll return with them in a minute."

"Thank you." Elissa recognized him as the same man who had been sent to Oxford to procure the replacement copy of *Theseus*. "We met the other day. I'm sorry, I didn't catch your name."

"It's Roger, miss."

"I'm sorry to be so much trouble, Roger."

He bowed deeply. "'Tis no trouble at all."

Elissa turned eagerly to her new treasure trove. She made some progress in getting things organized, but very little, owing to how often she began to read the books she picked up rather than shelving them. When Roger's knock came at the door, she was sitting cross-legged on the floor before the bookcase, absorbed in a volume of Theocritus.

"Come in," she called absentmindedly. She suddenly recalled that it was not proper to be sitting on the floor and turned to address the footman with a sheepish smile. "I'm afraid I haven't made much progress, but—oh!"

Instead of Roger bearing the last of her books, three of the most stunning young women she had ever beheld glided into the room. Elissa scrambled to her feet, juggling the book she'd had in her lap and frantically straightening her skirts.

She curtseyed deeply, for there was no need to ask who these ladies were. All three had Edward's otherworldly blue eyes. They had to be his sisters.

"I'm so sorry," she said, hastily laying Theocritus on top of a stack. "Your brother was kind enough to take me to the library, and I fear I was a bit, er, over-eager."

One of the blondes strolled over to inspect the piles of books. Elissa could not help but gape, because surely this woman was the Platonic form of the phrase "diamond of the first water." She was tall and graceful with a perfect figure, perfect features... perfect *everything*. Elissa knew nothing about London fashion, but there wasn't a doubt in her mind that this was the woman who set it.

"Greek, Greek, Latin, Greek." She rounded on Elissa. "Do you mean to tell me that this is your notion of a little light pleasure reading?"

Elissa felt herself flushing. "Er—yes?"

The blonde snapped open her fan as she turned to face her sisters. "This is the best news I have had in... La, I cannot even remember in how long!"

"She even has red hair!" squealed the other blonde, who looked a few years younger than her sister.

"I'm sorry, I—what?" Elissa said, baffled.

"Humph!" snorted the third girl, who bore less resemblance to her sisters. She was the female version of Edward, with glossy dark brown hair that made her blue eyes look startlingly intense. She was young, probably one of the twins, whom Elissa understood were eighteen, but already she carried herself with an unwavering confidence that Elissa knew she would never possess.

She strode over to the bookcase and wordlessly began

scanning Elissa's selections, removing three volumes from the stacks. She held them aloft. "These are also yours?"

Elissa peered at the titles. They were all novels, of the sort usually dismissed as "horrid." "Yes. I—" She swallowed, steeling herself for their derision. "I have somehow never read the *Castle of Wolfenbach.* But everyone likes a Gothic novel." She glanced around uncertainly. "Don't they?"

The dark-haired girl turned to her sisters and nodded crisply. "She'll do."

"It's *so* good," the younger blonde said, bouncing her way over to Elissa and clasping her hands. "I had nightmares for weeks after I read it, but in the best possible way. I'm Lucy, by the bye. It's so lovely to meet you at last!"

Elissa smiled, charmed, if a bit bewildered, by this reception. "I am so pleased to meet you, Lady Lucy. I am Elissa St. Cyr."

Lucy laughed. "Well of course you are! This is Isabella," she said, nodding toward the dark-haired girl, who inclined her head regally. "Izzie and I are twins. And this is Caroline, properly known as Lady Thetford."

"But you must call me Caro," she said immediately. "All my friends do. And I can tell already that we are going to be the best of friends."

"Anne will be here any minute," Lucy continued. "She wanted to look in on your sister."

From a few rooms over, Elissa heard a muffled knock, followed by the sound of her sister shrieking. "I would say she just did. That was a happy scream," Elissa hastened to reassure them. "Cassandra is a great admirer of Lady Morsley."

Lady Thetford smiled. "As are we all. Ah, here they are."

Elissa watched as a stunned Cassandra was led through the door by a tall, gorgeous woman with brown hair, brown eyes, and a beatific smile. She was rather obviously pregnant but was one of those women who carried it beautifully, the type who made you understand why pregnant women were sometimes described as "glowing."

"You must be Miss St. Cyr," she said warmly. "I am Lady Morsley, but I hope you will call me Anne."

"My lady," Elissa said, curtseying. She found herself at a loss for words, surrounded by the four Astley sisters, each of whom was more stunning than the next. She felt rather like a mortal who had taken a wrong turn and somehow found themselves atop Mount Olympus, surrounded by the goddesses.

Meanwhile, here she was, of average height and average figure with freckles on her nose and unfashionable red hair. As kind as the Astley sisters were, it was hard not to feel intimidated.

"No doubt you're wondering why we've invaded your room," Lady Thetford said. There came another knock at the door. "That should be the reason right there."

Three maids swept in, their arms overflowing with gowns. "Lay them out upon the bed," Lady Thetford said. She circled Elissa, studying her. "We'll start with the blue, the white, and then the yellow."

"I look terrible in yellow," Elissa said.

The viscountess's nose wrinkled when she smiled, as if she thought it adorable that Elissa had expressed an opinion. "Let's just try it on, shall we?"

CHAPTER 15

Two hours later, Elissa and Cassandra made their way downstairs in their borrowed finery. Lady Thetford had been correct, and Elissa was wearing the yellow gown. ("It's pale primrose you need to avoid, dear. See how *divine* you look in this saffron?") After forcing Elissa to try on every gown in the pile, the viscountess had written out a schedule detailing precisely what she was to wear for the next week.

The true miracle, as far as Elissa was concerned, had been the taming of her hair. As soon as the dresses were chosen, the Astley sisters began debating what to do with it. No appreciable progress was made until one of the maids, who had red hair herself, and who had slipped from the room as soon as the topic turned to Elissa's coiffure, returned bearing a little porcelain jar. "Stand aside!" she barked, then began poking through Elissa's curls.

"What do you think, Fanny?" Lady Thetford asked.

"It's gorgeous," Fanny declared. "I've been waiting for this moment my whole life, I have."

Elissa gave her an apologetic smile. "It's hopeless trying to do anything with it. My hair defies all attempts to tame it."

"Oh, is that so?" Fanny snorted. "We'll just see about that."

A half-hour later, Elissa peered at herself in the mirror in astonishment. Where her hair had always been a mess of frizz, it was now sleek and glossy, sculpted into a pile of curls atop her head. The whole thing was held in place with a bandeau in the same shade of yellow as her dress, with a few white flowers woven throughout for good measure.

"And that," Fanny concluded with a satisfied smile, "is the magic of coconut oil."

"Coconut oil?" Elissa asked, astonished. She had heard of coconuts, of course, but she had never seen one.

"That's right. You use it as a pomade," Fanny explained, replacing the lid on the porcelain pot and setting it upon the dressing table. "Use just a little—it goes a long way. This'll last you a month or two, but you'll want to get more."

Elissa gave a sheepish smile. "I fear we don't have coconut oil in Bourton-on-the-Water."

"Oh, you can find it in London," Lady Lucy hastened to say. "You can get anything there."

Elissa bit her lip, deciding it best not to mention that she had never been to London, and probably would never have occasion to go.

Now, as she and Cassandra followed a footman toward the dining room, Elissa gave her sister a tight smile. Cassandra's dark brown hair and cream complexion looked lovely with the rose silk wrap dress the Astley sisters had selected for her. The experience of getting dressed up for dinner, trying on a dozen silk gowns, having her hair arranged by a proper lady's maid instead of by one of her sisters, had been foreign for the girl who spent all of her pin money on books. But Elissa had quickly found herself relaxing and even enjoying herself thanks to the warmth and liveliness of the Astley sisters.

But now, passing through rooms so elegant they looked more fit for a palace than a mere house, Elissa could not help but feel out of place in her borrowed finery.

They finally reached a turquoise silk drawing room where the Astleys' guests were assembling for dinner. Elissa noticed two local families in attendance with whom she was acquainted, the Beauclerks and the Stavertons. The sons of both families had been her father's pupils. She and Cassandra were not nearly so high in the instep as the Beauclerk girls, whose grandfather was a duke, or the Stavertons, whose father was a baron. But two of the Staverton sisters smiled and nodded from across the room, and Henrietta Beauclerk, who was standing near the door, greeted them warmly and fell into conversation with Cassandra.

Elissa spied Edward across the room, and he smiled and inclined his head. He was speaking to a fair-haired man whom Elissa would probably have thought handsome had he been standing next to anyone else. Edward must have failed to attend to their conversation, because the blond man turned, then lifted an assessing eyebrow when his eyes fell upon Elissa. He turned back to Edward and said something, tilting his head in Elissa's direction.

An imperious voice interrupted Elissa's train of thought. "You must be the infamous Miss St. Cyr."

Elissa turned and gawped at the woman who stood before her, a woman who needed no introduction. She could not have looked more like her daughters, Lady Lucy and Lady Caroline, with her honey blonde hair and those stunning blue eyes.

Elissa remembered herself and dropped a deep curtsey. "Lady Cheltenham, thank you so much for inviting us."

The countess raised a single raised brow. "Yes, you seemed so grateful to have received the invitation."

Elissa blanched. "I—er—"

The countess took pity on her. "There, there, child, I do not bite. Except on Tuesdays, and then only if you displease me exceptionally." She turned to Cassandra. "You must be Mrs. Gorten."

Cassandra sank into a curtsey. "Yes, my lady."

Lady Cheltenham's gaze swept Elissa assessingly. "I look forward to learning more about you both."

A terrifying prospect from what Elissa could tell, but she won a reprieve from the butler, who entered the drawing room and announced that dinner was served. Lady Cheltenham floated off to the front of the line, and Elissa and Cassandra found their places toward the back.

Elissa felt her stomach drop again as she entered the dining room, which was large enough to accommodate the fifty invited guests and was decorated with gilt-framed mirrors upon red silk wallpaper. She had to force herself not to tip her head back to gape at the painted frescoes on the ceiling.

Nervous as she was, dinner went a good way toward assuaging Elissa's fears about mixing in such exalted company. She fell easily into conversation with her dinner partner, Mr. Peter Ferguson, a wealthy businessman whose father was Scottish and mother was from the Bengali region of India. He had russet skin and mischievous brown eyes, and, having grown up in India, spoke nine languages including High Persian. Elissa had dabbled a bit in High Persian, as she was fascinated by all of the great classical languages, and Mr. Ferguson was so obliging that he cheerfully conversed with her in High Persian and even assisted her with a few points of pronunciation.

It wasn't just Mr. Ferguson. Everyone seated around her

could not have been kinder or more welcoming. Elissa had never been in such convivial company, and by the time the ladies left the gentlemen to their brandy, she was starting to think that attending this house party might not be a complete disaster.

The ladies repaired to the portrait gallery. Lady Morsley and Cassandra fell into a lively discussion of the viscountess's charity, the Ladies' Society for the Relief of the Destitute. After a few minutes, Elissa excused herself to look at the artwork.

She strolled past paintings of the Madonna and Child and a naval battle she thought might be Cape St. Vincent, then paused before a pair of paintings, one depicting the Roman Forum as it looked today, the other imagining it in its full glory.

"Precisely where I expected to find you," a deep voice said from over her shoulder.

She turned and smiled at Edward. It appeared that the gentlemen had finished with their brandy. "Am I so predictable?"

"I did not mean to imply such. But these are my favorite paintings, and I suspected you might like them, too." He offered his arm. "How are you enjoying yourself?"

"Very well, thank you. I was nervous at first, but everyone has been so kind." She gestured to the skirts of her borrowed dress. "And thanks to your sister, I don't feel completely out of place."

"You look beautiful," Edward said. His eyes, full of sincerity, were midnight blue in the candlelight.

"Thank you," she whispered.

A bark of laughter from the far side of the room reminded her they were not alone, and she should take care not to gape. She turned to the painting of the Forum as it looked today, pointing to a string of columns that were still standing. "This was part of the Temple of Saturn, correct?"

"Just so. And here, to its left, is the—"

"Fauconbridge, there you are," came a slurred voice. Elissa turned and saw a gentleman with ruddy cheeks and more than a slight paunch.

"Uncle Mortimer," Edward said, turning to Elissa. "Miss St. Cyr, might I present my uncle, Colonel—"

"Oh, we can skip all that rot," the colonel said, waving his arm. This had the effect of throwing him off balance, and he lurched to the side before righting himself. "I need to borrow you for a moment."

Lord Redditch, whom Elissa recognized, came up behind the colonel and clasped him on the shoulder. "Leave him be, Morty. Can't you see he's found finer company than you?" He gave Elissa a wink.

"I've five quid laid against your father regarding a question of a mathematical nature," the colonel continued, undeterred. "They all say I'm wrong, but I won't accept their verdict. And why should I, when we have our very own Senior Wrangler on hand to decide it?"

Elissa felt Edward's arm twitch beneath her hand. She glanced up at him and found his expression completely blank.

Lord Redditch attempted to draw the colonel away. "Come, Morty. It'll keep."

The colonel rounded on Lord Redditch, swaying. "He can spare one minute for his uncle," he said, his voice rising. Along the length of the gallery, curious heads turned their way.

"I'll be right there, Uncle," Edward said. As Lord Redditch steered the colonel to the far side of the room, Edward turned to Elissa, his smile tight. "I am sorry. I will return momentarily."

Elissa squeezed his arm before releasing it. "There is no need to apologize. I quite understand."

Edward hastened across the gallery, and Elissa returned to her study of the paintings. After a moment, she heard the colonel bark, "What?" She peered over and saw that Edward had his hands up in a placating manner.

"Oh, dear. There goes the colonel again," a feminine voice drawled in Elissa's ear.

She turned to see an elegant young lady with dark hair and dark eyes. "Is the colonel often in his cups?" Elissa asked.

"Constantly," the girl replied. "I am Araminta Grenwood."

Elissa smiled as she sank into a curtsey. Truly, everyone was showing her such kindness. Look at Miss Grenwood, coming over to introduce herself as soon as she saw Elissa standing alone. "I am Elissa St. Cyr."

"The Viscount Grenwood is my father," Miss Grenwood added. Elissa got the impression that she was being warned against assuming they were equals just because they both had a 'Miss' before their names.

"Oh. How—how lovely," Elissa said, struggling to think of an appropriate response. "My father is Julian St. Cyr. He was Lord Fauconbridge's tutor."

"Ah, so that is how you came to be here." Miss Grenwood looked Elissa up and down. "That is a very fashionable dress you have on."

"Thank you." *See?* Elissa remonstrated herself. *Don't assume the worst.* Miss Grenwood meant well. "It is actually—"

"It belongs to Lady Lucy, does it not? How kind of her to have made sure you had *something* to wear. I imagine that none of your dresses would have done. *At all.* And it looks well enough on you." She laughed. "That is, as much as anything looks well with that garish ginger hair."

Elissa's smile was frozen. Well, perhaps not *everyone* at this house party was exceptionally kind. She cast about for a change of subject. "And how do you know the Astley family, Miss Grenwood?"

"My mother and Lady Cheltenham are the dearest of friends. Mama is godmother to the twins, you know. And my connection to the Astleys is about to grow even deeper."

"Oh? How so?"

Miss Grenwood laughed, but not in a friendly way. "Do you truly not know?"

Elissa shook her head, and Araminta Grenwood leaned in, looking her hard in the eye.

"I am to marry Lord Fauconbridge."

CHAPTER 16

$\mathcal{E}$lissa found herself incapable of speech. She shouldn't be surprised. She had known all along that the attentions some might interpret as a deeper regard were merely Edward's impeccable manners. The very notion that Edward Astley would ever be interested in the likes of her was ludicrous! She knew that.

But judging by the despair washing over her, her heart had allowed itself to hope.

Miss Grenwood was waiting for her to respond. "You are betrothed, then?" Elissa asked, trying to hold her voice steady.

"It is all but finalized," Miss Grenwood replied, dropping her voice to a whisper. "Before the house party, Lady Cheltenham told my mother that Lord Fauconbridge asked her to invite some young ladies, as he intended to select a bride this week. He asked his mother to choose the candidates." She gave a gloating smile. "As you can see, I am the only young lady of appropriate station who was invited."

"Oh!" Elissa was so taken aback that she blurted out the

first thing that came to mind. "But—but what about the Staverton girls? Their father is a baron."

Miss Grenwood snorted. "*A baron.* As if Lord Fauconbridge would even consider a mere *baron's* daughter."

Elissa frowned. "Well, there's also Henrietta and Mary-Elizabeth Beauclerk. Their grandfather is the Duke of—"

"Are you really so naive? Their father is the fifth son of the duke. Daughters of the fifth son of a duke are as common as cabbages."

Elissa bit her lip, remembering how warmly Henrietta Beauclerk had greeted them before dinner. "The Beauclerks are lovely girls. Lovely and kind. And I can assure you, there is nothing *common* about graciousness, a quality they possess in abundance."

"Loveliness, graciousness—praiseworthy qualities, to be sure. But Lord Fauconbridge doesn't need someone *lovely.* He needs a *countess.* Someone who can plan a gathering such as this without even blinking. Someone who knows that a Venetian breakfast should not start before three o'clock in the afternoon."

"Three o'clock? But... I thought you said it was a breakfast?"

Miss Grenwood gave her a pitying look and continued, "He needs someone he can present at court. Someone who can dance the requisite minuet before the king and queen without causing him disgrace."

Elissa blanched. She could barely manage a simple country dance, and a minuet was a thousand times more difficult. What was worse, the minuet was danced by one couple at a time, meaning that absolutely everyone would be staring at you, scrutinizing your performance and making note of every error. "Do you truly have to dance a minuet at court?"

"Oh, yes. Most places have abandoned the minuet, but they still dance them at court."

Elissa gave a nervous laugh. She had understood that she was unsuitable to the role of countess, but only now did she comprehend the full depth of her unfitness. "Well, I'm sure that the Staverton and Beauclerk girls are competent in all of those skills."

"I'm sure they are not." Miss Grenwood leaned in and whispered, "I was seated next to Henrietta Beauclerk at dinner. Did you know that she has never been to London?" Miss Grenwood shook her head. "No, Lady Cheltenham would never consider any of the young ladies present as a bride for her eldest son. Except for me. And so you see, I am the countess's choice for her future daughter-in-law. No doubt the formal announcement will be made before the end of the week."

"I—I see," Elissa sputtered.

Miss Grenwood's eyes narrowed. "But that is not what I wanted to speak to you about. I came over here to discuss your infatuation with Lord Fauconbridge."

Elissa's eyes flew back to Miss Grenwood. "My—my—what?"

Miss Grenwood rolled her eyes. "It's *obvious*. Everyone has been remarking on it. On how *pathetic* it is. Or, should I say, on how pathetic you are."

Elissa's cheeks felt very hot as she peered at Edward. He had slung his arm around his uncle's shoulders. His brother Harrington had joined them, and he said something that caused the whole cluster of gentlemen to burst into guffaws. Even the colonel started laughing, looking mollified.

Edward glanced across the room, his eyes finding hers.

His smile abruptly faded.

What a fool she had been. She'd never been any good at hiding her feelings. Of course her adoration must be obvious. And in a few short days, he would be announcing his betrothal to someone else.

No wonder everyone was saying she was pathetic.

Suddenly, Elissa knew she could face neither him, nor the other guests. Not tonight, when her feelings were so raw.

She turned to Miss Grenwood. "I apologize, but I feel a headache coming on. I should lie down."

Miss Grenwood's eyes were full of satisfaction rather than sympathy. "Yes, that's probably for the best."

Elissa managed to slip from the room without anyone noticing. She would explain to Cassandra what Miss Grenwood had said.

Tomorrow.

CHAPTER 17

For the next three days, beneath his impeccably calm exterior, Edward was seething.

He had felt a sense of foreboding the moment he saw Elissa engaged in conversation with the poisonous Araminta Grenwood. He'd extracted himself from his uncle with all possible speed, but Elissa had already fled the room, claiming a headache.

He could understand that well enough. Araminta Grenwood was enough to give someone with the constitution of a plough horse a megrim.

Try as he might, he couldn't seem to get a moment alone with Elissa to find out what had happened. The second he entered a room, Miss Grenwood attached herself to his arm like a barnacle. He thought he had made it plain after her leap from behind the potted palm that she should have no expectation of a future union. But neither that nor his cool behavior seemed to dissuade her.

Every time he managed to catch Elissa's eye, she would give him an unconvincing half-smile, then immediately avert her gaze.

What on earth could Miss Grenwood have said to her?

Then each evening, the order of precedence worked against him. As a future earl, his place near the head of the table was carved in stone. He was stuck entertaining the Dowager Viscountess Molesworth (which he actually didn't mind, for although Lady Molesworth was on the far side of seventy, she had a fine sarcastic wit). But an evening of repartee with Lady Molesworth was a cold comfort when he could see Elissa at the far end of the table charming everyone around her. Once, Harrington somehow contrived to sit next to her, and Edward was forced to endure the sight of her laughing at his brother's witticisms all night long.

How he longed in that moment to be the second son, *Mr. Astley*, who could sit where he bloody well wanted.

And so, upon the morning of the fifth day of the house party, Edward held out little hope that he would get to spend any meaningful time with Elissa. Still, when he saw her descending the portico's steps to the front drive where the company was assembling for a walking tour of the grounds, his heart gave a pathetic flicker.

He crossed to her immediately. "Good morning, Miss Elissa. Mrs. Gorten."

"Good morning," Elissa said, giving him that horrible smile-that-was-not-a-smile and dropping her eyes to the toes of her boots.

"What a lovely day for a walk," Cassandra observed.

"Yes, I only hope the weather will hold," Edward replied. Elissa was still staring at her feet.

Harrington strolled out onto the portico, along with Caro and her husband, Lord Thetford. Edward glanced around. The entire party was assembled, save Lady Grenwood and her daughter.

His mother clapped her hands. "It is now ten o'clock. Let's be off."

Edward glanced at his pocket watch. It was ten sharp. It was on the tip of his tongue to suggest they allow a few minutes for the Grenwood ladies to arrive.

He stopped himself. For once in his life, he was going to ignore what he should do, and do what he actually wanted.

He offered an arm to Elissa and one to her sister, but Caro hurried over. "Mrs. Gorten, would you walk with me?" She gestured to Thetford, who was standing with Harrington and Peter Ferguson, guffawing at some joke understood only by the three of them. "My husband is with his school friends, and you cannot imagine how incorrigible they become in one another's company. I should be so grateful for some civil conversation."

Edward happened to know that Caro could hold her own with absolutely anyone, any day of the week and twice on Sundays. But he wasn't about to point that out.

"I should be delighted," Cassandra said.

Caro cast Edward a wink as she linked arms with Cassandra and drew her away. The only positive about the fact that Elissa was still staring at the ground was that she missed his sister's rather unsubtle gesture.

"Miss Elissa?" he said, offering his arm.

She looked up at him then, her face a mixture of longing and despair, before dropping her gaze as she accepted his arm.

He wanted to ask what the hell Araminta Grenwood had said to her, but he could hardly do so when the group was so tightly packed.

So instead, he asked her if she had been enjoying her books from the library. This led to a halting conversation about Aristophanes, followed by a slightly less halting one about Horace. Then they rounded the corner and the Greek folly came into view. Elissa exclaimed over it before remembering herself and looking down.

She may have tamped down her reaction, but Edward knew he had her. He commenced with a full tour of the folly, showing her every detail. He described which temples the architect had used as his inspiration and confessed his disappointment that a grand tour had proved impossible due to the war with France. This led to a discussion of which Greek and Roman sites they each wanted to visit, of which there was a high degree of overlap, as they both wanted to visit them all. And by the time Edward showed her the little bench inside the folly and described how beautiful it looked by the light of the full moon, Elissa had given up staring at her feet. She was beaming at him again, and Edward could breathe for the first time in three days.

They spent so much time examining the folly that they fell behind the rest of the group, not so far away as to be improper, but well out of hearing range. It would be the ideal time to ask Elissa what Miss Grenwood had said to upset her, but Edward found himself hesitating. He didn't want to say anything that might bring their conversation screeching to a halt. It was more of a relief than he cared to admit to have Elissa speaking to him again, to see her wrinkle her nose when he teased her, to hear her quoting at length from the Eclogues of Nemesianus, to have her, just… being herself, in his presence.

They reached the top of the rise, and their destination came into view: Cranfield Castle, a glorious old ruin lying just over the boundary of the Astley estate on Lord Redditch's lands.

Elissa's reaction was every bit as rapturous as Edward had hoped it would be. "Oh, how glorious! Is that a—a—"

"A castle," Edward supplied, unable to suppress his grin.

"Yes, of course, but is it a—" She waved her hands, struggling to find the words. "Some people will *build* a brand-new structure to *look* like a ruin. Is it that, or is it—"

"It's a real castle," Edward hastened to reassure her. "It dates from the fourteenth century."

"A real castle!" She pressed a hand to her heart. "It is so perfectly picturesque, I couldn't be sure."

"Yes. When I was a child, it was my favorite place to play."

She seized his forearm in a surprisingly strong grip. "Do you mean to tell me that you played knights and dragons and unicorns in an actual castle?"

He barked out a laugh. "I cannot say I played *unicorns*."

She poked him in the arm, but she was smiling.

"As the older brother, I made Harrington be the unicorn," he explained solemnly. She laughed out loud, and it was as if the past three miserable days had never happened. "Come," he said, offering his arm, "I'll show you all of its secrets."

They made it up the hill in record time. In spite of his longer legs, Edward had to work to keep pace with Elissa in her excitement. They reached the base of the castle and began circling around, Edward showing her a mason's mark here, the remains of the rusted chain that had once hoisted the portcullis there. Elissa squealed aloud when he pointed out some scorch marks beneath a murder hole, the remnants of boiling oil employed during the War of the Roses.

Halfway around they reached the picnic area that had been laid out by Lord Redditch, with blankets spread in the shade of a grove of trees. As eager as Elissa was to continue exploring the castle, the day was warm and they had been walking for almost an hour, so they sat and accepted glasses of lemonade.

Lord Redditch joined them. "How are you enjoying the castle, Miss St. Cyr?"

"It is wonderful, my lord. Thank you so much for inviting us to see it."

"It is my pleasure." He nodded toward Edward. "Has Fauconbridge told you about the ghost yet?"

Elissa leaned forward. "There's even a ghost?"

Edward smiled. "I was saving that tale for you, sir. No one else can do it justice."

The earl began the story, glad to have found someone who hadn't already heard it a hundred times. Elissa made the perfect audience, gasping in all the right places and staring in rapt delight at the battlements where the ghost of the fifth Marquess of Redditch was said to appear when the moon was on the wane.

"It was the back right tower," Lord Redditch said, pointing, "where the assassin crept up behind him with the axe. Fauconbridge will show you when you go up."

Elissa's eyes flew to Lord Redditch's. "Are the battlements intact?"

Lord Redditch nodded. "The east walk fell two hundred years ago, and what's left is crumbling in a few places. But most of it is sturdy enough."

Elissa was already wandering, entranced, toward the gatehouse.

Edward glanced around. Lord Redditch hadn't been exaggerating when he said the battlements were crumbling; there was even a gap you had to jump. He didn't like the idea of Elissa going up there without someone to show her the hazards.

But up top, they would be out of view of the party. Elissa needed a chaperone, but he hated to ask Mrs. Gorten, who was absorbed in conversation with Anne.

He nudged his little sister. "Lucy, Miss Elissa wants a look around the battlements. Climb up with us, won't you?"

A look of panic crossed Lucy's face. Her eyes flew to their mother, and then back at Edward. "Oh, I couldn't. I'm, um— so exhausted from the walk!"

Edward frowned, as one minute ago, Lucy had been

bouncing around the meadow picking flowers. But he turned to Isabella. "How about you, Izzie?"

"Beg pardon, brother, but I find myself swept away by the atmosphere." She gestured to the verdant meadow. "I am envisioning a scene for my latest manuscript. I must memorize every detail before it slips away."

Edward frowned at the brilliant blue sky. Isabella's tastes ran to the macabre, and he was hard-pressed to recall a single scene she had written that did not take place on a dark and stormy night. "Is it not a bit… cheerful?"

"Precisely," she said in a rush. "The effervescence of the scene will make the discovery of Count Augusto's decapitated body all the more jarring."

"Er—right." As Edward turned to find another sister, he caught Mr. Nettlethorpe-Ogilvy trying to hide a smile by sipping from his lemonade. "Caro, how about you? I daresay it's been a few years since you've been up."

"I'm sorry, Edward, but I couldn't possibly go up in this dress," she said, fingering her skirts. "It's my favorite."

"I've actually never been inside," Thetford said, rising to his feet. "I'd quite like a look around."

"Of course, darling," Caro said. "But not just now."

"I'm sure we won't get a finer day than this," Thetford replied. "Come on, Ferguson. I know you want to see it. You're always droning on about medieval architecture."

"Of course I do." Ferguson gave his friend a significant look and tilted his head toward Edward. "But I'd prefer to see it *later*."

"Later?" Thetford's brow wrinkled. "Why later? Why do we not just—"

Caro grabbed her husband's arm, yanking him back down. "Henry, *darling*. I would be *bereft* without you."

She was staring hard into Thetford's face, and Edward could almost see gears turning inside his head. "I think I'll just... stay here, then?" he said, raising a questioning eyebrow.

Caro beamed at him. "Oh, thank you, my love."

Edward glanced about the party, searching for a suitable chaperone. He hadn't been planning to ask Anne, but judging by the glare Morsley was giving him, the suggestion that his nine-months-pregnant wife might like to climb the crumbling battlements would not be a welcome one.

"Darling," his mother called, "go up with Miss St. Cyr. It won't be improper, we're all just here. And I hate to think that she might miss the gap."

Edward suddenly recalled how, in her rapture, she had almost tripped over the statue of Hector in the rotunda. "Well, then," he said, rising. "If you're certain it's all right—"

A cacophony of voices called out for him to go.

Edward hurried up the stairs, and found her leaning against the crenellated parapets, gazing out over the surrounding countryside. She smiled as soon as she saw him, and he suddenly wished he were an artist so he could capture the way she looked in this moment, with her red hair and white dress, leaning against the golden stone wall, the deep blue sky and rolling green hills behind her. It struck him that his life two weeks before had been like a sketch in grey charcoal. But with Elissa in it, suddenly everything was painted in glorious colors.

Some mad impulse had him intertwining his fingers with hers rather than offering his arm as they started around the battlements. Elissa ducked her head, but her shy-but-thrilled smile was the opposite of the miserable grimace she had been sporting the past few days, and his heart sang to see it. It was windier up here, and when a sudden gust kicked up, she squeezed his hand as she caught her balance, then laughed.

"I've never been up this high," she confessed. "It appears I have a bit of vertigo."

"Wait until you see what's ahead."

They made their way across the front of the castle, pausing to enjoy the view from a corner tower. Halfway around the side, they came to the gap.

As the entire east side of the battlements were gone, the only way to reach the haunted tower was via the western wall. Most of it was still sturdy, but there was a gap of about four feet where the walkway had collapsed.

Four feet was hardly any distance at all. On flat ground, you scarcely even had to hop.

It was a bit of a different prospect when there was a twenty-foot drop below you.

Edward eyed Elissa. "You don't have to do it."

"No, I—I want to. It's really not that far, is it?" she said, studying the gap. "I'm not about to miss the haunted tower."

"In that case." Edward released her hand and cleared the gap with one big step. It didn't take him much effort, but of course, he was six-foot-two. Elissa only came up to his chin.

"Get a good running start," he called into the wind. "I'll catch you. I promise."

She looked nervous, but also determined as she took a few steps back and gathered her skirts in one hand. She rocked back onto her heel, then sprinted forward, taking the leap before she could change her mind.

It turned out she didn't need him; she cleared the gap with more than a foot to spare. But this had the fortunate effect of causing her body to go crashing into Edward's.

He caught her in his arms, pulling her flush against his chest. He hadn't been this close to her since the day he found her at the pond, but his body thrilled to the familiar feeling of her in his arms. He knew the gentlemanly thing would be to release her, but instead, he found one of his arms stealing around her waist and the other coming up to frame her face, and without even realizing he was going to do it, he leaned down and kissed her.

The moment his lips touched hers, panic set in. Because as much as Edward wanted to kiss Elissa St. Cyr, the truth was, he didn't know what he was doing. The handful of times he had been cornered and kissed, his focus had been on extricating himself, not learning what to do with his lips and tongue. Now he just... froze.

Elissa had frozen too. They were just standing there, their mouths pressed against each other, both of them as stiff as a board. He thought he needed to move his lips over hers, but he wasn't sure how, and he felt so *stupid* that he was seven and twenty and he didn't even know how to properly kiss a woman. He swallowed, trying to tamp down the failure rising like bile in his throat. What had he been *thinking*? This was a *disaster*. The only woman he truly wanted to think well of him, and he had made a complete and utter fool of himself!

But then, the most remarkable thing happened. Elissa made a sound, full of wonder, somewhere between a sigh and a moan. She absolutely melted into his chest. He realized she was trembling.

Suddenly he didn't feel like such a failure after all. He forced his lips to soften, to relax. He slowly opened his mouth and tentatively traced the outline of her lips with his tongue.

"Oh!" she cried, in what sounded very much like pleasure. So he did it again, and again after that. Hesitantly, she opened her own mouth, and her body jerked as if she'd been struck by lightning her when his tongue brushed hers.

By this time, she was shaking so hard that it was growing difficult to kiss, so he moved his lips to her cheek. He traced a path of kisses across her jawline, over to her ear, then down to the delicate, petal-soft skin of her neck. This did nothing to alleviate her trembling, but she continued making little sounds of pleasure.

He tried to kiss her again, but she was shaking so hard he couldn't maintain contact, so instead he gathered her to him, burying his face in her hair.

"I'm sorry, my lord," she said, her voice unsteady.

"Edward," he said without thinking. "Call me Edward."

"My—my Edward."

He groaned aloud, because surely that was the sweetest sound in the English language.

"It's just—" she shook her head, as if she were in a daze. "I've never been kissed before. I think my reaction is fairly normal. Isn't a girl supposed to tremble when she gets kissed by the man of her dreams?"

Her eyes flew open, and her characteristic oh-dear-what-have-I-done expression came over her features. "Did... did I say that out loud?"

He couldn't keep the joy from his voice. "Yes. Yes, you did."

She peered up at him, her cheeks scarlet. "I don't suppose you could forget I said it?"

He ran his thumb tenderly across her cheek. "Never."

And then he lowered his lips back down to hers, and although she was still trembling, they managed well enough. Her mouth was indescribably sweet against his, and his confidence grew with each sigh of pleasure that rose from her throat. She snaked her arms up around his neck, and when he traced his tongue across the seam of her lips, she opened for him. Her tongue hesitantly began to tangle with his, and now it was his turn to groan.

He was tracing his hand down the length of her spine, pulling her closer, when an unwelcome voice came wafting from the far side of the castle.

"Lord Fauconbridge? Lord Fauconbridge? Where are you?"

Edward had never in his life cursed before a lady, but he had to bite down the urge at the unwelcome news that Araminta Grenwood was bearing down upon them.

To his regret, Elissa took a step back and began smoothing her dress. Edward sighed and likewise began straightening his coat.

She reached up to tuck an escaped curl back in place. "How do I look?" she asked.

"Beautiful," he answered at once. Even more so, he thought, with the embarrassed-but-pleased smile that stole across her face.

"Elissa," he said urgently, "I don't know what she said to you the other day. But—" He struggled to find the words to explain how he felt, how awful the past three days had been. "Don't go. Stay with me."

She didn't have time to answer, because that was the moment Miss Grenwood came barreling around the corner, stopping short in front of the gap. "Lord Fauconbridge, *there* you are. Would you believe it, your mother told us the wrong time for the outing! We came down a full hour late. I must confess, I was very cross, and I did not hesitate to say as much to the countess. Then they said you had gone up here. Goodness, I had not expected it to be this grimy." She wrinkled her nose. "You would think that Lord Redditch would have had it properly scrubbed, knowing we were all coming. And it is in a shocking state of disrepair." She gave him an expectant look. "Well? Aren't you going to show me around?"

Edward sighed. It would appear that his idyll with Elissa was at an end.

CHAPTER 18

It happened that Miss Grenwood was unwilling to jump the gap. Edward informed her that they would be a few minutes, then led a silently giggling Elissa back to the haunted tower. This afforded him a bit more time in her company, albeit interrupted at frequent intervals by Miss Grenwood shouting across the bailey to ask if they were finished yet.

Eventually they were, and he and Elissa re-jumped the gap (Edward made a great show of catching her about the waist). He finished the castle tour with Elissa on one arm and Miss Grenwood on the other.

Back on the lawn, a picnic luncheon was being served. Miss Grenwood plainly intended to join Edward and Elissa on their blanket, in spite of her mother's embarrassed entreaty for her daughter to come and sit with her.

It was Graverley who saved him. "Miss Grenwood," he said, giving a tight smile, "I believe there is more room over here."

Araminta Grenwood was not about to pass up an invitation to sit next to the richest future duke in England, and the alacrity with which she abandoned Edward was almost embarrassing. Edward shot his friend a look of gratitude, which Graverley returned with an expression that said, *You owe me.*

As Edward settled down upon a blanket to spend the afternoon with Elissa, he silently agreed.

IN HIS ROOM THAT NIGHT, Edward reflected that it had been the best day he'd had in a very long time. Just being near Elissa made him so happy. She had such an open, easy manner. He wasn't one to drop his guard, but in her presence, the knots he tied himself up in seemed to loosen of their own accord, and it felt… good. He could get used to it.

He was, in fact, going to get used to it.

Because Edward had decided he was going to marry Elissa St. Cyr.

His decision would come as a shock to everyone who knew him. Well, perhaps not everyone. Judging by their rather unsubtle efforts to help him get Elissa on her own, his siblings had perceived his feelings and approved of his choice.

His parents would be another matter entirely. He knew what was expected of him, had known it almost from birth: to find a wife with position, propriety, and wealth. Elissa had none of them.

But Edward found that he didn't give a damn whether his parents approved or not. Which was entirely unlike him. But he just… needed this. He needed *her.* His life with Elissa in it was immeasurably better. That had been made clear to him these past few days.

He'd always tried so hard to do what was expected of him. He'd scarcely ever set a toe out of line. Could he not have just this one thing, Elissa as his wife, when she made him so happy?

He tossed his cravat onto his dressing table and crossed to the window, staring out into the night as shrugged out of his waistcoat. Of course, he was making an assumption—that Elissa would accept him. But perhaps he could be forgiven for getting ahead of himself after this afternoon. *The man of her dreams* was how she had described him, after all.

He noticed a flash of white out on the lawn. He leaned closer to the window to peer into the darkness.

There she was, as if he had conjured her. The night was cloudless and there was a full moon, so he could make out the red of her plait against a grey dressing gown.

What on earth was she doing outside, alone, in her dressing gown, at this time of night? She was headed south-west. There was nothing in that direction. Nothing except—

The folly. The folly which became a moonlight-drenched paradise precisely at midnight, as Edward had told her earlier today.

Surely it was fate that he had spotted her. He didn't bother with a cravat or waistcoat. He just threw his greatcoat on over his open-necked shirt and followed her out into the night.

Elissa knew it was foolish, being alone outside in the middle of the night. But she was too full of nervous energy to sleep.

The morning had been incredible. Edward Astley had kissed her. *Edward Astley.* It was like something out of one of her fantasies, one so impossible she would never admit to it, not even to Cassandra. She still couldn't believe it had actually happened.

But when they'd returned to the house, a letter from her mother had been waiting. Her father had collapsed again, this time in the middle of his classroom. With his past spells, he had roused himself quickly, but this time he had been too weak to rise from the floor, and they'd had to solicit help from the neighbors to carry him to bed. He had been up again the following day, but he remained weak, and her mother's anxiety was palpable. Her father's condition was worsening, and there was nothing the physician could do.

Her mother did not request that she and Cassandra return home to tend to their father. Having the two of them eating the Astley's food for another week was a welcome development in terms of the family budget, and besides, her parents were not the sort to have tender feelings that would be comforted by their daughters' presence.

Supper had provided a welcome distraction. But now that Elissa was alone in her room, she found herself pacing the floor. With her father's health failing, it was more important than ever that she win the contest, which would take place in just three days. She had been so distracted during her time at Harrington Hall, she had done nothing to prepare.

She knew she should put her shoulder to the wheel and complete a translation or two tonight, and it wasn't as if she lacked for appropriate material, having transported a significant portion of the Astleys' library into her room. But between her first kiss, her father's collapse, and her impending clash with Edward, her emotions were a jumble of elation and anxiety and everything in between, and her attempts to concentrate proved hopeless.

Glancing out the window, her eyes seized upon the folly. She wasn't going to get any studying done tonight. Deciding she might as well indulge herself in an hour or two of reminiscing about the more pleasant events of that morning, she threw her dressing gown over her shift and slipped out of her room before she had the chance to think better of it.

The folly truly was glorious with the moonlight pouring through the skylight. Elissa settled upon the stone bench at the center of the rotunda, drawing her knees up to her chest.

This was truly perfect.

The only thing that could make it better was if Edward could somehow be here, too.

"Elissa?"

She shrieked and spun around, her hand flying to her heart. And just like magic, there he was, standing between two columns. He swallowed thickly, and her mouth went dry as she realized that the reason she knew he had swallowed thickly was because he wore neither cravat nor waistcoat. His shirt was even open, revealing half his chest.

She couldn't tear her eyes from that bare vee of skin. Weren't men supposed to be… hairier? Not that his chest was entirely without hair. She could see a light sprinkling of it, but for some reason she had expected—

He cleared his throat. "I am sorry. I didn't mean to frighten you. I happened to see you crossing the lawn, and I —oh, never mind." He turned to leave.

"Edward, wait!" He paused, glancing over his shoulder. "You startled me, is all. At the moment you stole up behind me, I was staring off into space, thinking that the only thing that could make tonight better was if you were here."

He turned to face her again. "Were you truly?"

"I was. Here." She lowered her feet to the ground and shifted to make room for him on the bench. "Would you sit with me?"

He did just that. Slowly, giving her a chance to say no, he slid in close and draped his arm around her back.

She sighed, blushing as she leaned her head against his shoulder.

They sat that way for a moment. Elissa enjoyed the sound of his heartbeat, and the weight of his arm draped across her back. She could even feel the warmth of his skin through the thin linen of his shirt…

He broke the silence. "What was it Miss Grenwood said to you that made you avoid me for three days?"

"Oh. That. She said… " Elissa cringed. "She said the two of you were to marry—"

"*What?*"

"—and that everyone was mocking me because of my obvious infatuation with you."

His expression was one of outrage. "I would never speak ill of a lady, but right now I am sorely tempted." He took both of her hands in his and turned to face her on the bench. "Elissa, I have absolutely no intention of marrying Araminta Grenwood. I swear it."

"I know that now. I knew as soon as you kissed me. Because you would never dally with me if you were pledged to another. That's not who you are."

"Good." He looked pleased by her response. "And no one is mocking you. Judging by my sisters' blatant efforts to give us a chance to be alone, it wouldn't surprise me if there was some talk, but I expect it is of a friendly sort. Because *we* are so obviously infatuated with *each other*." He shook his head. "I can't believe she said that. I'd assumed it must have been something unkind about your father having been my tutor, or your having borrowed a few dresses from Lucy."

"Oh, well, she said both of those things, too. As well as a cutting remark about my hair."

"I love your hair." He ducked his chin. "I have a weakness for redheads."

Elissa's heart swelled. "Do you truly?"

"I do." He reached up to tuck an escaping curl behind her

ear. "In particular, beautiful redheads floating on ponds who quote Callisthenes at me."

She chuckled. "A quality prized by few men, I should think."

"A quality treasured by this man. The way I can talk to you… I don't have to put on airs or pretend to be anything I'm not." He closed his eyes. "Everything is better when you're with me. You've even made me forget—" He looked down, seeming to remember himself.

"Forget what?" She scooted closer to him. How ironic, that they had both come out here with thoughts they were eager to escape.

"It's nothing," he muttered, his shoulder twitching.

Elissa slid her arm around him and began stroking his back. After a moment she felt his muscles relax.

"Whatever it is, you can tell me," she said.

His head lolled to the side as she began to work a knot where his shoulder met his neck. "I wouldn't want to burden you—"

"You wouldn't be burdening me."

"I don't know—"

"Ed-ward," she said, drawing his name out.

"Fine," he grumbled. "I probably need to tell you anyway, if we're going to—" He cleared his throat. "It's about that contest. The one we're both participating in. At Oxford."

"Oh?" She felt her heartbeat ratchet up a notch, because of course, the contest was the root of her anxiety, too. "What about it?"

"It's just—I have to win it, Elissa. I *have* to. And I'm…" He trailed off.

Now her heart was all but flying. What did he mean, *he* had to win it? *She* was the one who had to win it. "Is there a particular reason why?"

"There is." He held her eyes. "I trust you will keep this in confidence."

"Of course."

"Harrington made a wager that I would win the contest. For fifteen thousand pounds."

Suddenly the folly was spinning, and Elissa had to clutch Edward's arm to stop herself from falling off the bench. *Fifteen thousand pounds?* That was more money than her father would earn in a lifetime. "Gracious, Edward! What are you going to do?"

"Win," he said grimly.

"It's a crippling sum."

"The money isn't even the worst of it. I mean"—he acknowledged her shocked expression with a nod—"it's *a lot* of money. It would be a hardship to pay it out. Not for me," he hastened to add. "I've got enough… boots and what not. But for our tenants. I have improvements planned for the cottages and fields. If we have to pay out fifteen thousand pounds, all that will have to wait."

She gave a nervous laugh. "What could be worse than that?"

He stared off into the shadows of the folly. "Harrington has this ridiculous idea that father disapproves of him." He shook his head. "I've never understood why he thinks this. He's the one that everyone loves."

Elissa frowned. "What do you mean, *the one?*"

Edward seemed not to have heard her. "But if I lose, Father will discover Harrington's imprudent wager. There will be no hiding such an amount. And…" He swallowed. "And Father has threatened to send Harrington to India if he causes one more scandal."

"India!" Elissa exclaimed. "Would your father really do it?"

"I believe he would. And Harrington is prone to attacks of asthma. The climate there is exceptionally unforgiving for

those who are unused to it. With Harrington's weak lungs…"
He looked down. "My brother would not survive it. I am sure
of it."

"You're doing it for your brother." Even though she
suspected he would rather not enter.

"Of course." He looked up, surprised. "I would do
anything for Harrington, or for any of my siblings."

He said it as if it were nothing, but Elissa knew better.
Such selflessness was rarer and more precious than rubies.

"So I *have* to win the contest," he said. "But—" He cut
himself off, turning to stare across the folly.

She squeezed his hands. "It's a lot of pressure to put on
yourself."

He squeezed his eyes shut. "It is a lot of pressure. And—"

"And?" she whispered.

"And I'm worried I won't be able to do it," he said in a
rush. "I haven't opened a lexicon in six years. And even if I
had…" He reluctantly met her eyes. "This mystery translator
—he's *brilliant*. He captures the spirit of the work in a way I've
never seen. Even if I were in practice, I don't know if I—" He
broke off, looking down. "My brother came to me. He asked
me for my help. And I'm going to let him down. I know I am."

Elissa wasn't sure how to respond. Her heart broke for
Edward. She was sympathetic to his predicament, to his
desire to help his brother. And yet…

She needed to be the one to win this contest. He had his
reasons, and they were good ones, but she had her own
reasons that were just as good.

No. That wasn't right.

Her reasons were better. Harrington was a man grown.
He didn't *have* to go to India. He could buck his father and
strike out on his own. A man could make his own way in the
world.

Her mother and sisters, on the other hand, could very well starve if Elissa could not support them. And it could happen sooner than she had supposed.

"I can't believe I told you all that," Edward said ruefully. "I didn't mean to burden you—"

"It's not a burden," she hastened to reassure him. "It's important to have someone in whom you can confide."

She meant it. She wasn't sorry Edward had told her about his problems, even if they made the faint hope that they could emerge from the contest with their budding affection unscathed even more untenable.

Beside her, Edward chuckled. "How did I veer so far off course? This is not what I came out here to talk about."

"What did you want to discuss?"

He lifted a hand to stroke her cheek. "Allow me to rephrase myself. I didn't come out here with a *discussion* in mind."

He threaded his fingers into the hair at the nape of Elissa's neck and slowly began tipping his head down to hers. She started to lean in, too, her own head tilting up, but then she froze.

He had just confided in her.

Should she confide in him, too? That *she* was the mysterious translator?

The very person he was so terrified to compete against?

He was likely to learn the truth at some point, either when she won the contest, or when one of the editors who had ultimately rejected her unveiled her identity.

She had always assumed that Edward learning her secret would be accompanied by his disdain.

But... Edward seemed to *like* the fact that she was clever. When she peppered her conversation with the perfect classical quotation, he would close his eyes, as if he were savoring it. He had extolled every one of her own translations she had shared with him.

He had even called her *brilliant*, and here he was, longing to kiss her in the moonlight.

What if she was wrong? What if he wouldn't despise her?

And yet... she could not help but recall his stilted response when she first told him she would be entering the contest.

You know better, Elissa. No man could abide a girl who was more intelligent than him.

Not even a man as wonderful as Edward.

"Elissa? Is everything all right, darling?"

What did it even matter? Here she was, worried her lie of omission would ruin her future with Edward.

But she had no future with Edward. Nothing she did or did not tell him tonight would change the fact that, although he might want to kiss her in the moonlight, she was not the type of woman he would ever marry.

She should enjoy tonight for what it was, should create a memory she would always treasure, even if she wound up old and gray and alone. There was no point in distressing herself over a future that had always been out of reach.

"Elissa?" His eyes were full of consternation. "You're distressed. I apologize. I should not have come out here. I would never want to put you in a compromising position."

"No." She grabbed his hand before he could rise. "This is what I want. To be here. With you."

And she leaned up and brought her lips to his.

CHAPTER 19

his kiss, Elissa thought, was very different from the one they had shared on top of the castle.

Then she had been surprised and unsure, and Edward had been so gentle with her. She knew she had made a fool of herself with the way she couldn't stop trembling, but honestly, Prince Charming himself had pulled her into his arms and kissed her, and on top of a castle to boot! Surely a girl could be forgiven for swooning.

It had truly been the perfect first kiss. This time, however, gentleness seemed to be the farthest thing from Edward's mind.

Not that Elissa was complaining.

He swept his tongue into her mouth, and she heard herself make an animalistic groan that would have been humiliating had he not been making precisely the same sound. She couldn't get enough of him, and it appeared that he felt the same way, because without warning he scooped her up off the bench and settled her in his lap.

This proved to be an *excellent* position for a number of reasons. Seated on his lap, she was only about two inches shorter than him, which made kissing quite a bit easier. She was now close enough to him that she was enveloped in the delicious smell of his bergamot shaving tonic.

But what Elissa enjoyed the most was the fact that her body was now pressed up against Edward's chest, separated by only the fine linen of his shirt. Clearly, he didn't spend all day holed up in the library, because he had the body of a demigod, with firm planes of muscle everywhere she touched. His shoulders were broad and his waist as flat as a board, and gracious, there were so many ridges in the muscles over his stomach...

Through the foggy haze that had descended over her brain, Elissa realized that the reason she was privy to this information about Edward Astley's physique was because she had all but crawled inside his greatcoat with him and was running her hands absolutely everywhere over his beautifully sculpted torso. She pulled back guiltily.

When he opened his eyes, they were unfocused.

"Please don't stop," he said, his breath coming fast. "Touch me, Elissa."

She was only too happy to comply. She found herself trembling again, but this time, it wasn't mere wonder that the man of her dreams was kissing her. No, this was pure, unadulterated lust. She could feel a pulse between her legs, as strong as a heartbeat, and judging by the hard bulge in the front of Edward's trousers that was pressing into her thigh, he felt it, too.

She had read enough Greek verse, much of which was shockingly frank, to know precisely what that bulge meant. An innocent young lady should be shocked and offended by his physical response. But she felt none of that. All she felt was wonder that she, of all people, made him feel this way.

Only half-aware of what she was doing, she found herself swinging one leg across his lap to straddle him. She gave a sigh of pleasure as the little rosebud between her legs came into contact with all of that delicious hardness. She glanced up at him to gauge his reaction and found his eyes filled with rapt wonder. But his gaze was directed not at her face, but lower.

That was when she noticed that her motion had caused the belt on her tattered old dressing gown to come untied, and that it had fallen open in the front. Elissa had been dressed for bed before coming out and was wearing only a shift beneath it. There was nothing but one layer of tissue-thin white linen separating her body from Edward's gaze. She could see her own nipples, and they were peaked not just due to the cold, but also because she was so aroused.

Edward ripped his gaze up to her face. "I'm sorry," he said, reaching for the flaps of her dressing gown and starting to pull them closed. "I just—*God*, Elissa, you're so beautiful."

She reached up and stilled his hands, blushing ferociously as she pulled them from the pilling grey wool. She wanted to place them over her own breasts, where her nipples were crying out for his touch, but she wasn't quite so bold.

Instead she brought them inside her patched old dressing gown, settling them on her sides. "Touch me," she whispered.

His hands swept around her waist. He made no move to kiss her, seemingly unable to tear his gaze away from the sight of her body through her thin chemise. She shifted in his lap, letting out a muffled cry as the little nub between her legs rubbed against his hardness.

Slowly, ever so slowly, he slid his hands up her torso. His gaze shifted to her face. He watched her carefully as he stroked his thumbs over the underside of her breasts, studying her reaction. She made a mewling sound. "Yes, Edward, please—"

That was all the encouragement he needed. His hands immediately cupped her breasts through the fine material of her shift, his thumbs caressing her peaked nipples. Now she was rocking back and forth against the bulge in the front of his trousers, and sounds of desire rose from both of their throats.

Slowly, deliberately, he brought his hand to the ribbon that gathered the neckline of her shift. He paused and looked at her, giving her the chance to tell him to stop.

She reached up and untied it for him. Elissa didn't know how far he was planning to take things, but it really didn't matter. She'd been in love with Edward Astley for half her life, and this would probably be the only chance she would ever have to be with him. If he wanted to take her virginity right here, right now, on this stone bench, she was ready and willing to give it to him, consequences be damned. What did it matter if she was ruined? It wasn't as if she had any marriage prospects.

"Elissa," he moaned, pulling the neck of her shift open to reveal her breasts. He reached out to cup them, his expression full of wonder. She felt herself jerk at the delicious feeling of his hands upon her bare skin.

He began kissing her neck, traveling inexorably downward. She wanted his lips on her nipples so badly, it was all she could do not to grab the back of his head and put his mouth where she needed it.

His lips were reverently brushing the upper swell of her breast when she heard the clip of boots on the marble steps of the folly.

As Elissa emerged from her lust-induced haze, she ascertained that the footsteps were getting louder.

Someone was *coming*.

Edward had noticed them, too. They both froze, staring at each other in horror. Then, as one, they began a mad scramble to put their garments back to rights.

Elissa yanked the neckline of her shift back into place and

hastily tied the ribbon. She made to slide off Edward's lap, but his hands grasped her about the hips, holding her in place. "Your dressing gown," he hissed, giving one last longing look at her whisper-thin chemise.

She was still straddling Edward, struggling to wrap the grey wool around her, when Archibald Nettlethorpe-Ogilvy came striding into the folly.

Considering the way he jerked to a halt and his mouth fell open, he was as surprised to see them as they were to see him. His eyes traveled from Elissa to Edward and back again. "Miss St. Cyr... Lord Fauconbridge, I—I'm sorry. I didn't know you were, er—"

Having finally managed to secure her dressing gown, Elissa slid off Edward's lap, blushing furiously. He whipped the flaps of his greatcoat closed to cover what was going on inside his trousers.

"What brings you here at this time of night?" Edward asked in a clipped voice.

"Something occurred to me regarding the de-carburization of pig iron." Mr. Nettlethorpe-Ogilvy's eyes took on a faraway look. "I was so excited, I couldn't sleep."

"And the de-carburization of pig iron could not wait until morning?" Edward asked. He said it lightly, but Elissa could tell he was annoyed.

"Look, Fauconbridge, I'm sorry. I wouldn't have walked in had I realized the folly was, er, occupied. I suppose I was in a bit of a trance. It just occurred to me that if we were to warm the puddled pig iron to *welding heat* and then *shingle it by hand* —" He rubbed the back of his head. "But I don't suppose you would care about that."

"No," Edward said, "no, we would not."

They fell silent for a moment. Elissa's mind was racing. It was embarrassing enough to be discovered in such an intimate moment. But the full risk of what she'd done now came crashing over her. If word got out, her reputation would be ruined, which mattered to her little, except that the contest was coming up. She couldn't imagine they would let a "fallen" woman through the hallowed doors of Oxford...

Edward cleared his throat. "If you would excuse us."

Mr. Nettlethorpe-Ogilvy gave him an aggravated look. "I didn't mean to stumble upon you. But surely you can appreciate that, now that I have, I cannot leave Miss St. Cyr in this, er, circumstance."

"It's all right," Elissa hastened to reassure him. "Truly, it is."

"You may trust that no one will hear of this incident from me." Mr. Nettlethorpe-Ogilvy's eyes were sincere, and Elissa relaxed a fraction. Their acquaintance was short, but he seemed like such a good man. Elissa was inclined to believe him.

"But," Mr. Nettlethorpe-Ogilvy continued, "if I stumbled upon you, the chance that someone else might do the same is too high." He shook his head. "No, I insist you allow me to escort you back to the house. I could never live with myself if you found yourself in trouble and I could have prevented it."

"There will be no trouble," Edward said, taking her hand.

"You cannot be sure of that," Mr. Nettlethorpe-Ogilvy insisted.

"There will be no trouble," Edward continued, his eyes fixed not on Elissa, but on Mr. Nettlethorpe-Ogilvy, "because I will marry Miss St. Cyr."

CHAPTER 20

*E*dward had already decided that he wanted to marry Elissa. But as soon as he spoke the words out loud, he felt immeasurably better.

It felt *real* now that he had declared his intentions aloud, before the whole world.

Well, before Archibald Nettlethorpe-Ogilvy. But the world would follow soon enough.

Elissa was going to be his *wife*. He would get to spend every day with her.

For the first time in years, he felt like everything was going to be all right.

He turned to look at Elissa, expecting to see her beaming at him, heart on her sleeve as always.

Instead, he found her staring down at her hands, her face a portrait of misery.

"Elissa?" he asked, shocked. "What's wrong, darling?"

"I—" She stopped herself, cutting her eyes to Mr. Nettlethorpe-Ogilvy.

Edward rounded on the man. "Could you perhaps give us a moment of privacy?"

Mr. Nettlethorpe-Ogilvy's gaze traveled back and forth between them. "No," he said, sounding affronted.

"I am not going to do anything untoward," Edward ground out. "I merely want the opportunity to make Miss St. Cyr a proper proposal."

He had a guess as to the reason for Elissa's distress. He had just issued not a proposal so much as a declaration that they were going to wed, and he had done so only after they had been discovered together.

She probably thought he was only offering marriage out of a sense of duty. Once he explained that he had already decided he was going to propose, that he wanted her in his life approximately the same amount as he wanted oxygen, she would look at him the way she had five minutes ago.

At least, he hoped to God she would.

Mr. Nettlethorpe-Ogilvy crossed his arms. "I should like to know," he said, "how one makes a 'proper proposal' without a chaperone's permission, at two in the morning, inside a Greek folly, while you are both dressed in your underclothes."

Edward had to admit that the man had a point.

Not that he had to like it. "Fine," he bit out, standing and offering Elissa his arm.

Mr. Nettlethorpe-Ogilvy promptly did the same thing, and so they made their way back to the house three abreast, in awkward silence.

Once they reached the foot of the staircase that would take Elissa back to her room in the southwest wing, Edward drew Elissa aside. Ignoring Mr. Nettlethorpe-Ogilvy looming behind him, he took both of Elissa's hands in his. "I'm so sorry, Elissa. I made a hash of things back there. That has to be the worst proposal that's ever been made."

If anything, she looked more miserable than before. "Oh,

Edward, I—" But again she stopped herself, glancing over his shoulder at Mr. Nettlethorpe-Ogilvy.

"Don't cry, darling," he whispered. The words "I love you" rose to his lips, but he bit them back How he wanted to tell her, to banish the distress from her eyes. But he couldn't quite bring himself to make such a declaration in front of Archibald Nettlethorpe-Ogilvy. "Everything is going to be all right. I promise."

She swallowed thickly, then nodded.

"I'll be in the library all morning, waiting for you. And I promise I'm going to give you the proposal you deserve."

He kissed her knuckles then released her, and she fled up the stairs.

He scowled at Mr. Nettlethorpe-Ogilvy as he ascended the opposite staircase that led to his own room, even though the man had done nothing he wouldn't have done himself.

But he didn't have time to dwell on Archibald Nettlethorpe-Ogilvy.

He had a proposal to plan.

THE FOLLOWING MORNING, Edward arrived in the library at six o'clock sharp. He didn't expect Elissa to appear for hours, but there had been little point in remaining abed considering how little sleep he was getting.

A little after eight o'clock there was a knock at the door. "Come in," Edward called, springing to his feet and hurrying across the room.

But when the door opened, it proved to be Harrington.

Edward's shoulders sagged, and his brother grinned. "Expecting someone else?"

"Perhaps. I certainly wasn't expecting you at this hour."

Edward returned to his seat behind the desk. His eyes strayed back to the door.

"Don't worry," Harrington said, taking the chair opposite him. "I'll make myself scarce if the lovely Miss St. Cyr should arrive. Wouldn't want to interfere with your proposal."

Edward's head snapped back to his brother.

Harrington was grinning. "Oh, come on, Edward. I know you better than anyone. I've been expecting this all week."

Edward settled his features into his best big brotherly glower. "If you suspected I would be proposing at this exact moment, then may I inquire as to what the hell you're doing here?"

"I'm here to help."

"God save me," Edward muttered.

Harrington laughed. "Trust me, brother, this is one thing I can do for you that you cannot do for yourself." He withdrew a stack of four tiny envelopes from his pocket and pushed them across the desk. "These are for you."

Edward arched a skeptical eyebrow at his brother before opening one. Inside he found a tube of paper-thin, white, almost translucent material, closed at one end and with a pink ribbon around the opening of the other.

He blanched, realizing what it was. "Harrington," he hissed, stuffing it back inside its envelope and shutting the flap, "is this a—"

"A condom," Harrington said cheerfully and at full volume, as if this were a completely normal conversation to be having with one's brother at eight o'clock in the morning.

"What am I supposed to do with this?" Edward hissed.

"You put your prick inside, tie the ribbon, and—do you need me to explain the rest?"

"I meant," Edward ground out, "why would you think I need it?"

Harrington's eyes were sympathetic. "Given your reputation as the golden boy of Gloucestershire, I know you can't exactly walk into a shop in town and ask for them behind the counter. At least, not without causing a storm of gossip. Whereas I, the scapegrace of the family, can do so without anyone batting an eye."

Edward frowned. "You're not a scapegrace—"

"Oh, come off it. We both know I am." Edward started to protest, but Harrington cut him off. "In any case, seeing the two of you beaming at each other yesterday, it was clear you were going to propose at first opportunity. It's also clear that you don't stand a prayer of making it the three weeks it will take for the banns to be called. And knowing how you would hate the scandal of an eight-month baby, I thought this was an area where I could assist you."

"A rather astonishing series of assumptions," Edward grumbled.

Harrington raised a single eyebrow. "Are you saying you don't want them?" he said, reaching for the stack of envelopes.

Edward snatched them away, stuffing them inside his coat pocket. "I want them," he muttered.

"Ha! I knew it. Now brother, allow me to give you some advice. When your darling Elissa gets here, what you need to do is heed the immortal words of the poet Addaeus."

Edward peered at his brother suspiciously. He would have wagered a great deal that Harrington did not recall a single line of Greek verse. Edward had personally completed just enough of his brother's schoolwork to prevent him from getting sent down. "What do you know of Addaeus?"

"'She's pretty?'" Harrington quoted with a florid gesture. "'Then strike while the iron's hot. Just grab your balls and state your case—'"

"Thank you, Harrington!" Edward said, cutting his brother off before the torture could continue.

Harrington grinned as he rose from his chair and strolled toward the door. "You'll want to soak the condoms in some water before using them."

He was halfway out the door when Edward called out, "Harrington?"

His brother paused, leaning back inside. "Yes?"

Edward forced himself to look him square in the eyes. "Thank you."

Harrington grinned. "You're welcome. Good luck, brother. We all like her, you know."

AT NINE O'CLOCK, Elissa stood nervously outside the library door. She had managed a scant few hours of sleep, tossing and turning and worrying about the conversation she was about to have.

She still could not wrap her head around the notion that *Edward Astley* intended to propose marriage to *her*. It was beyond comprehension.

But now that she understood that his intentions were serious, it meant she had made a serious blunder in not telling him the truth. She needed to tell him that she was the anonymous translator, and she needed to do it before he made his proposal.

And then she was going to have to live with whatever his reaction might be.

She was so anxious as she knocked at the door, she worried she might be physically ill. "Come in," Edward called. She heard the muffled sound of hurried footsteps upon the carpet.

He reached the door just as she stepped through it. "Elissa," he breathed, "I'm so glad you're here." He shut the door behind her, then cupped her face and gave her a kiss that was almost reverent in its gentleness.

He stepped back immediately, taking her hand and leading her to the sofa. "I've been waiting for you all morning." He gave her a sheepish grin. "I all but leapt out of my skin every time someone walked past the door."

He settled her on the sofa and sat beside her, still holding her hand. "Would you like some tea?"

She swallowed. "No, thank you."

His smile was rueful. "That's probably for the best. I had to move the table back so I would have room to go down on one knee."

Oh, but this was awful. He was so, so *wonderful*. She wanted to marry this man *so badly*.

And in a few minutes, he was probably going to despise her.

She gathered her courage. "Edward, there's something I need to tell you—"

"I know, darling. I know. There is so much that we need to say to each other."

"It's not that," she said hastily. A look of uncertainty crossed his features, so she added, "I mean, it is, but"—he swallowed—"but first—"

"But first," he said, speaking over her, "before you say another word, you must allow me to apologize for my behavior last night." His eyes were sincere. "I should never have put you in such a compromising position." He shook his head. "It is a poor excuse to say that I was overwhelmed with wanting you. But it's true."

"There's no need to apologize," Elissa said, squeezing his hand. "I wanted you just as much."

His face lit up, and she wished she had not said it, not because it was untrue, but because the conversation was veering off course. "But Edward—"

"But then," he said, seeming not to have heard her, "there is the matter of my proposal. Or should I say, my dictate." His eyes were miserable. "I am so, so sorry, Elissa, for behaving like a pompous brute, declaring that we would wed, when really I should have been down on my knees, begging you—"

"Edward," she said gently, "I wasn't upset about that. Mr. Nettlethorpe-Ogilvy caught us both off guard. I know you only meant to reassure me with all possible haste."

He shook his head. "It was unacceptable. You were upset last night, Elissa. Do not deny it, I could see it in your eyes. And no wonder. Not only did I speak for you, but I fear the unfeeling way in which I did led you to believe that I was only offering marriage because we had been discovered. Out of a sense of duty, rather than affection, when nothing could be farther from the truth." He closed his eyes, grimacing. "Never have I been so disgusted with myself."

Elissa peered at him. Indeed, he looked disgusted with himself; she could not think of a time when she had seen him so upset. It hadn't been the most romantic declaration, but that was only because of Mr. Nettlethorpe-Ogilvy's unfortunate timing. "Truly, you have nothing for which to apologize—"

"I do. My behavior was execrable in every regard. I want you to know that if you do me the honor of accepting my hand, you can expect better of me in the future."

She blinked up at him. "Are you always this hard on yourself?"

He blanched, his shoulder giving a sharp twitch, then cleared his throat. "No more than is warranted. But we have far more important matters to discuss." He took her hand in both of his, then sank to the carpet, going down on one knee. "My darling Elissa—"

"Wait, Edward!" She cringed at the hurt and confusion

that swept over his face. "I—I'm so sorry to interrupt, but before you proceed, there's something I need to tell you."

He gave a tight smile, trying to hide his annoyance. "More important than us spending the rest of our lives together?"

Her voice shook as she said, "Before you ask that of me, there is something you deserve to know."

His blue eyes clouded with wariness. "What is it?" he asked softly.

"The translator. Of *On the Sublime*." Elissa swallowed, gathering all of her courage. "It was me."

$\mathcal{E}$dward froze. He was kneeling on the carpet, his gaze fixed upon the striped cushions of the sofa, struggling to figure out how he felt about what Elissa had just told him.

Elissa was the translator. He... he could see it now. She had this talent for picking up the meter from the original Greek and giving her translations the same feeling. Not fully, of course. The languages were too different for that, but even that hint of the meter was more than he'd seen anyone else manage.

Excepting the anonymous translator of *On the Sublime*. He had been able to do it, too.

But, of course, not he. *She.*

He should have seen it, should have known at once. It seemed so obvious, in retrospect...

Elissa's wobbly voice managed to penetrate his foggy brain. "I know you must be very upset."

Was he? He... he honestly wasn't sure. On the one hand, he'd felt slightly nauseous ever since he found out she would also be taking part in the contest. The last thing he wanted was to compete against Elissa.

But… this was slightly different. She had published a successful book, one he knew to be deserving of its brilliant reception. That did not reflect in any way on *him*. Her book was not in competition with his own, and the fact that she had succeeded did not mean that he had failed.

Was he jealous of her? He probed his feelings. He—he didn't think he was. The misery that welled up inside him whenever the thought of Robert Slocombe being named First Classical Medalist… it wasn't there.

It might be different if his book had come out around the same time as hers. The reviewers might have compared them, expressed a preference for one over the other. One would have sold more copies than the other. Those thoughts made him feel a bit twitchy.

But that was never going to happen. He certainly wasn't planning on publishing any more translations.

And, as his viscountess, neither would she.

He needed to answer her. "I wouldn't say I'm upset. Surprised, perhaps? But also…" He shook his head, struggling to find the right words. "I already knew you were brilliant. So I'm surprised, but also… not surprised. At the same time. If that makes sense?"

After all, the true issue was the upcoming contest, and the odds of him losing to her (and subsequently having an unworthy reaction, which she would witness, thereby ruining her good opinion of him) had not increased just because she was the anonymous translator.

Sure, he felt a familiar wave of nausea at the thought of competing against her. But it seemed that was a separate thing.

He chanced a glance at Elissa and saw that she was crying.

"I'm sorry, Edward," she said, her voice breaking. "I'm so

sorry. I should have told you earlier. I wanted to, but I—I was so afraid—"

He shook himself. She was sobbing and here he was, rooted to the floor, doing nothing to comfort her. He rose and sat beside her on the sofa, taking her hand. "Why were you afraid, darling?"

She told him. She told him about her father's heart troubles and about her cruel uncle who would cast them from their home. She told him how she had always felt responsible for saving her mother and sisters, because she was the one who had failed to be the boy her father had wanted, the boy who could have saved them all. She told him how no one had ever taken her seriously as a scholar, how she had been mocked and ignored on the days Edward wasn't present in her father's classroom, which didn't come as much of a surprise. He'd seen the strange indifference the other students, and even her own father, had harbored toward her. And she told him about all the publishers who had rejected her manuscript as soon as they found out she was a woman.

"That's why no one can find out." She gave a sad sniff, and Edward handed her his own handkerchief, taking her soiled one and tossing it on the end table. "Not unless I win the contest, that is. My identity will come out eventually. I submitted my manuscript to enough publishers that one of them is bound to talk, and they'll probably do it immediately before my next publication. To s-sabotage me. And I can tell you just what will happen next. The reviewers will mysteriously find that it did not move them in the same way my first book did. They will decide, in fact, that their original opinion is the one that is wrong. That I was never really that talented after all." She glanced up at him, her eyes pleading. "Unless I can win the contest. If I've defeated all of the most talented scholars in England head-to-head, then maybe, *maybe* that will serve as my shield. That they won't be able to dismiss me."

"You probably have the right of it. There are a great many stupid people in this world." He waited for her to finish dabbing her eyes and made sure she was looking at him before he continued. "But I hope you understand that I am not one of them. I *love* the fact that you're so clever. It's one of my favorite things about you. The conversations we have, the way I can talk to you…" He shook his head. "I *never* thought I would find something like this. Someone like you."

For some reason, this made her cry all the harder. "I should've known this would be your reaction. Most men cannot abide a woman who is as intelligent as them. But you've never been anything like those louts from my father's classroom, and I should have trusted you from the start. I—I *love* you, Edward," she said, her voice breaking.

Hearing her say those words was like stepping from a cold, dank cellar into a sunny meadow awash with spring flowers. Edward felt his chest expand, his neck relax. "And I love you, Elissa," he said, leaning down to give her a kiss.

It wasn't as passionate as their kiss last night, as Elissa was still crying, although Edward fancied they were now happy tears. He settled back on the couch and wrapped an arm around her, rubbing her back while she cried on his shoulder.

The more he thought about it… this was actually a good thing. Because the fundamental reason Elissa wanted to enter the contest was so she could provide for her mother and sisters.

But that was no longer a concern. Once they were married, Edward would take care of her family. The financial factors that had motivated her had just disappeared. And besides, it was unseemly for members of the nobility to publish books for profit, so Elissa's publishing career would have to end, regardless.

This meant that Elissa could drop out of the contest. She could drop out of the contest and Edward wouldn't have to compete against her! She wouldn't even need to go to Oxford. In the event that he lost (probably to Robert bloody Slocombe) she wouldn't be there to witness whatever unworthy reaction he might have.

Suddenly Edward felt better than he had in weeks.

He gave her shoulders a squeeze. "Don't cry, darling. Everything is all right. It's better than all right, in fact. I will obtain for us a bishop's license so we can be married with all possible haste."

She laughed, tossing his now-soiled handkerchief atop the one already on the end table, then gave him a watery smile. "There is nothing I would like better."

He took her hands in both of his. "Perfect. I'll go today to see about that license. And tomorrow, you can drop out of the contest."

CHAPTER 22

*E*lissa blinked at Edward.

"Drop out?" She shook her head, certain she must have misheard. "I can't drop out. I'm the reason there *is* a contest."

He was smiling at her as if everything was normal and he hadn't just suggested that she give up on her dreams. "There is no reason for you to participate now. You no longer need the five-hundred-pound prize, or a credential for your publishing career. I'll take care of you and your family from now on. Come." He stood and started toward the door. "The closest place to get a marriage license will be Gloucester. I'll secure one straightaway. We should also send word to your parents and your older sisters."

"Edward, wait. It's not about the prize. It's about proving myself against the most talented men in the country. Showing that I deserve be taken seriously, that my translation wasn't a fluke."

He glanced over his shoulder, surprise registering on his face. He backtracked to stand in front of her. "I know that, Elissa. I know you're as talented as any man who will be in that room, myself included. As I said, it's one of the things I love about you."

She took his hand and squeezed it. "Then you understand. You understand how important this is to me."

His eyebrows flew up. "Surely you're not still thinking to enter?"

"Of course I am! Why would I not?"

He gaped at her. "Well for one, there's the fact that my estate—which is soon to be *your* estate—stands to lose fifteen thousand pounds if I don't win."

She set her jaw. "If I win this contest, I can earn us that much and more. It will take me two more translations, perhaps three, but I'll do it."

He blinked at her as if she were speaking Bengali. "As the Viscountess Fauconbridge, you cannot publish *any* translations."

She recoiled. "Why not? You did."

"That was entirely different. The proceeds from my translation were donated to Anne's Ladies' Society. What is improper is for someone of our station to work for money."

Elissa was reeling. She knew there would be some changes to her life if she were to marry Edward. That she would have to put on a fancy dress and parade about London on his arm, pretending she was viscountess material and trying not to trip over a candelabra and set somebody's hair on fire.

But she had assumed that the majority of her time would be spent the way she spent her days now: sitting around the library, her nose stuck in a book, working on whatever translation or composition had struck her fancy. She had thought the only differences would be that she would be in Harrington Hall's library instead of her father's, and that she would have Edward working alongside her.

It appeared she had comprehended very little.

A solution occurred to her. "I will continue to publish anonymously. No one ever need know that it's me."

He spoke through clenched teeth. "They're going to reveal your identity if you win the contest. You won't be anonymous anymore. Which is, again, why you can't enter!"

She felt tears forming. "You don't understand. You don't understand how important winning this contest would be to me."

"Not more important than it is to me, I assure you."

Now she felt annoyed. Edward had won dozens of contests and awards at Cambridge. She'd never even had the chance to enter. "How could it possibly be more important to you?"

Edward's voice was tight, and his wrists flexed backward. "You seem to be forgetting the fact that *my brother* will be packed off to his death in India if my father finds out about his wager!"

Elissa stood. "I understand that you are concerned for your brother. But your father cannot *force* him to go to India. He's not going to tie him up and drag him onto a ship."

"No, but he can refuse to aid him in making a start in another suitable career. Without my father's support, both financially and through his connections, Harrington will never be able to secure an appropriate position."

Elissa crossed her arms. "So, he'll have to make his own way—that's no different from what everyone else has to do. What *I* have managed to do, with the disadvantage of being a woman. And I think you're selling your brother short. Harrington has so many wonderful qualities. With his wit, he would make a splendid playwright, or—"

"A *playwright*?" Edward recoiled, looking so horrified, one would have thought she'd suggested his brother take up a career in highway robbery. "He is the son of an earl!"

"Why should that matter? He would be good at it."

"Suitable careers for the son of an earl include the army, the Royal Navy, the law, the clergy—"

"The *clergy?*" Elissa closed her mouth, which she found was gaping open. "I do not mean this as an insult to your brother, but surely it is apparent that Harrington is ill-suited to life as a vicar."

Edward waved a hand in acknowledgment. "It would not be my first choice for him, either. But if a lucrative living should become available, it might be the best option for him."

Apparently Elissa understood *far* less about life in the aristocracy than she'd realized. "How can his best option be to spend the rest of his life doing something he hates?"

Edward looked affronted. "It is a respectable career for a gentleman!"

Elissa shook her head. "The point is, Harrington is a man grown. He is more than capable of making his own way. And I do not think it unreasonable to expect him to face the consequences of his own actions."

"The point is that there is no longer a need for you to enter the contest, and that, due to the risk of your identity being revealed, it is no longer appropriate for you to do so." Edward turned on his heel and strode toward the door. "I will advise the organizers upon my arrival that you changed your mind and will not be participating."

Elissa stalked after him and grabbed him by the elbow, spinning him around. "You will tell them no such thing, because I have no intention of dropping out of that contest!"

Now it was Edward's mouth that fell open. When he spoke, his voice was clipped. "Is this how little you value our future together? That you would… would throw it all away so you can enter some stupid contest?"

"Throw it all away?" What on earth was going on? When had the conversation taken such a drastic turn? "Who said anything about throwing it away? Of course I want a future with you, Edward!"

"You have a strange way of showing it!"

"I'm not the one talking about calling off our marriage over something so trivial! If anyone is throwing it away, it's you."

"Don't be ridiculous. I just asked you to marry me!"

Elissa's hands curled into fists. "And in the next breath, told me I have to change who I am!"

He spoke through gritted teeth. "All marriages require some degree of compromise."

"Some degree of compromise, to be sure! I am willing to wear whatever clothes your sister tells me are befitting. To practice pouring tea with your mother. But I am a classical scholar. That is *fundamental* to who I am." She dabbed at her eyes with her sleeve, realizing they were suddenly damp. "And I am not willing to—to—" Her voice broke, and she gave a great sniff. *Perfect.* Now her nose was starting to run. She reached for one of the soiled handkerchiefs from the end table but hesitated when she saw how damp it was.

Edward was glowering out the window. "There are some clean handkerchiefs in the desk drawer," he said, his voice clipped.

"Thank you," she muttered, crossing the room and pulling it open.

As she reached to retrieve one of the neatly stacked handkerchiefs, her hand brushed something cold and hard that made a metallic clink. "What's this?" she asked, pulling it out.

It was a large, gold coin, about the same size as a crown piece. The image showed a man in collegiate robes kneeling before a Muse, who was enthroned upon a dais. The Muse held a lyre under one arm and with the other, reached forward to crown the kneeling man with a wreath of laurels.

There was an inscription in Latin, which Elissa translated aloud without thinking. "Praise has its own rewards."

She flipped the coin over. The reverse side showed a man in the sort of curly wig that had been popular during the previous century. "Sir William Browne," she read absent-mindedly, then gasped as she realized what it was.

"Edward! Is this one of your Browne Medals?" Elissa had followed his academic career at Cambridge assiduously in the newspapers and knew very well that he had won four of them, two for Latin composition and two more for Greek. "Surely you don't keep your Browne Medals loose in your desk drawer!"

But it seemed that was exactly what he did, because digging around, her hands felt more large, cool, coin-shaped objects. She pulled a handful out and laid them on the desk. There were two more Browne Medals and a few smaller ones she didn't recognize.

It seemed that Edward hadn't been attending, but the clank of the medals on the desk snapped him from his stupor. He hurried across the room, his eyes so wide they were showing more white than blue. "What—what are you doing?"

"No wonder you don't understand," Elissa spat, pulling out another fistful of medals. "You've won so many awards, they don't even mean anything to you. You've just tossed them in a drawer!"

"Put those back!" Edward snapped. His shoulder twitched violently as he yanked the drawer open. The medals made a great clatter as he swept them back inside, then slammed the drawer shut.

One of the medals was still in Elissa's hand. It was different from the others—bronze and almost the size of her palm, far larger than the others. There was another goddess upon a dais, this time addressing a cluster of students. In the background was a building with a columned portico. The inscription was again in Latin. "For classical studies. From the liberality of Thomas Holies, Duke of Newcastle... *Chancellor* of the University!" Her fingers were trembling as her gaze snapped to Edward. "Do you mean to tell me that you keep the *Chancellor's Classical Medal* shoved in the back of a drawer?"

He spun around, making a feral sound, something she had never imagined Edward Astley capable of. "*Give me that!*" he shouted, lunging for the medal.

Elissa took a step back. "I won't! Not if you're going to throw it in that drawer to clatter around and get damaged." He tried to snatch it from her grasp, but she held it out of his reach. "I'm surprised at you, Edward! You should take better care of this. Do you have *any idea* how much it would mean to me to have a Chancellor's Classical Medal? It would mean everything, absolutely *everything*! But I never had that chance. I've never been permitted to cross the hallowed thresholds of Oxford or Cambridge." Tears were streaking down her face, and she was fairly certain her nose was running again, but she didn't care. "You should *treasure* this! You shouldn't keep it loose in a drawer. You should have it on display!"

"*Display?*" he shouted. His eyes were wild, and his shoulder was positively spasming. "I will *never* put it on display! I hate the sight of that bloody thing! Because that is not the Chancellor's Classical Medal, Elissa, and I am not the Chancellor's Classical Medalist. *Robert Slocombe* is the Chancellor's Classical Medalist! I am the Chancellor's *Second* Medalist, and I can assure you, there is a *world* of difference!"

Never in her life had she seen Edward Astley lose even an inch of control, but here he was, shouting, hands shaking uncontrollably, a sheen of sweat upon his brow. His eyes were frantic, and as annoyed as she was with him at the moment, it tore at her heart.

All at once he seemed to realize himself. Horror swept across his face, his cheeks flushed, and he hastily turned away, crossing the room and staring determinedly out the window.

She set the medal down upon the desk and trailed after him. "Edward." He refused to meet her eye. She tried to lay her hand on his arm, but he shook her off. "You don't truly berate yourself for that, do you?" He said nothing. "For coming in second? Out of everyone at Cambridge? That is an achievement. Not something you should be ashamed of."

He glared out the window, his jaw iron. Suddenly certain things he'd said to her over the past two weeks came flitting across her mind.

"—everything I used to love about classical verse—"

"—Harrington is the one that everyone loves—"

"—I think it is common enough for authors to see nothing but the flaws in their own work—"

"—being around me is often a burden—"

"—I wouldn't want to burden you—"

"—I didn't mean to burden you—"

Burden.

Burden.

Burden.

She could hear the note of desperation in her own voice as she said, "You do know how wonderful you are, Edward, both as a scholar and a person. Don't you?" He still wouldn't look at her, so she grabbed his arm with both hands. "Don't you?"

He jerked away from her. For a fraction of a second, his eyes met hers before he looked down, and the humiliated sadness she saw in them broke her heart.

He stalked across the room and opened the library door. He did not look at her as he held it open expectantly.

She crossed to stand beside him but didn't go through the door. "No. We need to discuss this."

His gaze was fixed on the far wall. "There is nothing to discuss."

"There is. This is important."

He swallowed thickly, a muscle working in his jaw. "You still mean to enter the contest?"

"Y-yes. I do."

"Then we are at an impasse."

"We're not. We can get past this. I know we can. If you would just—"

"I would like for you to leave." He enunciated each word, as if he wanted there to be no possibility she would fail to understand. He made a sweeping gesture toward the door.

Numb, Elissa stepped into the hall. "Edward, wait. Don't do this. Don't—"

"I wish you good fortune in the contest, Miss St. Cyr."

She couldn't see anything through her tears, but she heard the click of the door.

CHAPTER 23

$\mathcal{A}$fter he was sure Elissa was gone, Edward stormed from the library, past the footman stationed outside the door (who no doubt had heard everything), and went straight to the stables.

He could not believe he had slipped in such a manner. Here he'd been so worried that an unguarded look or a careless word would cause Elissa to guess at his inner troubles. Well, there was no need for her to guess, as he'd gone and shouted them at her!

He couldn't face her now. He absolutely couldn't. He had never told *anyone* how devastated he'd been to lose the Chancellor's Classical Medal. He was always so careful to maintain a strong front. But even worse, Elissa had immediately perceived how deep his feelings of worthlessness truly went. *You do know how wonderful you are, Edward, both as a scholar and a person. Don't you?*

She had said it out of kindness. Or possibly out of pity, a thought so horrible it caused the gorge to rise in his throat. But no one really wanted to hear about his sorrows, to be burdened with his problems.

He spent the rest of the morning and the better part of the afternoon pounding out his bitterness on horseback. Even a challenging cross-country route with plentiful jumps wasn't distracting enough to drown out the voices in his head, which were bent upon replaying the scene in the library over and over. Still, it was better than being completely at loose ends, and at least out here there was no one to witness his misery.

But by early afternoon, Edward became cognizant that even a horse like Bucephalus couldn't go indefinitely. There was also the fact that he hadn't informed anyone of his plans to stay out all day. He was fortunate someone had strapped a canteen to his saddle, but he had no food, and his growling stomach was doing nothing to improve his mood. And so he reluctantly pointed Bucephalus back toward the house.

As he rounded a bend and the stables came into sight, he saw a rider approaching at full gallop. He hastily reined Bucephalus in.

It proved to be Harrington. "Where the devil have you been?" he snapped as he brought his bay gelding to a halt in the middle of the road.

Edward was in no mood to put up with whatever temper his brother was in. "And good afternoon to you, too."

"Don't you give me that sanctimonious nonsense. This is no time for niceties. We've got a crisis on our hands!"

Oh, Harrington thought *he* was having a crisis? Edward raised a skeptical eyebrow. "And what is the nature of this crisis?"

"She's left!" Harrington spat.

"L-left?" Suddenly Edward's head was swimming. He hastily masked his features. "To whom are you referring?"

"You bloody well know who I'm talking about. Miss St. Cyr! What on earth did you say to her?"

Edward glowered. "That is none of your affair."

"The hell it's not! If you think I'm going to sit back and watch you throw away the best chance you've ever had at real happiness, then you don't know me at all."

"The best chance I've—" Edward looked down, suddenly feeling an urgent need to dislodge a twig from Bucephalus's mane. "What nonsense. I'm perfectly—"

"Miserable. Don't deny it. I know you better than that. But when you're with her..." Harrington waved a hand. "I haven't seen you this happy in *years*. And there isn't a chance in hell I'm letting you walk away from that! Now, you're going to pull your head out of your arse and tell me what happened, and we are going to figure out what to do."

"I—" Edward bit back a curse. As soon as Harrington said Elissa was leaving, a piercing ache had started in the center of his chest. It showed no signs of abating. He shouldn't be surprised that she'd left. Hell, he'd been the one to tell her to go!

But it would seem that he wasn't nearly as prepared to see Elissa St. Cyr walk out of his life as he had supposed.

Edward shook his head. "It's too late. I—I've ruined everything."

"As a noted expert in making a hash of things, I doubt that very much. It takes a real concerted effort to ruin *everything*."

"I can't face her," Edward said in a rush. "Not after I... I... "

"Start at the beginning."

Edward paused. Elissa had trusted him with her deepest secret. Even though she probably hated him now, he didn't mean to break her confidence. "I was trying to propose, but she stopped me. She had some, er, surprising news that she thought she should tell me first."

Harrington snorted. "What, is she the secret translator of that book everyone's going on about?"

Edward froze.

The truth must've shown on his face, because Harrington's eyes went wide. "She is?" He barked out a laugh. "Good for her! Is that it, then? You didn't take the news well?"

"No, I think I did. She was expecting I wouldn't." Edward gave Harrington a hard look. "It is very important to Elissa that her secret not come out. You can't tell anyone. Not even Thetford."

"What a shame, because all Thetford and I talk about is Greek poetry." Harrington rolled his eyes. "So, if that wasn't the problem, what was?"

Edward paused. He didn't want to tell Harrington that their argument had started with Edward's insistence that Elissa drop out of the contest. He didn't want Harrington to feel bad, so he decided to skip forward a bit. "She was crying. With relief, I think, that I wasn't put off that she was the translator. And I was, you know, patting her on the back and what not. And she needed a fresh handkerchief, and I told her there were some in the desk drawer."

Harrington looked perplexed. "Um, all right?"

Edward swallowed. "It is the same drawer where I keep some of my old awards from Cambridge. And when she reached in there to get a handkerchief, she happened to pull out the Chancellor's Second Classical Medal."

A swift, horrified comprehension swept over Harrington's face. "Oh, *shit!*"

Edward rubbed an eye with the heel of his hand. Apparently, Harrington was more observant than he'd given him credit for. "Oh, shit," he agreed.

"That could not have gone well. What happened?"

Edward sighed. "She was chastising me for keeping it in a drawer. Going on about how I should be proud of it."

"She happens to be right about that."

He narrowed his eyes at his brother. "In any case, we

started arguing about it. She was actually quite upset, because of course she wasn't allowed to go to Cambridge and try for any awards. And she kept going on about how I should treasure it, how I should put it on *display*." His whole body gave a horrified shudder. "And I—I snapped. I started ranting about how I hated the sight of the bloody thing, and... and screaming about Robert Slocombe—"

"Oh, my God!" Harrington threw his head back, squinting at the sky. "You even brought up Robert bloody Slocombe!"

Edward scowled. "Do you even know who Robert Slocombe is?"

"Of course I do! Do you truly think I don't know the name of my own brother's nemesis?" Harrington's eyes turned sympathetic. "Look, Edward, it doesn't take a Senior Wrangler level of intellect to figure out you were berating yourself for not winning First Classic. You think I haven't noticed how quickly you change the subject whenever someone mentions your time at university? I know you like to bury these things and pretend nothing's bothering you. But I'm your brother. And every time Slocombe's name came up, you'd go so stiff you looked like you were dying of tetanus."

"Right." Edward cleared his throat. It would appear he wasn't nearly so good at concealing his feelings as he had supposed. "Well, suffice to say, I made a great fool of myself. I'm sure her good opinion of me has been destroyed. Forever."

Harrington was studying him. "Did she say that?"

"Not in so many words, but—"

Harrington pointed his riding crop at Edward. "Quit prevaricating. What did she say?"

"I, uh, I can't recall—"

"Yes, you can! Tell me! Right now!"

Edward glowered across the field. "She said I was wonderful, and she wanted to make sure I understood that."

Harrington clinched his hand into a fist. "I knew it! *She* isn't the one who thinks you're not good enough. You think that, to be sure."

"I—I—"

"But you're wrong. Utterly wrong. You're the best man I know."

Edward rubbed his eyes. "You don't understand."

"Yes, I do. You didn't ruin things. Not at all. You're just embarrassed, and because you have absolutely no experience in making a complete and total cake of yourself and then having to get up the next day and carry on, you're imagining it's worse than it is. It's not. Take it from someone who's an *expert* in these things. It'll be fine."

"No, it won't be. I—I cannot possibly face her."

"You can and you will. Come on." When Edward made no move, Harrington leaned forward and tried to grab Bucephalus's reins. Bucephalus responded by laying his ears back and snapping at his brother's hand.

Edward sighed. He had, in fact, been on his way back to the house, so there was no point in being stubborn about it. Deciding to spare his brother's fingers, he gave Bucephalus the signal to walk.

"There's a good chap," Harrington said brightly. "Look, I know you're embarrassed. But being embarrassed is the worst reason imaginable to spend the rest of your life without the woman you love."

Edward grunted. Harrington did have a point. However much he was dreading it, the dull pain in his chest suggested that living without Elissa might be the one thing worse than facing her.

"You said she left. Do you have any idea where she was going?"

"My information is from Roger the footman. He said she left on foot. What worried him was that she was carrying all of her luggage. She wouldn't say where she was going and declined his offer to summon the carriage. She set off toward town."

Edward groaned. This was going to be *mortifying*. But there was nothing for it. "Then town is where I'm heading. I hope to God I'm not too late." He cut his eyes to his brother. "Thank you."

Harrington made some reply, probably wishing him luck, but Edward had already urged Bucephalus into a gallop and didn't hear anything over his horse's pounding hooves.

CHAPTER 24

*E*dward's mind raced as Bucephalus flew down the graveled drive leading toward the main road. As best he could figure, Elissa probably meant to pick up the mail coach at the Plough.

He wondered what time the mail coach departed. Of course, he hadn't the faintest idea, as he'd never had to take the mail coach in his whole bloody life...

A blur of white caught his eye as Bucephalus rounded a curve. There was something in the grass, in a little grove of trees near a picturesque bend in the stream.

He squinted. It proved to be a woman in a white dress, lying on a blanket.

A woman with red hair.

A woman with red hair and a book propped open on her chest.

He pulled a sharp right, reined Bucephalus in, and vaulted off before his horse had even come to a full stop.

Bucephalus gave him a strange look, then wandered over to the stream for a drink.

Elissa was so absorbed in whatever she was reading, she gave no sign of noticing him. He plopped down beside her on the brown plaid blanket she had spread out on the grass. "I didn't really want you to leave."

Her whole body jerked, and a characteristic look of befuddlement crossed her features. "Edward?" she said, sitting halfway up.

He was breathing hard, and he knew he should apologize for having startled her, for having told her to go away that morning, for being covered in mud and smelling of horse, for having in the past twenty-four hours issued not one but two of the worst proposals in the history of mankind... for an alarmingly long list of offenses, now that he thought on it.

He knew what he should say, but every time he tried to speak, the words died in his throat. He was in agony waiting for her to get her bearings. To give him some indication of where he stood.

And then, she did it.

She smiled at him as she pushed her way up to sitting. It was her real smile, as if she were delighted to see him (*how was that possible?*). "I'm so glad you're here," she exclaimed, laying aside her book.

"You—you are?" He gave a furtive glance around, half-expecting to find someone else, the person to whom she was speaking, sitting beside him on the blanket, but there was only Bucephalus grazing nearby.

"Of course." He noticed then that she had removed her bonnet, gloves, and half-boots, which were arranged neatly along the edge of the blanket. There was also a tea towel covered in crumbs with two biscuits on it.

His stomach gave a great rumble, reminding him that he hadn't eaten since breakfast.

"Are you hungry?" she asked as she tucked her stockinged feet beneath her.

"I am," he confessed. "I've been out riding ever since we parted."

"Perfect!" She reached into her leather satchel, which he now recalled was both 'all of her luggage,' and also a reasonable receptacle for a book, a blanket, and a picnic luncheon. She pulled out a canteen and a large tea towel that had been tied into a bundle. "I asked the kitchen to pack something for me. Wait until you see how much they sent!" She laughed as she picked at the knot. "I thought it excessive at the time, but now that you're here, it feels fortuitous."

His stomach growled again as two rolls and a wedge of cheese came rolling out of the bundle. Elissa handed him a roll and quickly sliced him some of the cheese. "Oh! And you'll be wanting some lemonade," she said, passing him the canteen.

He devoured the roll in three bites, which earned him a giggle. She hastened to unpack the rest of the food. He felt so grateful upon being handed a chicken and leek hand pie he could've kissed her stockinged toes. While he ate the pie, she carefully applied butter and jam to the second roll, then went to work peeling him an orange.

The worst of his hunger sated, Elissa cheerfully helped him remove his boots, "So you'll be more comfortable." She was just so *kind*. Edward was accustomed to being the one who looked after everyone else, the one no one thought to assist. And he knew this was his own doing. He was the one who rigidly maintained an image of self-sufficiency at all times. But considering the way his heart lurched as Elissa smiled up at him, proffering her orange slices, perhaps there was something to be said for letting this particular woman take care of him sometimes, too.

By the time he polished off the slice of pound cake Elissa presented for dessert, his stomach was feeling significantly better.

The rest of him was feeling relieved, as Elissa was rather obviously not furious with him, but also a bit stupid. Because clearly he had overreacted that morning.

She brushed a few crumbs of pound cake into the grass, then settled on the blanket facing him. She took his hands in both of hers. "So… I wasn't leaving."

"I see that now," he said, gesturing toward the blanket with an elbow, "although it would be my fault if you were."

Oh, how he wanted to close his eyes, to stare off across the field. But he forced himself to meet her gaze as he said, "I am very sorry for what I said this morning. I shouldn't have told you to go away. I thought I meant it at the time, but as soon as I heard you'd left, I realized I'd made a horrible mistake." He swallowed. "I handled the conversation in the worst way imaginable, and for that, I am truly sorry."

She ran her thumb over the back of his hand. "It's all right, Edward. I've been thinking about it all morning, and the thought I keep coming back to is that when I saw your medals, all I could see was an opportunity I would have loved to have had, but was always denied." She bit her lip. "But that's not what they represent to *you*. Is it?"

She understood. She understood perfectly.

The thought made him queasy. "That's correct."

"For you, they represent not something you wanted to do, but something you felt you *had* to do. Do I have the right of it?"

"It became that, by the end." He cleared his throat. "As you saw this morning, I am not at my best when discussing the Chancellor's Classical Medal. But if you can find it within yourself to grant me another chance, I promise I will never mention it again."

One corner of her mouth quirked up. "Never mention it again? I believe we should take the opposite approach."

Sweat broke out on his temples. "I disagree. Strongly."

"And yet, after this morning, I do feel that I deserve an explanation. Especially if there is to be any discussion of our marrying. How can I properly consider your offer if I don't understand you, Edward?"

He slouched on the blanket. "I wish you didn't have such a reasonable argument."

He volunteered nothing. If she wanted to have this horrid conversation, she could take the lead.

After a moment, Elissa squeezed his hands. "So. It is clear that you have been very hard on yourself for failing to win the First Classical Medal. Why was it so important to you?"

Was it not obvious? "I've been determined to win it ever since I was a boy. Everyone expected it of me."

"Everyone expected it of you." She tipped her head to the side. "Who is this 'everyone'?"

"Absolutely everyone. My family. My friends. My tutors, including your father."

"And they were not proud that you worked hard and became a fine classical scholar? That you won a medal, albeit the one for second place?"

He had to repress the urge to snort. "Not in the least. I am expected to achieve the highest standard, at all times, in all situations. It is what my family requires of me."

"Is that so?" She stared across the sweep of lawn a moment, lost in thought. "And by your family, do you mean your parents? Or do you include your brothers and sisters in that number?"

"All of them." Edward cleared his throat. "Is that sufficient explanation? May we move on?"

"Not quite yet." Elissa gave him a smile. "I do not doubt that you're right about your tutors being anxious for you to win such an award. It would have been a feather in my father's cap to have one of his students named First Classic, and he would have bragged on it incessantly. I do not know your parents well enough to say what their expectations might have been. But I wouldn't be so sure that your siblings care about what academic honors you did or did not achieve."

"They do. They expect me to be the best, and I was not."

"Hmm."

She lapsed into silence. He didn't care for the way Elissa was studying him, noting his every reaction.

She squeezed his hands. "Did you know that your siblings have been trying to 'sell' me on you all week? The number of times I've heard the words, "the best big brother in the world" is in the dozens, possibly the hundreds." She laughed. "Little did they know that I've been sold for years. Would you like to know what they've been telling me?"

"Probably that I was Senior Wrangler, or—"

"Not a word. Although I am curious—did winning Senior Wrangler not soften the blow of not being named First Classic? Almost everyone considers it the greater honor."

"No. The truth is, it was just an accident that I won Senior Wrangler."

Elissa bit her lip. "How does one accidentally be named the top student in mathematics at Cambridge?"

"It was merely a quirk of the exam process," Edward said in a rush. He had never admitted this to anyone before. "The exam lasts for three days, the first two of which consist of a written exam. The examinees are then sorted into groups based on their performance, and you dispute against those in your group on a series of mathematical propositions. Because I was more focused on the classics, nobody was expecting me to test into the top group. But it happened that one section of the exam required us to calculate square and cube roots by hand."

"Calculate square and cube roots?" Elissa's brow was creased.

"Only to three decimal places," he reassured her.

"Oh, is that all?" She gave an incredulous laugh. "That sounds impossible."

"It's not hard if you know the trick of it. It happens that my childhood tutor had taught me how. But nobody else knew how to do it, and so I performed better on the written exam than anyone anticipated. And, of course, having focused on the classics, my Latin was a bit stronger, and I had a good deal of practice in disputations. So it is perhaps not surprising that I performed well on the third day. But the truth is, I have no particular facility for mathematics."

Elissa blinked at him a few times. "Allow me to make sure I understand. Your argument that you have 'no particular facility' for mathematics is based on the fact that you can calculate square and cube roots by hand?"

"Precisely."

Elissa rubbed her forehead. "I must confess that I do not find your argument as convincing as you seem to think it. But leaving that aside, let us return to your siblings and the qualities *they* found praiseworthy. Lucy told me about the time she broke her ankle when she was five and you carried her around on your back all summer so she wouldn't be stuck inside while the rest of you were out playing."

"Anyone would have done that for their little sister."

She didn't contradict him, but her eyes were skeptical. "Anne told me how you agreed to publish your translation of *Prometheus Unbound*, even though you didn't want a soul to see it, and donate the proceeds to her Ladies' Society. She said you were the reason she was able to get her charity off the ground."

Edward frowned. "Wait—she said that? That I didn't want anyone to see it?" *Perfect.* First Harrington somehow managed to figure out about Robert Slocombe, and now Anne knew about his dread of anyone reading his translation.

He realized that he had gone tense and was gripping Elissa's hands in a way that was probably uncomfortable. He forced himself to relax. It appeared he wasn't as inscrutable as he thought. He needed to be much more careful, to make sure he wasn't giving away even the most subtle sign of these base feelings.

Elissa continued, "Isabella told me that you were the only one willing to read her early stories, of which I am given to understand there were *many*. She said that without your help and encouragement, she would never have been able to become the writer she is today."

"That was nothing—"

"Caro believes you strong-armed Lord Graverley into asking her to dance at her debut ball to guarantee her success." Edward attempted to maintain a tactful silence. She nudged him with her knee. "You did, didn't you?"

Well, of course he did. "She's my little sister. It was the least I could do."

"I'm curious—why did you not do the same for Anne?"

"Whereas Caro longed to be the toast of London, Anne would've been petrified to have so many eyes on her. I would've asked Graverley had it been something she wanted."

Elissa shook her head and made a wistful sound. "So thoughtful. But my favorite was the story Harrington told me, about the one and only time you were paddled at Eton."

Edward groaned. "Oh. *That.*"

"Yes. *That.* Would you prefer to tell it?" His only response was to narrow his eyes at her, so she continued, "I'm given to understand that Harrington was on the brink of being sent down when *someone* left an anonymous poem entitled 'The

Love Song of Jonathan Davies' upon the headmaster's podium. Harrington thinks it was someone named Percival Thistlethwaite who ratted him out."

"He's probably right." Edward shook his head. "That little weasel."

"Headmaster Davies summoned the entire school to upper chamber, where he levied his accusation against Harrington and told him to go and start packing his trunk. But before he could move, you stepped forward and declared that Harrington must be innocent, because *you* were the author of the poem."

Edward scowled across the lawn. After a moment, Elissa continued, "I am given to understand that an argument ensued in which Headmaster Davies tried to prove that you could not possibly have penned such a work." She made her voice deep. "'You wrote this, Fauconbridge? About my quest for *gratification*? Amongst Farmer Anderson's drove of goats? Misspelling the word *lascivious*?'"

Edward's stern expression cracked. Her imitation of Harrington's imitation of Headmaster Davies was remarkably good.

Elissa chuckled. "That was my favorite part. Harrington described the pained look that came into your eyes when you were forced to own to his misspellings, but you didn't so much as flinch. You just said, 'So it would seem.'"

"That part was worse than the paddling. In truth, everyone knew I hadn't written it. But still, it rankled."

"Of course it did. But you did it anyway. Not only did you take a paddling for your brother, you gave up your spotless record of having never misbehaved in order to save him." She stroked her thumb across his knuckles. "Do you have any idea how much that meant to Harrington?"

"He has this ridiculous idea that Father is ashamed of

him." Edward shook his head. "He couldn't be more wrong. Harrington is inherently loveable."

"He's not the only one." She scooted over to sit beside him, looping her arms around his chest. "I'd like you to consider, Edward, that your siblings, at least, don't have the same high expectations for you that you have for yourself. That they love you for the many acts of kindness you've shown them over the years, and that they don't care in the slightest that you didn't win the *First* Classical Medal."

Edward shook his head. "They were disappointed that I didn't get first place. I know they were."

"Have you considered that the reason they were disappointed is that they knew how badly you wanted it? That their true desire was to see the brother they love achieve his dream?"

Edward frowned. "I—I don't think so."

"Ed-ward." She poked him in the side. "Are you truly trying to convince me that Harrington thinks it an embarrassment that his brother was only recognized as the second-best classical scholar in all of Cambridge?"

Edward paused. He'd participated in enough disputations to know a losing argument when he saw one, and the notion that Harrington gave a fig about academic accolades was hopelessly indefensible.

And truth be told, he was having difficulty forming arguments for his other siblings as well. It was impossible to argue that Anne and Lucy, two of the kindest people on the face of this earth, despised him for his failure. If Caro prized academic achievements, she probably wouldn't have married Thetford, and the only time Edward could recall horrifying her was when she'd caught him leaving the house in a five-year-old jacket (she had only calmed down when he explained he was on his way to inspect the pigs.) Freddie seemed to be following more in Harrington's footsteps than

Edward's, regarding school as a place to make friends and pull pranks. And as for Izzie…

If Izzie wasn't reading a Gothic novel or writing a Gothic novel, she was daydreaming about one. Izzie was scarcely aware of the world around her. He would be surprised if her thoughts had strayed to his academic achievements, or the lack thereof, in years.

He sighed. Elissa *might* have a point.

"That may be true of my siblings. But my parents have expectations for me. They've made that very clear."

"I find it interesting that you dismiss Harrington's concerns that your father is ashamed of him, even though he has misbehaved to the point that the earl has threatened to cut him off. Please do not mistake me—I think your brother is wonderful. But there seems to be no mistake he could make that would render him unlovable in your eyes, yet you censure yourself over the tiniest imperfection."

She didn't understand. She didn't understand at all. "Harrington is different. *Completely* different. Harrington is the one—"

"—who everyone loves," she said along with him. "You said that to me last night. It broke my heart, but I hoped you had misspoken. Now I know you meant every word."

He knew it. He bloody well knew it. She saw past all of his defenses, saw all of the things he tried desperately to keep hidden so she wouldn't despise him.

She hugged him tighter, resting her head upon his shoulder.

There was a sudden roaring in his ears. Because —because—

Elissa *saw those things.*

She *already knew.*

And she—she *didn't despise him.*

That couldn't be right. That couldn't possibly be right.

And yet, Harrington knew about his problems. And Anne, too.

And they loved him. He knew they did.

But they don't know the whole truth whispered that little voice in his head, the one that never really went away. *If they knew everything, they would cast you out.*

Elissa squeezed him again. "I know how much you hate this. But I want to understand. For some reason, you believe that you're unlovable. But you're wrong. And the only way to overthrow this misguided belief is for you to tell me whatever it is that you think is so horrible and see that I still love you. Because I will still love you, Edward. I promise I will. And then maybe you'll finally understand that you're worthy of love."

Edward couldn't bring himself to respond. His thoughts were flying away from him like horses that had shied. They were now carrying him far afield, to places he'd never meant to go.

He couldn't tell her about *the incident*, the day he had learned with absolute certainty that his father did not love him in the same way he loved Harrington.

Obviously, he couldn't tell her. It had occurred almost twenty years ago, but he'd never told *anyone* about… about…

But… what if he was wrong? What if he was wrong and Elissa was right?

What if he didn't have to hate himself?

The thought should've cheered him, but paradoxically, there was nothing more terrifying than hope. Because there was nothing worse than letting yourself believe, only to have everything come crashing down around you.

"Is it because you're the heir?" Elissa asked. "Is that why you believe the expectations are so different for you and Harrington?"

He couldn't believe he was even considering it. But the thought of telling her… it was strangely tempting.

It was also completely terrifying. And yet…

"There is that. But there's also…" He cleared his throat. "There was also…"

"Yes?" Elissa said encouragingly.

He drew in a breath, steeling himself to tell her.

CHAPTER 25

$\mathcal{E}$lissa stroked her hand across Edward's back, which had gone stiff as a plank. He didn't look very well; frankly, he looked like he might cast his accounts.

She looped her arms around his chest again, mostly for comfort, and only a bit because his eyes were darting around frantically, and she feared he might leap to his feet and take off running across the grass.

"I was..." he began haltingly. "We were..."

"Yes?" She rubbed his back encouragingly.

It happened suddenly. His body seemed to deflate, his spine going from ramrod-straight to slumped in an instant. He squeezed his eyes shut and rubbed at the creases on his forehead. When he spoke, his words came out in a panicked rush. "I can't, Elissa. I can't tell you. I'm sorry, but I—I—"

Some instinct told her that this was not the moment to push him. "It's all right."

He opened his eyes, and they were slightly wild. "I thought maybe I could tell you, but... but..."

"Please do not distress yourself." She laid her head upon his shoulder. "You'll tell me when you're ready."

He nodded tightly. She just held him and waited for his panting breaths to slow.

After a few minutes, he turned his head and gave her a cringing grin. "I realize that my first two attempts at proposing marriage have not done a great deal to recommend me. But I do want to marry you, Elissa. If you'll have me."

Elissa bit her lip, because she'd been thinking about this all morning, too. "I hope we can marry, Edward. But there are a few things we need to discuss. You said this morning that, as your wife, it would not be permissible for me to publish any translations."

It pained her to see the worry steal into his eyes. "That is correct. And again, I must apologize for the way the conversation went this morning. I did not explain myself properly. There are certain rules that, as the heir to an earldom, society expects me to follow. Not working in trade, including publishing, is one of them. And while I might privately agree that many of these rules are nonsensical, there are consequences if I do not follow them. And those consequences would affect not just me, but my entire family."

Elissa sighed. She had hoped so desperately that he would say he'd changed his mind, that it didn't matter. But that didn't seem to be the case. "What sorts of consequences?"

"Any improper behavior from me—or my wife—would hurt Lucy and Izzie's marriage prospects." He shook his head. "I could never do that to my little sisters." He looked up, his blue eyes entreating. "And so I would have to ask you to make some sacrifices. Some of which I know would be significant to you. But if it means we could be together, I—I hope you will consider it."

"You also said it would not be permissible for me to enter the contest."

"Well..." Edward paused, thinking. "That was because you

had announced your intention to continue publishing anonymously. And, of course, you would lose your anonymity if you were to win. But if you were to agree to cease publishing following our marriage, I—I suppose there would not be any impediment to your entering the contest," he said stiffly.

Elissa studied him a beat. "Although you would prefer I not do so."

Edward's shoulder gave a violent twitch. "What makes you say that?"

"How I wish I had a mirror. Your face has turned positively chartreuse." She laughed as he shifted uncomfortably. "Given your reaction to finishing second to Robert Slocombe, it isn't much of a deduction."

Edward took her hand in his. "All right, I admit it. The thing I came to understand this morning, when you told me you were the translator..." He waved his free hand, as if searching for the right words. "I do not mind that you are good. I meant it when I said that I love the fact that you're so intelligent. What I mind is when I am bad."

She squeezed his hand. "You're never bad, Edward."

"But you understand my meaning."

"I think so. If we're competing head-to-head, my victory might be the cause of your defeat. And you worry about how you might react."

"Precisely. I'm not proud of it," he said in a rush. "I wish I didn't feel this way. And I wish I could be the one to drop out of the contest in order to avoid the conflict. I would do it gladly were it not for my brother's predicament."

"I'm sure you would. I'm guessing you would rather not enter at all."

"You have the right of it." A silence fell, interrupted only by the song of a skylark fluttering in the branches above them.

Edward cleared his throat. "So. Would you be willing to compromise? To give up your publishing career so we can be married?"

"The problem," she said carefully, "is not giving up my publishing career per se. The problem is that I am a duck."

The befuddlement that crossed his face was actually quite adorable. "You are… I'm sorry, I think I must've misheard."

"I am a duck," Elissa repeated. "I float around in ponds. I trip over pigs. I once became lodged in chest-deep mud over at Bicklebury Bog, and Farmer Broadwater had to fetch his plough horse to pull me out. I am a clumsy, inelegant duck. But you do not need a duck, Edward. What you need is a swan."

"Ah!" Comprehension dawned on his face. "But I can help you with that. I will steer you around pigs and bogs and whatever else—"

"Alas, my duck-qualities run far deeper than my propensity for wandering into blackberry brambles. Every single thing I would have to do as your countess makes me want to run and hide. The only thought more horrifying than that of attending a London ball is of *planning* one. It isn't merely the fact that I would constantly do the wrong thing, although I assure you, I would. I am just not the girl who gets excited over a trip to the dressmaker, or who spends her afternoon trimming a new bonnet. I am the girl who misses not only luncheon but also dinner because I'm absorbed in a two-thousand year-old manuscript. The one who emerges from the library bleary-eyed with my hair in a tangle, much like a hermit emerging from his cave. The girl who has freckles on her nose and ink on her elbow, and sometimes, I fear, the reverse."

She pressed his hand, her eyes beseeching him to understand. "The true issue is that the tasks that would fill my days as your countess are not merely things I'm terrible at. They are things I detest. I just—" She broke off, looking down. "I'm a duck, Edward. I'm not a swan. I'm just not." She forced her eyes up to his. "I'm so sorry."

Edward's brow was knotted, but his eyes were not bereft of hope. "But Elissa, I do not want you to give up your duck qualities! Your duck qualities are the very things I love about you. And more than that"—he glanced in every direction, then dropped his voice to a whisper, even though there was no one around for miles—"I am also a duck. I am merely *pretending* to be a swan. And that is what we shall do. When it is just the two of us, we shall indulge in all of our favorite duck activities. Get ink on your elbow. Barricade yourself in the library. Never give a thought to your wardrobe. Have Caro design it all for you."

He was warming to his theme and rose to pace across the blanket. "It will only be during the London Season that we need to pretend to be swans. That's just six or seven months out of the year. And whenever my mother is hosting guests here at the house. So, another month or two. And on those nights when company comes to dinner. And whenever we're in public." He turned to face her, wearing a hopeful smile. "But you will see that doing the things we hate will be ever so much more tolerable, because we will be doing them together!" His smile faltered as he realized what he'd just said. "Er, allow me to rephrase that…"

"Edward!" She gave an incredulous laugh as she grabbed his hand and tugged him back down onto the blanket. "I believe you phrased it perfectly, and that you understand how ridiculous it sounds. If we are both truly ducks, we should be ducks together. We should try to do *more* of the things that make us happy, not fewer."

"But I—I don't have a choice, Elissa. Were I a younger son, I would not be under so much scrutiny. But I am the heir. And as I said, it would reflect poorly upon my family if I were to flaunt society's standards, and it would cause difficulties for my little sisters in particular."

She closed her eyes. She had been steeling herself for this moment ever since they parted in the library. Deep down, she had always known she wasn't what Edward Astley needed.

It didn't make it hurt any less.

She opened her eyes, and he was regarding her sadly. "Does this—" He swallowed. "Does this mean you won't marry me?"

"I'm so sorry, Edward." Her voice broke. "But I cannot change who I am. Not even for you."

The misery in his eyes was devastating to see. He started to look away, but she caught him under the chin. "Wait, Edward. Look at me. I cannot be your wife."

She gathered all of her courage and said, "I will have to settle for being your lover instead."

CHAPTER 26

*E*dward was certain he had misheard. He became conscious that his mouth was hanging open. "Elissa, I—I think I misunderstood—"

"We can start tonight. Will you come to my room?"

Now he knew he was gaping at her. "You want me to—to—"

Her face flushed as red as her hair. "Unless you do not want to. I had assumed that you did, but if you do not—"

"Of course I *want to*." Edward rubbed his temple. Of all the ridiculous notions. "But I want you to be my *wife*. I wasn't trying to coerce you into some… illicit affair."

She leaned forward, squeezing his hand. "I know that, Edward. I would never think that of you. But if this is all we can ever have, we will at least have this much."

"I suppose I feel the same way. Although…" He cut himself off. She had already declined his proposal. As much as he wished she would change her mind, it was unseemly to badger her.

He cleared his throat. "Very well. I will come to your room. Tonight."

By then the sun was starting to slant low in the sky, reminding them it was time to dress for dinner. They packed up the picnic and headed back to the house together.

As Edward headed up to his room, his thoughts were consumed with one thing.

Tonight.

Tonight would be the night. He was finally going to make love to a woman. And not just any woman.

To *Elissa*.

He had been longing for this moment for half of his life. But mixed in with the longing, he felt terror in equal measure, because he had only a vague idea about how to make the experience good for her.

He had always thought he would hold himself aloof on his wedding night. He would go through the motions in a perfunctory manner, never confessing to his bride that this was his first time doing them.

But he couldn't imagine doing that with Elissa. She would never allow him to close himself off, for one, but more than that… he didn't want to.

Yet, at the same time, the thought of confessing that he was a virgin? That he didn't know what he was doing?

Impossible.

Edward sighed as entered his room. Why couldn't he look forward to losing his virginity like everyone else?

EIGHT HOURS LATER, Elissa paced her beautiful bedroom, barefoot, waiting for Edward. She wore nothing but her shift, the nicest one she had, which was hopefully more alluring than her tattered old dressing gown.

Not that it mattered what she wore. It would all be coming off as soon as he arrived.

Her arms seized at that thought, shrinking to curl against her chest. She willed her knotted wrists to relax. It was natural to be nervous, but she wanted this. She wanted him.

She had lit every candle in the room. She did not care that this was shameless. She was quite looking forward to seeing Edward Astley in the altogether.

There was a soft knock at the door, and Elissa scurried on tiptoes across the room. She opened the door without thinking to check that it was him, but it was, and the next thing she knew, Edward was slipping inside.

His dressing gown wasn't pilling, grey wool. It was made of midnight-blue silk brocade, and he looked heart-stoppingly handsome in it, as those brilliant blue eyes devoured the sight of her in her chemise. She hastily shut the door and turned to smile at him. "G-good evening," she stuttered, fidgeting with her plait.

"Good evening," he answered, his voice pitched a half-octave lower than usual.

They stood blinking at each other. Elissa found herself at a loss. She had assumed he would take the lead, but after a moment of standing there, she reached out, took his hand, and led him nervously toward the bed. He was carrying a glass of water, which he set down on her dressing table as they passed.

She stopped at the foot of the bed and turned to face him. She found him staring unseeingly across the room. He made an emphatic gesture, then another one. Had the circumstances been different, she would have thought he was... rehearsing some sort of speech.

"Edward?" she asked tentatively. "Do you want to, er—"

He nodded, and his eyes snapped to hers. "I presume you have read Ovid?" he asked abruptly.

She blinked at him once... twice... three times. "Ovid?"

"Ovid," he confirmed.

"I... I... of course," she replied, bewildered.

He began pacing the room. "I do not refer to his *Metamorphoses*."

"Um... do you not?" Was it her imagination, or were his cheeks slightly flushed?

"I refer," he said, turning to face her at the far end of the room, "to *The Art of Love*."

"*Oh*," she said, comprehending. Now she was the one blushing, because Ovid's *Art of Love* was... quite explicit. "I—I have read it."

"Good," he said in a clipped voice. "I have read it as well. You see—" He broke off, cringing.

His pacing had brought him back to where she stood at the foot of the bed, and Elissa reached out and caught both of his hands in hers. "Edward?" she asked tentatively.

"It's just—" He was looking everywhere but at her. "You know me well enough to know that I'm not the type to go around cornering the housemaids."

"Of course not."

"Or visiting a—a brothel."

"Indeed, no."

"So the truth is... the truth is..." He swallowed thickly and closed his eyes, then said in a rush, "The truth is that I have never done this before."

"Oh!" She was surprised, because it was her impression that most men did not wait for their wedding night, and he could not have lacked for opportunities.

But she wasn't displeased.

Edward, however, seemed to regard this as a source of some embarrassment. His eyes remained squeezed shut. "I want you to know, Elissa, that I intend to do everything within my power to please you." She felt her heart melting, because *of course* that would be his worry, whether he could make this good for *her*. And also because she could see how hard this was for him, to admit something he perceived to be a weakness. She could tell how important it was to him that he succeed in this. Edward Astley expected himself to be good at everything, and he looked terrified that he might fail her tonight.

He opened his eyes but still didn't look at her. Instead, he stared resolutely over her shoulder as he said, "And although I do not have any firsthand experience, as I said, I have read Ovid. I therefore know that there is a particular spot somewhere between your legs where 'a woman loves to be touched.'" He shook his head, staring off into the corner. "If only I knew the precise location of this spot."

Elissa swallowed, her heart suddenly flying. She was terror-stricken to speak one of her most closely guarded secrets out loud, but she had to help him. "I—I know where it is."

"If we can but find it," he said, seeming not to have heard, "it will greatly increase the chances of our success."

"Edward," she said, squeezing his hands until he looked at her. She could see her own reflection in the dressing table mirror behind him, and her face was every bit as red as her hair, but she forced herself to say it again. "I know where it is." He was staring at her, bewilderment etched across his features. "The spot," she clarified, trying not to cringe. "Where I, er, love to be touched."

His eyebrows shot up halfway to his hairline. "Oh! You mean to say that you—that you like to…"

She swallowed, fortifying herself. "I do."

She was in agony awaiting his reaction. Because she could not have confessed to something more taboo. On this matter the church was clear: self-pleasure was strictly forbidden. Yet it was one thing for a man to admit to such a failing. It was still thought wrong, but it was a common enough sin. Men were allowed to have desires. They were *supposed* to. Women, on the other hand…

She peered at him uncertainly, trying to glean any emotion other than shock from his expression. Oh, but this was awful. He probably thought her the worst kind of strumpet. His good opinion of her had just been destroyed in an instant. He would want nothing to do with her now. He would leave, and she wouldn't even have tonight to look back upon.

"Thank *God*," he said, his voice shaking.

"Wha—what?"

"That is the most wonderful news!"

"It—it is?" she asked, befuddled.

"Of course it is." He looked down at her then, his eyes full of relief. "Elissa, *you can show me what to do*. To please you." He let his head loll back. "Never have I been so relieved."

She gave a nervous laugh. "I was afraid you would, er, think poorly of me."

He snorted, dropping his gaze to hers. "Well, that would make me a rank sort of hypocrite, now wouldn't it?"

"Do you mean that you—that you—" She trailed off, unable to say it.

His expression was incredulous. "I am a *twenty-seven-year-old virgin*." He said this as if it explained everything, but seeing her blank look, he added, "I would have absolutely lost my mind if I didn't… you know."

"Oh! I—I see," she said, even though she did not. She cleared her throat, gesturing to the bed. "Shall we, er—"

"Let's," he said, and she giggled at how formal and awkward they were being. He sat upon the bed, and Elissa climbed into his lap, looping her arms around his neck.

He enveloped her in his embrace, and then they were kissing. She could tell he was trying to go slowly, to be gentle. But his hands trembled as they framed her face, and when her thigh brushed the insistent bulge in the front of his trousers, he broke off his kiss with a moan. Elissa found his artless fervor more arousing than the most practiced seduction could ever have been.

Elissa delved inside his dressing gown to trace the broad planes of his chest through the fine linen of his shirt. He could tolerate only a minute of that and soon rolled back upon the bed, taking her with him so they were lying side by side. It was becoming more real now. They were lying together on her bed. *They were going to do this.* Slowly, reverently, his hands began stroking her breasts through the fine fabric of her shift, while hers had worked their way under his shirt to caress his bare back. Impatient to feel more of him, she struggled to tug his dressing gown down his arms. He shrugged it off onto the bed, then, seeing her efforts to pull his shirt up, he rose to sitting and obligingly removed it.

Elissa propped herself up on one elbow, staring at him in awe. Not that she had seen so much Greek and Roman sculpture, but she couldn't imagine that there existed anything out there as exquisitely sculpted as Edward Astley. His shoulders were broad, his waist trim, and every inch of him was firm planes of muscle. As she had ascertained the other night, he was not overly hairy, just a sprinkling of dark hair across his chest, and a thicker trail extending below his navel and disappearing beneath the waistband of his trousers. She reached her hand out tentatively to stroke him. His skin was surprisingly smooth to the touch, the texture of silk when it was warm from the iron.

She caught him looking at her, and she took it by the hungry expression in his eyes that he was keen for her to return the favor. She sat up nervously. "Have you ever seen a naked woman before?"

His reply was guttural. "No."

She smiled in spite of her nerves. He must have been

longing for this moment for years. She was happy to be the one who got give it to him.

She tugged the hem of her chemise up around her thighs. "Wait," Edward said, reaching out and taking the end of her plait. He untied the cord and began awkwardly unravelling her hair. "Do you mind?" he asked belatedly.

She felt her heart squeeze. "Not at all. Here," she said, reaching up and taking over for him.

He said only one word as he drank in the sight of her in naught but her shift, her red hair tumbling in waves past her waist, and that word was, "*Siren*." The admiration in his eyes gave her the confidence to peel her shift up over her head and cast it aside. That was the limit of her courage, however, and she squeezed her eyes shut as she laid back down upon the bed. It took her a moment to work up the nerve to open her eyes, but she was so glad when she did. She knew at once that she would never forget the expression in Edward's eyes in the moment she lay naked before him for the first time, a potent mixture of longing, reverence, and awe.

He reached for her, then paused. "Elissa…" He swallowed thickly as his hand came to cup her breast. "You're so beautiful. You're the most perfect thing I've ever seen."

Hesitantly, he stroked down her side, and she shivered. She wanted his hands all over her, but he seemed to need a moment to drink in the sight of her, so she bit her lip, trying to tamp down her impatience.

He didn't make her wait long. After a moment, he lay down beside her and took her into his arms. They both moaned aloud in the moment his body pressed against hers, overwhelmed by the delicious sensation of so much skin-upon-skin.

"*God*, that feels good," he groaned.

"*So* good," she confirmed.

Then they were kissing again, and Elissa got her wish,

because Edward's hands were everywhere—stroking down her arms, caressing her shoulders, sweeping down along her waist, then finally coming up to cup her breasts. He leaned down and took her nipple in his mouth, and her back arched so hard at the pleasure she almost dislodged him.

He chuckled, and his voice shook as much as his hands when he said, "You like that, then?"

She was breathing hard. "*Yes.*"

"Good." He looked cautiously pleased with himself. "I suppose I should do it some more."

He proceeded to do just that, experimenting with soft, teasing flicks of his tongue as Elissa tangled her fingers in his silky, dark hair. He then tried gentle suction, and when this caused Elissa to cry out, he gave her a deep pull that made her hips buck up off the bed.

By now, there was a heartbeat pulsing between Elissa's legs. Figuring she was as ready as she was ever going to be, she reached for the placket of his trousers. He snagged her hand, then brought it to his mouth and kissed her palm.

"Edward, I'm—I'm ready," she said, her voice emerging in short pants.

"Thank God," he murmured, but when her hand strayed down across his stomach, he captured it again, a vein popping out at his temple. "I need those on, darling."

"But why?"

He scooped her up and lay her across his lap, so that she leaned against one of his shoulders. His body felt rigid beneath hers. He wiped his palm upon his trousers, then moved his hand to the juncture of her thighs. "We will be pleasuring you first," he said firmly.

She felt her cheeks flush. "You don't have to—that is—"

"Yes," he said firmly, "I do." He drew in a shuddering breath. "Now, if you would be so kind as to show me what to do."

Elissa thought she might die from mortification, but she spread for him, and she felt his groan as it trembled through his chest. She swallowed her discomfiture and parted her folds with her left hand, then brought her right hand tentatively to the little rosebud at the juncture of her thighs, just as she would if she were alone, pleasuring herself. "It's just here," she explained, demonstrating the circular motion she liked best. She glanced up at him. He was watching her, enrapt. Flushing, she took his hand and guided it to the little nub. "That's it," she said when his fingers found the right spot. "If you touch me there, it will—it will make me come."

"Here?" he asked, rubbing her hard enough that she shrieked, slamming her legs shut.

She tried to make her features neutral, but she could tell he had understood her reaction perfectly. "I, uh, usually start off slowly. Gently," she explained, opening her thighs again.

"Like this?" he asked, stroking her tentatively.

"Yes, that's much better." It was much better, but it was also far from ideal. After a moment, she cleared her throat. "Sometimes I use a little of my hand cream. It's there on my nightstand, in a little jar."

He was already padding across the room to get some. "Ah, here it is."

He was back in an instant, resuming their former position. Elissa tried to relax as she spread her legs again, but she found herself feeling… pressured. She knew Edward wanted desperately to make this good for her, and somehow knowing how anxious he was made it that much more difficult for her to let go and enjoy herself.

She inhaled, expecting to detect the familiar honeysuckle scent of her hand cream. Instead, she smelled… nothing. Oh dear, this was going worse than she'd thought. What could he have mistaken for her hand cream?

"Let's try this again," Edward said with a tight smile,

returning his hand to the spot between her legs. He resumed his gentle circling motion.

And then, the strangest thing happened.

Elissa knew at once that whatever he had found on her dressing table, it was not her honeysuckle hand cream. She was extremely familiar with the lubricating properties of her honeysuckle hand cream, and whatever it was Edward was using on her, it was *far* superior. His fingers were so slick and light as they moved over that sensitive little nub between her legs, and it felt… it felt…

Nothing had ever felt like this. Nothing had ever felt so good, and Elissa found herself moaning aloud as dozens of sleeping nerves sprang to life.

"Is that good, then?" Edward asked, eyes crinkled with consternation.

"Oh my *God*, Edward. *So* good," she panted.

"Really?" he asked, hope stealing across his face.

"Really. Please don't stop. In fact—" She drew in a shaky breath. "You can go just a touch faster."

He was all too happy to comply, and soon, Elissa was squirming in his lap. Finally, she was able to relax. She forgot her embarrassment, her nervousness, the pressure to come. She knew nothing but the exquisite pleasure he was giving her.

Suddenly, he lifted her off his lap and lay her upon the bed. He slid down between her legs. "There's something I'd like to try."

"Yes?" she breathed.

He stroked his hands up and down her calves. "I am given to understand that you will like it."

"According to Ovid?"

"According to Ovid," he agreed with a grin. He pressed a kiss into the inside of one of her thighs, merely inches from her pulsing core. "But if you would rather I not—"

"No! That is to say—" Goodness, could her face get any hotter? "I think you're right, and that I will... uh... like it. Very much."

After all, she *had* read Ovid, as well as a variety of ancient authors who were equally explicit, and she had been touching herself for years. She'd honestly never thought she would receive such a gift, but the thought of Edward kissing her on that special spot? She shivered in anticipation.

He gave her a crooked smile. "Let's see, shall we?"

And then he lowered his mouth. She felt his warm breath against her intimate skin, and she couldn't help but squirm. He kissed her reverently, as if there was nothing else in the world he would rather be doing, as if this was something he had dreamed of. He kissed every inch of her inner folds before settling his mouth over the special nub between her legs. Glancing up at her with those brilliant blue eyes, he began stroking her with his tongue.

And—*oh good gracious heaven*—the swirl of his tongue over that sensitive little spot... This must be what it felt like to be drunk on ambrosia, because it felt like the nectar of the gods was running through her veins. She was writhing on the bed, babbling nonsense, and she felt his hands upon her hips in a touch that was partly a caress, and partly to hold her in place.

She glanced down at him, and those blue eyes were still upon her, studying her every reaction, homing in on the strokes that pleased her the most. Elissa could tell by the crinkles around his eyes that he was enjoying her uninhibited reaction, but he didn't stop, not even for a second, he was so intent on pleasing her. He increased his pace, flicking his tongue light and fast over her nub, and nothing, nothing in the whole entire world, had ever felt so good.

She tossed her head to the side and encountered the soft satin of his dressing gown against her cheek. And there it was—*bergamot.* The scent of all her hopeless girlhood dreams that tonight were coming true pushed her right to the brink. He held her on that edge, where the pleasure was most exquisite, for the space of a few heartbeats, and then the wave crested and she cried out. Her legs began shaking uncontrollably, and she felt everything between them pulsing again and again in the most beautiful pleasure she had ever known.

Eventually the room stopped spinning, and Edward's dimples swam into focus. While she'd been busy convulsing, he'd slid up the bed and now hovered beside her. He looked boyish, almost giddy. "I did it!"

She laughed. "You did!" She looped her arms up around his neck. "Thank you, Edward. That was *wonderful.*"

"Truly?"

"Truly." She kissed him, then pulled back, blushing. "Better than anything I have ever known."

He looked tremendously pleased, but as her hand began tracing the contours of his chest, he groaned.

He surprised her by climbing off the bed. He shucked his trousers, then crossed to her dressing table in two steps and fished something out of the glass he had brought with him. This gave Elissa an impressive view of his backside, which was so taut it had a fascinating little dimple in the side of it.

When he turned around, her mouth fell open. Of course, being an innocent, she hadn't been quite sure what to expect. But she hadn't realized that his member would be so… so…

Elissa swallowed thickly. Nothing she had read in Ovid could have prepared her for this.

EDWARD BLOTTED the sheath he had removed from the glass on a towel then slid it over his straining cock, tying the ribbon with hands that shook. He glanced over at Elissa, who was peering at him with huge eyes from the bed. "Is everything all right?"

"Yes!" she squeaked.

His brain wasn't functioning so well, because he had reached this moment in which he was finally, *finally* going to make love to a woman, and not just any woman, but his beautiful, beloved Elissa. But he registered that she was nervous. Having secured the sheath, he lay down next to her and hugged her close. In spite of her anxious expression, she immediately rolled onto her back, pulling him on top of her and spreading her legs for him. A feral groan emerged from his throat. There was some primal recess of his brain that liked having Elissa naked beneath him, that liked it *very much*.

He felt a vein pop out on the side of his neck, but he took a deep breath, studying her for any sign of uncertainty. "You're sure about this, Elissa?"

She nodded tightly. "Completely sure."

"Because if you're not, we don't have to—"

"I want to do this with you, Edward."

"It's just that I would never do anything to hurt you, or dishonor you, or—"

She framed his face in both of her hands and brought her lips up to meet his. "I love you, Edward. Make me yours."

He really couldn't deny himself any longer after that. He reached a shaking hand between her legs and felt around until he found her opening. He guided his cock there and slowly began to press forward.

She was so *tight* and so *slick*. He heard himself moan as he inched forward, because from his perspective, everything about this moment was pure, unadulterated bliss, from the soft folds caressing the sensitive head of his cock to the intoxicating feeling of Elissa's delicate curves beneath him.

But some hazy corner of his brain reminded him to see how she was doing.

He found her brow wrinkled and her eyes squeezed shut. Edward paused, his cock halfway inside her. He reached up and stroked her cheek. "How is it, darling?"

She bit her lip as she opened her eyes. "It—it doesn't hurt, per se. If you could just give me a moment to—to adjust."

He was physically shaking, so desperately did he want to thrust into her, but he drew in a ragged breath. "Take all the time you need," he said with forced lightness before his lips descended upon hers.

It was agonizing, being so close and having to wait, but Edward would never have considered doing otherwise. There probably wasn't much art to the way he was kissing her, nor the way his hands were roaming clumsily over whatever parts of her body he could reach, but he did the best he could. And it seemed to help—after a few minutes Elissa gave a pleasurable sigh, and he realized she had relaxed beneath him.

"You can go ahead," she said, breaking off their kiss. "It's better now."

He resumed his agonizing progress, studying her face the whole time. To his immense relief, he was able to seat himself fully within her. "Is that all right?" he asked. "Can I—"

She leaned up and kissed his throat. "It's fine. Go ahead, my Edward."

He slid carefully out and then in, then repeated the maneuver twice more for good measure. Seeing no discomfort on her face, he groaned and increased his pace. The sheath he wore dulled his sensation significantly, and thank God for it, because otherwise he would have embarrassed himself by climaxing on the third stroke.

As it was, he barely lasted a minute before the pleasure

overwhelmed him. He heard himself making guttural sounds, the only comprehensible word of which was Elissa's name, uttered like a prayer in the moment that he came.

He collapsed on top of her, his body trembling as he came back down to earth. He became conscious of Elissa's hands stroking patterns across his bare back. He hesitated, because he had been so lost in the moment, he'd paid scant attention to how she was feeling, and he was nervous of her reaction. He slowly lifted his head, bringing a hand up to frame her face.

She looked so happy, happier than he could ever remember seeing her (and this was saying something for the girl who radiated joy just looking at his front lawn). It was entirely contagious and he felt the corners of his mouth rising. Probably it didn't hurt his mood that he had just made love to a beautiful woman, but Edward felt unfamiliar emotions washing over him. Joy. Contentment.

Trust.

"How are you?" he asked, reaching up to brush her hair back from her face.

"I've never been better. That was *wonderful.*"

"It certainly was for me. It wasn't too painful for you?"

She shook her head, her expression holding a touch of wonder. "Much less than I was expecting. It was a bit"—she paused, searching for the right word—"tight, at first. But then I managed to relax." She smiled sheepishly. "I—I actually quite enjoyed it."

"Good," Edward said, his chest expanding with relief.

He withdrew and rolled to the side of the bed. As much as he hated to leave her, the sheath was now rather full, so he padded to the washstand to clean himself up.

He was already completely hard again by the time he rejoined Elissa upon the bed, which was embarrassing. He might be a virgin—

Well. Not anymore.

He might be *green*, but he didn't want her to think he was *that* green. He certainly wasn't going to trouble her for another go-round tonight, as he was given to understand that she would be too sore. He might be dying to make love with her again, but he was a gentleman, damn it, and besides, this was Elissa. He would never do anything to hurt Elissa.

So as he took her into his arms, he sought to leave enough space between their lower halves that his arousal wasn't completely obvious.

Elissa promptly ruined his plans by curling herself into him. He was momentarily overwhelmed by the mind-bending pleasure of every inch of her petal-soft skin pressed up against his, but the exclamation she gave as his jutting erection poked her in the stomach managed to penetrate his foggy brain.

"Oh!"

Edward cringed. "Ignore that, darling."

She laughed. "Ignore it? How am I supposed to ignore something that big?"

His cock gave a pulse, interpreting this as a compliment.

He cleared his throat. "What I meant is that you needn't worry. I don't intend to bother you again this evening."

"Bother me? I assure you, you're not bothering me." She sat halfway up, peering over his shoulder. "Which jar did you get the hand cream from?"

"The hand cream?" He struggled to think about anything other than her breasts looming above him, petite, pert, and perfect, with nipples the precise same shade as her freckles. "It was in the little porcelain jar with the flowers."

"Aha," she said, slipping out of the bed and padding over to her dressing table. "That explains it, then."

Edward frowned. "That explains what?"

Elissa turned to face him, fully nude and holding the jar. "This one isn't my hand cream. It's coconut oil, for my hair."

"I'm sorry," Edward said, feeling like a fool. "I didn't know the difference."

Elissa laughed as she climbed back onto the bed to kneel beside him. "I'm not the least bit sorry, because it worked a thousand times better than my hand cream! In fact"—she paused, biting her lip—"I thought I might try some of it on you. Seeing as you're, um, ready again."

Edward was stunned into silence, as a thousand tempting images of Elissa *trying things* on him flitted across his mind. She misinterpreted his silence. "That is—if you would like that. If you're not too sensitive… Do you feel sensitive afterward, too? After you, you know—"

"After I climax?" he asked, finally managing to form something resembling a sentence. He filed the fact that Elissa would be sensitive after her own peak away for future reference. "I do." He cleared his throat, then added in a rush, "But I don't think I'm too sensitive right now."

A smile broke over her face. "Excellent!" She opened the jar and scooped out a dab of the coconut oil, smoothing it over her palms. She fumbled the jar with slick hands as she attempted to place it on the bedside table. "Ooh, that is slippery. Now, let's see, should I just—"

"Here." Edward rolled onto his back with what was perhaps an unbecoming alacrity and flipped the bedclothes back. "Help yourself."

It was agony, those seconds in which she tried to figure out how she was going to touch him. She would reach a hand out toward his purpling cock, then hesitate, shaking her head, then approach from a different angle, but again pause just shy of touching him. By the time she finally wrapped one hand around the side of his shaft, Edward had all but wrung the bedsheets into knots.

He saw *immediately* what she meant about the coconut oil, because the slide of her hand along his length was *deliciously* slick. And Elissa's hands were so soft and tiny and sweet, different in the best possible way from his own rough, clumsy hand.

She was stroking up his shaft, slowly, tentatively, experimentally. Edward's jaw was like iron. Part of him wanted for this to never end, for her soft little touches to go on forever. But another part of him yearned to cover her hand with his own and urge her to stroke him faster and harder, to give him the release his body was crying out for.

She had been sliding up and down along the middle of his shaft, but her hand slipped and she came up to cup the head of his cock. He made a strange sound, somewhere between a groan and a bleat.

Elissa's eyes flew to his face and her hand froze. "I'm sorry! Should I not touch you there?"

He felt his cheeks burning. *How humiliating.* But the last thing he wanted was for her to stop, so he forced himself to say, "No, that was a good sound. That's where I'm most sensitive, near the tip. It—it felt good."

"Did it? How about this?" she asked, cupping him and rubbing his head with her thumb.

"*So... g-good...*" was all he could manage, as the pleasure overwhelmed his brain. Elissa gave a bright giggle as she redoubled her efforts.

Edward knew he should feel embarrassed to be so out of control, but he was having difficulty summoning the willpower. The sight of Elissa kneeling next to him, naked, alluringly curtained in her red hair, a delighted smile on her face as she stroked up and down his cock, was better than any erotic fantasy he'd ever had, and he found himself unable to focus on anything else.

She tried a new motion, stroking down his cock and then

coming up to swirl her soft little hand over his head, and he made another sound that was more animal than human. "Does that feel good?" she asked eagerly.

"Oh, my God!" he gasped. "You have n-no idea."

Elissa giggled, delighted, and a teasing expression came into her eyes. "I think I know something you'll like even better."

"Not possible," he bit out.

"I'm not so sure. You see"—she grinned as she scooted down so that she was *kneeling between his legs*—"I, too, have read Ovid."

"Elissa?" he asked uncertainly. Because the lurid direction his thoughts were taking—it was crazy. Of course, *of course*, she couldn't be thinking of—of—

"How I would hate for you to conclude that my understanding of Ovid was not as thorough as yours." She leaned forward onto her elbows so that her sweet pink lips were mere inches from his cock, so close he could feel the whisper of her breath against his head. "As I'm sure you recall, he made some suggestions that were rather… intriguing."

"Elissa, you—you don't have to do that. If you'd rather not."

She was studying him with those sea-glass green eyes. "Would it feel good?"

He swallowed, his gaze straying to her hand where it was slowly stroking up and down his shaft. "I'm sure it would."

"And would it make you happy?"

His eyes flew to hers, surprised. "I—yes. Yes, it would."

She pressed a lingering kiss to the tip of his cock. "I want to make you happy, Edward."

He couldn't manage to reply, not only because the softness of her lips on the place where he was most sensitive was beyond *anything* he could have imagined, but because those words… He felt as if his chest had been ripped open, his beating heart bared before her. *It's all right. Go ahead and take it. It's yours.*

And now she was kissing her way down the side of his shaft, then shifting around to come up the opposite side. With each kiss he felt the tentative exploration of her tongue, and even these shy caresses were enough to bring him to the brink of insanity.

As she came back up and positioned herself directly above him, she gave him a bashful smile. And then she wrapped her lips around him and took him into her mouth. She swirled her tongue right over his head, and Edward could hear himself making animal noises, but he was too far gone to get hold of himself.

He wanted to ask her to use her hand on him at the same time in the same motion he used when he touched himself. But he would have to show her next time, because he knew with absolute certainty that he was going to come in a few scant seconds.

"Elissa... Elissa *darling*, that feels so good, my love, and you're going to—you're going to make me—" She brought her lips up and began focusing on his head, and he made a strangled sound as he passed the point of no return, where the pleasure was *so intense.* "Elissa, I'm about to—if you don't move I'm going to—I'm going to come." She did not seem to take his meaning, for she continued her maddening minis-trations. "In your mouth," he added in a rush. "I'm going to —" Instead of lifting her head, she began swirling her tongue all the faster, and— Oh. Oh! *Oh!*

His vision blurred from the intensity of his climax. When it swam back into focus, what a sight greeted him! Elissa was gazing up at him, positively *beaming.*

He drew her up so her head rested on his shoulder, then kissed her deeply. "Thank you, Elissa. That was..." He struggled to find the words. It wasn't, he realized, merely the physical pleasure, although that had been overwhelming.

He recalled the expression on her face when she had pressed that first kiss to him. *I want to make you happy, Edward.* She truly meant that. To the man who always looked out for everyone else… his throat constricted.

His voice, when it emerged, was a touch unsteady. "It felt wonderful. And the fact that you were willing to do that for me… it means *everything* to me, Elissa."

"You are most welcome. I loved making you feel good." She smiled as she snuggled into his chest. "I'm so happy. This is the best day of my life."

Edward could not imagine a context in which he would consider a day in which the woman he loved refused his offer of marriage, he accidentally revealed his most closely guarded secret to her in the most humiliating manner imaginable, and then found out that at least two of his siblings already knew that same secret as anything other than the worst day of his life.

And yet… it somehow hadn't been nearly as bad as he would have supposed. To be sure, he hoped Elissa might change her mind and agree to marry him after all. And he still felt twitchy at the thought that Elissa, Harrington, and Anne (and God knew who else) knew what he was really like on the inside.

But the cataclysmic after-effects he had always assumed would come to pass—*they will all despise me*—had simply… not occurred.

And the conclusion of the day, making love to Elissa, definitely fell under the best-day-of-his-life category, in spite of the fact that he'd made the mortifying confession that he was a virgin, then proceeded to prove it with a lovemaking performance that he knew had been the opposite of suave.

And yet, Elissa had not seemed to mind. It had actually gone surprisingly well.

He paused. To put a finer point on it, the reason making love to Elissa had gone so well was *because* he had made that confession. That was why she had helped him, had shown him how to please her. He could tell she had been terrified to reveal that she liked to touch herself and embarrassed to show him how. But because he had trusted her, she had trusted him in return.

Her words from that afternoon suddenly echoed in his head. *The only way I can think of to convince you that you're worthy of love is for you to tell me whatever it is that you think is so horrible and see that I still love you.*

Maybe… maybe she did have a point.

And although the angry voices in his head were shrieking in protest, he found himself saying the words he never thought he would speak aloud. "I was eight years old when it happened."

Elissa looked up from where she had been resting on his chest, her expression content and sleepy. "Hmm?"

"Harrington would have been seven. I fear I was a bit of a rascal in those days, and we were throwing rocks."

Understanding dawned in Elissa's eyes, as she realized that this wasn't just any story.

"We weren't throwing them at anyone," he hastened to add. "At least, not intentionally. We were aiming for trees, fence posts, things like that. But we weren't being mindful, and we didn't notice one of our tenant farmers, Mr. Pearce, riding up the lane."

He studied the swirling ornamentation on the ceiling. "One of our stones caught his gelding in the flank. We both threw at the same time, so we'll never know whose it was. But the horse shied and Mr. Pearce fell off, breaking his arm."

Elissa said nothing but stroked his chest.

"It is a serious thing for a farmer to have a broken arm, and just before harvest time. We were very fortunate that the break healed cleanly and there was no lasting damage. We both apologized, and Father hired someone to help with the physical labor while Mr. Pearce recovered. Harrington and I had to pay the hired hand's salary out of our pocket money, which we absolutely should have done."

"Oh, Edward." He glanced down from the ceiling and found Elissa's eyes full of sympathy. "You did make a mistake, but you were eight years old. And you made things right. Can you not forgive yourself?"

He probably could have, if that had been all, but he had not yet reached the difficult part of the story. "There's more," he said, his voice gruff. "That evening, my father asked to speak to us one at a time. Harrington went in first. Father received him in the library. I was left to wait my turn in the sitting room next door. Both rooms have doors that open onto the west balcony. I slipped outside. I knew just where to sit so Father wouldn't be able to see me through the French doors. And…" He trailed off.

"Did you overhear your father's conversation with Harrington?" Elissa asked.

"I did."

He fell silent, unsure how to continue, because he was coming to the shameful part.

After a moment, Elissa asked softly, "Was it awful?"

"It wasn't awful at all," Edward said in a rush. "When I chanced a glance, Father was smiling at him and they were both laughing. I remember Father mussed Harrington's hair and told him he was a rapscallion. Then he told him to go to his room, but he was smiling fondly the whole time, and…"

Elissa said nothing but gave Edward a squeeze.

After a moment he continued, "Then it was my turn. I honestly wasn't worried about it. I thought it would go more or less the same way for me. But instead—" He drew in a shaky breath, because this was the part of the story that cut him to the quick.

"Instead?" Elissa whispered.

He had to close his eyes. "Father yelled at me for a good ten minutes. He said that he had expected better of me. That as the oldest, it was my responsibility to set an example for Harrington and the others, to keep them out of trouble. And that I had disappointed him. Tremendously."

He felt Elissa's hand caressing the side of his face. "Oh, Edward—"

"And so you see," he said, cutting her off, "I am not the same as the rest of my siblings. There is something about Harrington and all the others that is inherently loveable. But I do not possess whatever quality that is."

"You do." Elissa reached up to wipe away a tear that was making its way across her cheek.

He'd gone and made her cry. *Perfect.* He knew he shouldn't have burdened her with all of this.

"I promise that you do," Elissa continued. "You are the most loveable person I've ever met. I didn't stand a chance of not loving you."

He stroked his hand up and down her arm while she sniffled against his chest.

After a moment, she'd regained enough composure to speak again. "I can understand why you reached that conclusion. Especially because… God, you were eight years old, Edward. But tell me this—did your father have any idea you were spying on his conversation with Harrington?"

"I do not believe so, no."

She bit her lip. "I have not known your brother for very long. But my impression of him is that he could make a dead man laugh."

"He could. Harrington has an effervescent personality. He

immediately lifts the mood of everyone in the room the second he walks into it. Well—" A ghost of a smile crossed his lips. "Excepting Graverley. Graverley despises him. He's been on the receiving end of too many of Harrington's pranks."

"And has Harrington always been that way?" Elissa asked. "Able to make people laugh?"

"Always. Even as a very small child."

Elissa seemed to be weighing her words carefully. "Please do not mistake me, because the last thing I want to suggest is that your feelings were unreasonable. I think you drew a logical conclusion. But have you ever considered that your father's intention might have been to give Harrington the same lecture he gave you? But Harrington, being Harrington, spoiled his plans by making him laugh at every turn?"

Edward frowned. Elissa's suggestion had never occurred to him. On the one hand, he had seen Harrington cut up in an attempt to get out of trouble any number of times.

But still, that couldn't be right.

He cleared his throat. "I do not think so. After all, Harrington went first. Why would he not have matched my lecture to his?"

"But you said your father didn't know you had been listening."

"That... that is true." Edward was finding it difficult to form counterarguments. His brain felt sluggish and overfull.

She laid her head against his shoulder. "I only ask that you consider it."

"I... I will." And he meant it. He would consider everything Elissa had said.

Later.

Without warning, he flipped her onto her back and came to rest on top of her, pinning her to the mattress. "But right now, I have a more pressing concern."

She gave a startled giggle. "Oh?"

He caressed her breasts with both of his hands. "It's just that, earlier, you displayed such a thorough understanding of Ovid."

"Did I?" Her voice had taken on a breathy quality.

He slid down far enough to press kisses against her breast. "You did. And it is so rare for me to have the opportunity to analyze Ovid with a scholar whose level of understanding matches my own." He moved over to lave her other breast with his tongue.

"Is that so?" Her breath was growing labored.

He glanced up at her and found her pink and panting. "And what's more, you now know of my competitive nature. You have gifted me with two climaxes, while I have only given you one. That simply will not do. I must therefore beg your indulgence as I explore a few of Ovid's suggestions in more depth."

Her head fell back against the pillow, making a soft *thunk*. "I will allow you to make your argument. But make no mistake—this competition is not over. I intend to return fire."

In the end, it was a tie. But for the first time in his life, Edward didn't mind.

CHAPTER 27

As the first glimmer of dawn broke through the window, Edward slipped reluctantly from Elissa's bed. She made a sleepy sound of protest, but he forced himself to go. As much as he longed to linger, he couldn't risk discovery by the servants, who would soon be starting their morning tasks. He padded silently back to his own room, thankfully encountering no one.

He would've liked to do something he never did, which was sleep until noon, but as the contest was to be held the following day, they needed to depart for Oxford that morning.

After a scant three hours of sleep, he piled into the carriage along with Elissa and Cassandra. His and Elissa's exhaustion was such that they slept for most of the bumpy carriage ride and were awakened by Cassandra only as they pulled into the yard of the Angel Inn where they had reserved rooms.

Edward arranged for them to sup in a private dining room. While Cassandra was busy speaking to the propri-etress about the available fare, Elissa stole up beside Edward.

"Do you want me to come to your room tonight?" she whispered.

He had to tamp down his reaction, given that her sister was just across the room. He murmured, "As much as I would like that, it's probably unwise."

She nodded. "You're right. We need to get a good night's sleep before the contest."

"I was thinking more of the risk to your reputation were we to be discovered."

"I suppose there's that, too. I was just thinking it was a good opportunity. We probably won't have many chances to make love in an actual bed." At Edward's quizzical look, she added, "We'll have to be clandestine in our future meetings. I'll leave the house on the pretense of reading outdoors, as I often do. You'll ride out and meet me in some glen. More often than not, we'll probably be making love on the forest floor."

Making love on the forest floor. For God's sake. Edward rubbed at his forehead. "Can't we please just get married? I want to spend every day with you. I want you in my bed every night. I don't want to see you a scant few times a month and make love to you on the forest floor, throwing ourselves upon the dubious mercies of the English weather."

"I wish we could, Edward. Truly, I do. But—"

Cassandra suddenly appeared at her sister's side. "Mrs. Spencer recommended the roast goose in oyster sauce, so I took the liberty of ordering it. Will that be acceptable, my lord?"

"That will be lovely. Thank you, Mrs. Gorten."

The conversation moved on, but really, there was no need for Elissa to finish her sentence. The word *but* told him everything he needed to know. She still could not marry him, not even after what they had shared last night, because marrying him would force her to give up everything she loved and become someone she was not. And he couldn't fail his family by being anything other than the perfect future earl.

He gave a tight smile as a servant appeared bearing the first course. In truth, he was worrying about nothing, because by this time tomorrow, he would no doubt have ruined everything.

~

THE FOLLOWING MORNING, Edward made his way to their private dining room at the Angel Inn and found Elissa and Cassandra already inside. In spite of her sister's entreaties to sit and eat, Elissa was pacing the room, wringing her hands and looking as green as her dress, which was the same woolen one she had worn to the dance.

Edward managed to choke down some coffee and toast, then they made the short walk to Oriel College, which had lent its hall to host the contest. Cassandra accompanied them as far as the quadrangle, then turned to her sister. "They won't let me in since I'm not competing, so I'll leave you here." She took Elissa's hands. "You can do this, Elissa. You belong here. You do," she insisted when Elissa's hands began to tremble. "And whatever the result, I will be so very proud of you."

Cassandra kissed her sister on the cheek and then stepped back, wiping her eyes. She turned to Edward. "I wish you good fortune as well, my lord," she said, then turned and headed back toward the inn.

Edward offered Elissa his arm and they proceeded across the quadrangle. He tried to admire the gabled buildings that made up the courtyard, but his thoughts were frayed.

Across the lawn, a familiar diminutive figure with wheat-blond hair and spectacles was approaching hall's porticoed entrance. Edward's shoulder gave a sudden spasm. *Robert Slocombe.* He'd known Slocombe would have received an invitation, had fully expected him to be here, but seeing him in the flesh sent his pulse racing.

Having spied him across the quad, Slocombe nodded and touched the brim of his hat. Edward returned the gesture.

Elissa was peering up at him. "Is that—"

"Robert Slocombe," Edward said tightly.

Seeing Slocombe somehow made the disaster that was about to unfold seem real. Even after the passage of years, he couldn't even look at the bloody man without breaking out in a cold sweat. Which was bad enough when it was Robert Slocombe, who lived in some godforsaken corner of Lancashire and whom Edward was unlikely to ever see again.

But what if Elissa beat him today? Was he going to have the same reaction? He didn't want to, but to his immense shame, he could not be completely certain he would not. He didn't want to loathe Robert Slocombe, after all, and yet here he was.

He could not live with himself if he had the same unworthy reaction toward Elissa. *Oh God.* He was going to ruin everything. He knew he was.

They mounted the stone steps. *If only there was some way to get out of this.*

A bespectacled man in academic robes stood outside the doors, holding a sheet of paper. "Ah, Lord Fauconbridge. A man who requires no introduction." He made a mark on his list, then gestured to Elissa. "Women are not allowed inside the college, of course, so you'll have to say your goodbyes out here."

Elissa lifted her chin. "I believe you will find my name on your list as well, sir. I am Elissa St. Cyr."

"You?" The man dropped his chin to peer at her over the

tops of his spectacles, regarding her with bald skepticism. "That's impossible."

Her cheeks had turned pink. "I pray you, sir. Consult your list, and you will see that my name does indeed appear."

"Nonsense," he said, but he did scan his paper. "There is no mention of a... Well. There is an *E.* St. Cyr, but—"

"That is me. The 'E' is for Elissa."

The man frowned. "I had assumed E. St. Cyr was the son of Julian St. Cyr."

"You are very close. I am his daughter."

"Well, as I said, women aren't allowed in the college."

"But I received an invitation—"

"No women allowed. Lord Fauconbridge, you may proceed."

The man was waving the person queuing behind them forward, clearly annoyed that they were blocking the way, but Edward was too stunned to move. After coming all this way, Elissa would not be allowed to participate after all. He... he wouldn't have to compete against her.

This was it. This was what he had wanted.

He glanced down at Elissa, saw that her face had crumpled, and—*No.*

This was not what he wanted.

Not in the slightest.

Scarcely able to believe what he was about to do, he rounded on the man. "I can assure you that Miss St. Cyr is the equal, if not the superior, of every man on your list. She has been invited to take part. You cannot turn her away."

The man looked shocked. "Come, my lord. Be reasonable."

"I am not being the least bit unreasonable. Miss St. Cyr's name is on your list. You must allow her to compete."

The man studied him a beat. Seeing that Edward was not about to bend, he muttered, "Let me speak to the dean."

He retreated inside. Elissa was blinking up at him, her expression uncertain. "Edward?" she whispered.

"It will be all right," he murmured, pressing her hand where it rested upon his arm.

The man reappeared with an older gentleman, also wearing black robes, in tow. "Lord Fauconbridge, my apologies, but it's as Wickham here says. This is a hallowed space. No woman can pass through these doors."

"How odd," Edward countered. "Here I was under the impression that female servants pass through them every day."

The dean shifted uncomfortably. "That's different."

"Is it? Pray, enlighten us as to how."

"It is one thing to let the bedmakers and the laundresses in to clean. But to allow a woman to participate in an academic exercise?" He shook his head. "A woman's brain was not designed for these rigors. In the end, it would be a cruelty toward the lady. Miss St. Cyr would stand no chance against men such as yourself."

Edward snorted. "Were you to speak with her for three minutes, you would discover how mistaken you are."

The dean peered at Elissa, baldly skeptical. "Even assuming you are correct, I am dean of this college, and I have a duty to uphold its reputation. And no woman will be passing through these doors on my watch." He turned, beckoning Edward forward. "Come, my lord. The competition will be beginning shortly. You'll need to take your seat."

"I will not be going anywhere," Edward snapped.

The dean looked over his shoulder. "Whatever do you mean?"

Edward leaned forward. "I mean that if Miss St. Cyr is to be denied the opportunity to compete, then I will not be taking part either."

A sheen of sweat shone upon the dean's brow. "But you're

one of the premier entrants. Every writeup I've seen in the papers has mentioned that you are taking part. You have to compete."

He glanced down at Elissa. She was staring up at him, stunned.

And in that moment… he just knew. What Elissa wanted, Elissa was going to have, if it was remotely in his power to give it to her. There was nothing he would not do for this woman.

Nothing.

His voice, when it emerged, was firm. "Any contest in which a scholar as fine as Miss St. Cyr is denied the opportunity to compete is a travesty, and I will have nothing to do with it. Good day, sir."

The dean's voice rose half an octave in pitch. "But if you do not participate, everyone will be asking why."

"And I will have a fascinating story to tell them, now won't I?" Edward turned to Elissa. "Come, Miss St. Cyr. We will waste no more of our time with these small-minded fools."

"Wait," cried the bespectacled man who had been manning the door. Edward turned to regard him with one eyebrow raised. He swallowed. "If we allow Miss St. Cyr to compete, then you would as well, my lord?"

Edward made his expression nonchalant. "I suppose."

"Excuse us a moment." He pulled the dean aside, and they began to converse in harsh whispers.

Edward leaned down toward Elissa's ear. "Are you all right?"

She gave a sniff, and he hastily fished his handkerchief from his pocket and pressed it into her hand. Her smile was wobbly as she dabbed at her eyes. "We'll find out in a few moments, I suppose. Thank you so much for standing up for me, Edward. It means everything to me. Especially as I know you'd prefer I not enter."

"You have the right to be here today, and those feelings are my problem to work through."

She squeezed his arm. "But what if they refuse to bend? What about your brother?"

He gazed down at this unexpected, magnificent woman, who had changed his life irrevocably. "I will have no regrets. This is the right thing."

The two men returned. The dean was red in the face, but he said, "Very well. As her name is on the list, then I suppose Miss St. Cyr must be allowed in. You may proceed."

Elissa's head tipped back as they stepped inside the hall. Edward knew this was an important moment for her, to be permitted to enter this shrine of learning. It was a high-ceilinged room whose white walls were dominated by huge stained glass windows. Dark wood beams crisscrossed the roof, and long wooden tables, usually used for dining, had been cleared to make room for the scholars.

Edward found them seats together. Just as they finished laying out their inkwells and quills, Oxford's vice-chancellor, Dr. Whittington Landon, rose to address the fifty-some-odd assembled. "Thank you so much for coming today. We are so pleased to offer this competition in partnership with Mr. George Martindale of the publishing house Martindale and Carruthers. Today, we shall test the mettle of Britain's finest scholars. Tell us, Mr. Martindale," he said, gesturing to a slim man with chestnut hair, "is your mysterious translator of *On the Sublime* in attendance?"

Mr. Martindale's eyes flicked toward Elissa, but not long enough to give her away. "I can confirm that the translator is in this very room."

Excited murmurs filled the hall, and the participants

craned their necks, wondering which one of them it might be.

Once the room quieted, the vice-chancellor gestured to some stacks of papers on the table behind him. "Your task shall be as follows: here you will find passages from ten different classical works. Works that are all fragmentary in nature. You will translate the extant passages and compose original verse, in both the original language and in English, to fill in what is missing. Your choices are Aristotle's *Protrepticus*, Euripides's *Andromeda*..."

Edward bit back a groan. So his absolute least favorite task, putting words in the mouth of an ancient great, was the very thing he would have to do.

Perfect.

Having finished his list, the vice-chancellor continued, "One more matter before we begin. Write your name upon a sheet of paper, then fold it into quarters and seal it. If the mystery translator would be so kind as to indicate as much after the first fold. You will place this within your composition. In this way, your entries will be judged anonymously, and only the winner's name will be revealed. The remaining names will all be burned."

Edward had participated in contests that employed this system to ensure that entries remained anonymous before, but he hadn't known the judges would be using it today.

The judges would only open the name of the winning entry. This meant that no matter how atrocious Edward's attempt might be, no one would ever know that he had been the one to create it.

His shoulders unknotted. As rusty as he was, that tiny detail came as a considerable relief.

They all filed to the front of the room and selected one of the ten works to translate. Back at their table, Edward and Elissa exchanged a quick smile, then settled down to work.

CHAPTER 28

Two hours later, the contest concluded. Elissa folded her entry into a packet around the sheet of paper bearing her name and added it to the growing stack on the table before the Dean of Oriel College. Edward offered her his arm, and they headed outside.

There was now a two-hour break during which the judges would select the winner.

Edward was strangely relaxed. "We may as well take in some of Oxford's famous sights while we wait," he said, leading her across the grassy quadrangle. "Let's start with the Bodleian Library. It's just across the street."

Elissa tried to attend to the things Edward was showing her. Really, she did. But she was so anxious, she couldn't seem to stop babbling about the translation she had just completed.

"… and I'm fairly certain I rendered it in the indicative imperfect, when of course it should have been the optative aorist—"

Edward pressed her hand where it lay upon his arm. "I'm sure your translation was wonderful. With such limited time, nobody's submission will be completely free of errors." He gestured down the street. "The gardens of Magdalen College are particularly fine. Would you like to see them?"

Elissa peered up at him. "Why are you so calm? I would have thought you would be in agony over the outcome."

"I am, a bit. Part of it is that I've given up. I have no realistic chance of winning."

"Edward!" She squeezed his hand. "I don't believe that for a second."

"I do. I told you I haven't opened a lexicon since I left Cambridge. I didn't even manage to study these past few weeks. I just wrote from my gut. It won't be the same quality as the other submissions, but at least the judges will toss it into the fire and no one else will ever read it. Although…" He gazed down at her, and his blue eyes were so tender, she forgot to breathe. "Maybe I'll try to re-create it, just for you to read. You see, I chose Sappho 31."

Elissa gave a startled laugh. Sappho 31 was arguably the most romantic poem in all of classical verse. "Did you truly?"

"I did. And I reworked the missing section to dedicate it to you."

Elissa could feel that she was blushing, the curse of being a redhead. "I would like to read that."

"It's not very good. But I'd like for you to read it. I realized something back there. I realized—"

"Yer blocking the pavement!" barked a man approaching with a wheelbarrow laden with vegetables.

Edward stepped back, frowning as he drew Elissa out of the way. "That is no way to speak to a lady," he muttered.

Elissa's heart was still racing. She tugged on Edward's sleeve. "What was it you realized?"

He glanced up and down the crowded street. "I'll tell you once we reach the gardens."

"As you prefer." She allowed Edward to steer her down

the pavement, but after a few steps, her body stiffened as she came to another unfortunate realization. "Oh, my gracious— I am fairly certain that I rendered the word 'sky' in the *third declension—*"

"Careful, darling," Edward said, gently but firmly pulling her back up onto the curb. "Oncoming carriage."

"Oh! Thank you, Edward." They had taken all of three steps before her mouth resumed babbling of its own accord. "The third declension. Of course, it should have been the *second* declension."

Edward made a sympathetic sound. "Quite tricky, those declensions."

She shook her head. "Not for a masculine noun. How could I have made such a rudimentary error?"

Edward bore her prattling with good humor. She knew it had to be irritating, but she couldn't seem to stop. He never once complained. He alternated between murmuring reassurances and trying to take her mind off the contest by pointing out Oxford's notable sights. None of it worked, but she appreciated his efforts.

"And I think I might have used the pluperfect tense on…" Elissa broke off, noticing they were approaching the Church of St. Mary the Virgin, where the award ceremony was to be held. "Do you mean to tell me it's time for the results already?"

"It is." Edward led her through the wrought-iron gates. "Time to learn our fates."

Elissa fell silent as they entered the nave, the soft clip of their footsteps on the black-and-white tiles discernible over a few soft whispers from those already gathered. The frontmost pews had been reserved for the entrants, but as they made their way up the aisle, she saw Cassandra, who gave her an encouraging nod. Harrington must have ridden up from Cheltenham that morning to learn his own fate, for he was there, too, seated between Cassandra and a young man Elissa did not recognize.

Other than Cassandra and a lady whose face Elissa could not see due to her wide-brimmed hat, she was the only woman in the room.

They claimed seats in the third row. After a few minutes' wait spent in nervous silence, Dr. Whittington Landon, the vice-chancellor of the university, emerged from the wings and made his way toward the altar. He was a portly man, and the severe black of his academic robes was interrupted only by the two white flaps of a plain jabot collar. The silence in the church crackled with tension as he slowly made his way up the wooden steps of the raised pulpit.

He turned to face those assembled. "I will not leave you in suspense. There were many worthy entries today. But there was one that rose above the rest." He reached inside his robes and withdrew a sheet of paper. "I will now read aloud the submission of the winner."

He cleared his throat.

BY THE SECOND LINE, Edward knew.

The winner had opted to translate a fragmentary poem by Simonides of Ceos about a mother and child trapped on a ship in a maelstrom and the mother's terrified certainty that they would not live out the night. Never had he heard such a poignant translation of this work. The mother's despair at her inability to save her child was heart-wrenching.

And the translator had even managed to infuse the work with just a hint of its original meter.

He glanced at Elissa and found tears streaming down her face. He pulled out his handkerchief and handed it to her. "Congratulations," he whispered.

She looked startled for an instant, then accepted his handkerchief and busied herself dabbing her eyes. "How did you know it was mine?" she murmured.

He gave her a wry look. "You think I don't recognize your style?"

They listened in silence for a moment. Elissa's translation was superb, as was the original verse she had composed to complete the poem, whose ending was missing. Her fears that she had used the indicative imperfect instead of the optative aorist were unfounded, as was her worry that she had been mistaken in her use of the pluperfect tense. To be sure, she did render *sky* in the third declension, but it was scarcely noticeable, and overall, it was an outstanding work.

After she managed to stanch her tears, she peered up at Edward nervously. "How are you doing?"

"I am… disappointed. To have let my brother down," he said haltingly. "But…" He paused, searching his feelings. "I'm doing better than I would have thought. I'm—I'm holding up." He was surprised to find that he meant it.

She bit her lip. "Do you hate me?"

He looked at her beautiful face, more precious to him than all the lost plays of Aeschylus. "I could never hate you." He gave her a wry smile. "It seems that I am capable of feeling more than one thing at a time. Because amidst my disappointment, I am genuinely happy for you."

She was crying again, and he wanted to take her in his arms, but he couldn't do that in this public setting. He settled for taking her hand, holding it down on the seat of the pew in a way he hoped wasn't visible to those around them.

Once she had calmed a bit, he leaned down so he could whisper in her ear. "So, I was thinking. There's a dower house about two miles from Harrington Hall that's not currently in use. It's a reasonable size—twenty-three rooms.

Yellow stone, of course, and charmingly situated. You'll love it. It even has its own little pond."

She gave him a curious look, and he continued, "We can stay there year-round. You'll never have to go to London unless you wish to. You won't have to attend any society functions. You will dictate how you spend your days."

She was squeezing his hand so tightly it stung. "Edward, are you asking me to—to—"

"To marry me," he murmured. "You can read outdoors on the pond. Get ink on your elbow. Publish a thousand translations. Be precisely yourself, because that is who I love."

She was back to crying. "But—but what about your sisters?"

"I've been giving them some thought. Any man who is weak-minded enough to be put off from marrying Lucy does not deserve her. And I daresay Izzie will do a better job scaring off her suitors than I ever could. But I also feel quite certain that, were I to ask them, they would both say they wanted me to be happy. And my happiness lies with you."

She dabbed at her eyes as she gave him a smile that was as radiant as it was watery. "Yes. A thousand times, yes. But… when did you decide this, Edward?"

"Before the contest. When that lout tried to deny you entry."

She gave a silent chuckle. "Then why didn't you ask me earlier?"

"I did. Twice, actually. Do you remember when we were in the gardens of Magdalen College, and you asked me why I was crawling around in the dirt?"

"Yes, that was most peculi—" She gasped, squeezing his forearm. "Wait, were you… down on one knee?"

"I was. You were rather distracted, darling."

She rubbed her temple. "So it would seem. I'm so sorry, Edward."

He stroked his thumb over the back of her hand. "There's no need to be sorry. There's no need to be anything other than precisely who you are."

Murmurs filled the church. Edward realized with a start that Vice-Chancellor Landon had finished reading Elissa's poem. He heard someone behind him whisper *brilliant*, while the man seated next to him chose *outstanding* as his descriptor.

On the other side of the aisle, someone spoke. "It's the translator. The translator of *On the Sublime*. I'd recognize his style anywhere."

Murmurs of agreement filled the room. "Let's see, shall we?" Dr. Landon pulled out a second piece of paper, this one folded into a tiny square.

He undid the first fold. "You are correct. It is the anonymous translator." His eyes gleamed as they swept around the church. "Whose identity we are all about to learn."

Excited whispers filled the room. Dr. Landon held up a hand for silence, then opened the final fold. His mouth fell open, and his whole body froze for a beat before he said, "Miss Elissa St. Cyr."

Suddenly the sacred church was as noisy as a tavern. Everyone was talking at once and craning their necks to get a look at the slip of a girl who had bested them all.

Elissa's publisher, Mr. Martindale, rushed to the foot of the pulpit. He held both hands out placatingly. "Yes, that is correct. I can confirm that Miss St. Cyr is the translator of *On the Sublime*, as well as the winner of today's contest."

Edward squeezed Elissa's hand as he glanced around the church. It had fallen silent once more. Absolutely everyone was staring at her. A few looks were admiring, but others were openly hostile. The largest number seemed wary, as if they were making up their minds. Elissa managed to keep her chin up, but her lower lip was quivering, and he could read her face well enough to know that one cross word would send tears spilling across her cheeks again.

On the far side of the aisle, Robert Slocombe rose to his feet. He turned to face Elissa. And then, ever so slowly…

He began to clap.

At first, each of his claps echoed in the vaulted stone room. But on the sixth clap, someone seated behind them joined him, and then another person joined in, and another. Soon the room was filled with applause, and a whistle came from behind them, the shrill kind that Harrington was particularly good at.

He glanced at Elissa and there were tears in her eyes, but this time they were of a happy sort.

Edward turned and caught Robert Slocombe's eye. He inclined his head in gratitude, and Slocombe smiled as he returned the gesture.

He'd always been a good sort, Robert Slocombe.

Once the applause died down, a few of the entrants made to stand, but Dr. Landon held up a hand. "Before you go, there is one thing more. Although the judges agreed that Miss St. Cyr's poem was the winner, there was one more entry of such exceptional quality, we thought you would all wish to hear it."

He pulled out a second sheet of paper and began to read.

PEER OF GODS he seemeth to me, the blissful
    Man who sits and gazes at thee before him,
    Close beside thee sits, and in silence hears thee
       Silverly speaking,
    Laughing love's low laughter.

. . .

BESIDE HIM, Elissa's spine had gone stiff as a ramrod, because of course she recognized the famous opening lines of Sappho 31. "Edward?" she whispered. "This… this is yours. Is it not?"

"Yes," he confirmed. His shoulder was spasming nonstop, to the point that he had to place his free and upon it to get himself under control. *Oh, God.* This could not be happening. He knew he should be honored to have his poem read before such company. But the thought of all of these people, all of these *scholars*, listening to his sloppy verse, to think how they would pick his work apart, *judge* him… And even worse, what was to come: his original verse, the words he thought no one but the judges would ever read, in which he had all but ripped open his chest and laid his beating heart bare…

He felt the gorge rise in his throat.

Dr. Landon was still reading.

OH THIS, this only
  Stirs the troubled heart in my breast to tremble!
  For should I but see thee a little moment,
    Straight is my voice hushed;
  Yea, my tongue is broken, and through and through me
  'Neath the flesh impalpable fire runs tingling;
  Nothing see mine eyes, and a noise of roaring
    Waves in my ears.

SOMEONE SEATED BEHIND THEM WHISPERED, *incandescent,* and his companion murmured in agreement. Edward swallowed thickly as Dr. Landon continued,

SWEAT RUNS DOWN IN RIVERS, a tremor seizes
  All my limbs, and paler than grass in autumn,

Caught by pains of menacing death, I falter,
  Lost in the love trance.
But all this will I bear, my darling Elissa—

THE CROWD, which had been hanging on every word, erupted as the dedicatee of this rendition of Sappho's famous ode to her beloved was revealed. Now it was Edward's turn to be stared at, as of course he was the one sitting next to Elissa, holding her hand, and, apparently, being less-than-subtle in the looks he was giving her.

After a minute, the room quieted enough for Dr. Landon to continue reading.

FOR ALTHOUGH ALL *I yearn for in this life*
  Is to spend each day with you,
  I will cherish whatever crumbs of your attention
  You might choose to give me
  As manna from the gods.

FOR IN YOU *I have found a prize beyond compare:*
  Your heart, as kind as Eleos.
  Your mind, sharp as Achilles' spear,
  And your will, forged from adamantine.
  And, if you will let me, I will treasure you every day,
  For the rest of our lives.

YOU COULD'VE HEARD a pin drop in the church. Oh, but this was agony. He never thought there was a chance anyone would hear this drivel, save the judges to whom he would be anonymous, which was the only reason he'd let his emotions flow unfiltered onto the page.

The tortuous silence was broken by a voice from the front row. "By Jove, I wonder who wrote that one?"

Sniggers filled the room. Edward chanced a glance around him. To be sure, everyone was laughing, and some people were openly jeering. But most of those assembled seemed to be laughing in a friendly way.

He made an effort not to look at them, to focus instead on Elissa. She was glowing. There was no other word for it. She was looking at him as if he were some sort of demigod.

"Is that truly how you see me?" she whispered.

"It is," he said softly.

She squeezed his fingers.

Dr. Landon unfolded the folded piece of paper bearing the author's name and confirmed, "It is indeed by Lord Fauconbridge."

Edward cleared his throat. "Miss St. Cyr has recently done me the very great honor of agreeing to be my wife."

Good-natured murmurs filled the room. Amid the sea of amiable faces that surrounded them, Edward picked out one scowl. He realized it was William Ricketts, Elissa's old schoolroom tormentor.

In an instant, Edward understood that Ricketts' taunts had not been borne of hatred. That he had been one of those young fools who would say anything to get the girl he fancied to look at him and didn't care if, in doing so, he made her cry.

Meeting Edward's eye, Ricketts' glower deepened. "It was a bit maudlin for my taste," he said in a voice loud enough to carry.

"Ah," Dr. Landon said from the pulpit, "but so was the original. Lord Fauconbridge matched the spirit of the work remarkably well. The poem is sentimental, to be sure, but that is the reason it is so beloved." He gave Ricketts a pointed look. "It takes courage to write something so raw, and I daresay that is the reason the esteemed judges selected Lord Fauconbridge's poem to be read aloud, and not yours."

Dr. Landon began descending the steps, marking the conclusion of the ceremony, and those assembled began filing out of the church.

CHAPTER 29

Outside, the participants milled about the green of Radcliffe Square. Edward smiled as he watched Cassandra fight her way through the swarm of well-wishers so she could catch her sister in a hug. "I knew you could do it! I'm so proud of you." Cassandra dabbed beneath her eyes with a handkerchief. "How I wish Mother and Father had been there to see it. I thought they were going to come up for the ceremony."

"I did too," Elissa said. "But it doesn't matter."

Everyone wanted to meet Elissa, so Edward spent the next half-hour introducing her to his former school friends and professors. When the crowd finally started to thin, Harrington strolled up.

Considering he had just lost a fifteen-thousand-pound wager and was about to face the wrath of their father, his brother looked strangely jovial.

"Congratulations, Miss St. Cyr," he said, bowing over her hand. "I very much look forward to having you as my sister."

"Thank you," Elissa said. "The feeling is entirely mutual."

"I'm sorry, brother," Edward said. "I tried. There was just no besting Elissa today."

Harrington laughed. "There's no need to apologize. It happens that you did precisely what I needed you to do."

Edward cocked his head. "But… I lost."

Harrington's eyes gleamed. "Happily for me, I did not wager that you would win. I wagered that your poem would be read aloud in University Church by the vice-chancellor of Oxford University on the first of April. Which it was." He gave a triumphant laugh as he reached into his breast pocket. "Avery was a tremendous sport about the whole thing. He's already handed over the bank draft. See?"

"You don't mean—" Edward peered at the document in Harrington's hand, which was indeed a bank draft for fifteen thousand pounds.

"This has turned out better than I could've imagined," Harrington crowed. "I spent all morning worrying that I was going to be thrown in debtor's prison. Instead, I've gained a fortune!"

Edward scowled. "You worried all morning? I've been panicking for the last month. Besides which, I did all the work. I think we should donate that money to Anne's charity."

"Not a chance. I already have plans for it."

He was interrupted by a feminine voice. "Do you, now?" Edward glanced over his shoulder and saw an elegant woman in a wide-brimmed hat.

She lifted her head and was revealed to be their mother.

"Am I to understand," Lady Cheltenham asked, joining their circle, "that you wagered fifteen thousand pounds on the outcome of the contest?" She pinched the bridge of her nose. "You're lucky your father isn't here."

Harrington blanched. "You won't tell him, will you, Mother?"

"Gracious, no," the countess replied. "But nor am I inclined to let you fritter such a sum away in some seedy gaming den."

"Not *all* of it," Harrington grumbled.

Edward caught his mother's eye. "You were present for the ceremony?"

"I was." Lady Cheltenham turned to Elissa. "Congratulations, my dear. As a mother, I found your poem ever so affecting. I'm not too proud to admit I shed a tear."

Elissa curtseyed. "Thank you, my lady."

Edward peered at his mother. She seemed strangely nonchalant. "Then you also heard my announcement that Elissa and I are to wed?"

"Of course, darling." The countess smiled fondly as she took Elissa's hand and pressed it. "Not that it came as a surprise."

"Did it not?" Edward exchanged a glance with Elissa. "We thought you might, er—"

"Fauconbridge, there you are." Edward turned to see Elissa's father approaching, his wife on his arm. "One of the stagecoach horses threw a shoe, which is why we..." He trailed off, noticing Lady Cheltenham.

"Mother, allow me to present Elissa's parents." Introductions were completed in short order. Elissa's mother seemed flustered to be in the presence of a countess.

Her father was more composed. He turned to Edward. "So, what happened? Did you win?"

"I did not," Edward replied.

Mr. St. Cyr shook his head. "Ah, that's a pity. We came all this way for nothing."

Edward was torn between fuming that Mr. St. Cyr did not even consider the possibility that Elissa might have won, and the anticipation of having such an obvious example of his daughter's talent to throw in his face.

Mr. St. Cyr shook his head. "I suppose the prize went to that anonymous translator."

"Indeed, it did," Lady Cheltenham confirmed, a gleam in her eye.

"Who was it, then?"

Edward smiled fondly at Elissa. "Why, your brilliant daughter, of course."

"What?" A look of shock crossed Mr. St. Cyr's face as he rounded on Elissa. "You?"

Elissa took a deep breath. "Yes, Father."

"You—you won the contest?"

"I did."

"And you're the secret translator?"

She lifted her chin. "I am."

Her father's face had fallen completely slack. "But that's… that's impossible!"

Edward clapped his former tutor on the shoulder. "Don't worry, Mr. St. Cyr. I, too, felt exceedingly foolish when first she told me. In retrospect, it was so obviously her style, I cannot believe I didn't figure it out for myself."

Elissa's father was apparently stunned speechless. Mrs. St. Cyr shook off her stupor. "This is dreadful, absolutely dreadful! You had to go and flaunt your unnatural infatuation with topics best reserved for men in such a public manner. Now everyone will know you to be the worst kind of bluestocking." Mrs. St. Cyr rubbed her forehead. "We will never marry you off now."

"As much as I hate to contradict you, Mrs. St. Cyr," Edward said with a grave sincerity he did not feel in the slightest, "Elissa will be marrying, and sooner than you think. You see, I have asked her to be my wife."

"And I have accepted," Elissa added.

Mrs. St. Cyr's jaw was hanging open in a manner that was not particularly becoming. "You… you…"

Edward patted Elissa's hand. "She will be my viscountess. And one day, the Countess of Cheltenham."

"The Countess of…" Mrs. St. Cyr shook herself, then turned to Edward's mother. "My lady, I know I will come to regret what I am about to say. But as a Christian woman, I feel honor-bound to tell you the truth. My daughter will make a terrible countess."

Lady Cheltenham raised a single eyebrow. "Oh?"

"Of a certainty," Mrs. St. Cyr said in a rush. "She cannot dance. She cannot sew. She cannot plan the most basic gathering—"

"Do you know who is very good at planning parties?" the countess drawled. "My daughter, Caro—Lady Thetford, as she's properly known." She smiled fondly at Elissa. "She is beside herself with excitement at the prospect of arranging yours as well as her own."

"But… but…" Mrs. St. Cyr sputtered, "Elissa is the worst sort of bluestocking—"

"Original," Lady Cheltenham interjected.

"Origi—what?" Mrs. St. Cyr asked.

The countess fanned herself nonchalantly. "Whether or not your daughter is a bluestocking is beside the point. She is an *original*. That is how society will regard her."

"Oh, no!" Mrs. St. Cyr laughed. "An original is someone who is unique in the *right* way. Who is confident and beautiful. Whereas my daughter—"

"I beg your pardon," Lady Cheltenham said. "Did you just imply that I lack the influence to persuade society to accept my future daughter-in-law as an original?"

"N-no, my lady! I did not mean—"

The countess leaned forward, her eyes fierce. "No one will say a word against her. *No one*. Because *I* would cut them dead, and then *Graverley* would cut them dead. You do know that he is Edward's dearest friend, do you not?"

Mrs. St. Cyr's eyes had gone wide as dinner plates. "The Marquess of Graverley? Is—is he truly?"

"Certainly he is. And after that, their social demise would be irrevocable. I therefore do not expect to hear one word spoken against your daughter." Lady Cheltenham gave Mrs. St. Cyr a very pointed look. "From *anyone*."

This was sufficient to stun Mrs. St. Cyr into silence. Elissa's father shook himself. "I say, Elissa. Wasn't there some prize money associated with this contest? What was it— twenty pounds? Thirty?"

"Thirty pounds?" the countess said. "Gracious, no." Quick as a jaguar, she plucked the bank draft from Harrington's grasp. "The prize was fifteen thousand."

Harrington's hand instinctively reached for the bank note. Realizing he couldn't very well wrestle it away from his mother, he curled his fingers into a fist. "I believe you are mistaken, Mother. Is the prize not *fourteen* thousand pounds?"

Edward took the bank draft from his mother, carefully positioning his thumb over the name of the recipient as he showed it to Elissa's father. "No, Mother has the right of it. The prize is definitely *fifteen* thousand."

"Fifteen thousand pounds!" Mr. St. Cyr exclaimed. "You don't say! By rights, such an amount should go to your father for safekeeping."

"*No,*" Elissa said forcefully. She cleared her throat and continued in a softer tone. "If it goes to you, it will become part of the estate. But if it stays in my name, then Uncle John can never make any claim to it."

"You marvelous girl!" Mrs. St. Cyr burst out. "Why, you have saved us all! And a countess. A *countess*! I do not pretend to understand it. Never did I dream that *you*, of all people, would—"

"You must be tired and thirsty after your journey,"

Edward interjected, not caring to hear how his future mother-in-law would finish that sentence. "Why do you not head to the Angel Inn for some refreshment?"

Cassandra stepped forward. "Some refreshment—what an excellent suggestion." She hooked her arms through those of her parents, tugging them along. "Come, I shall show you the way."

Elissa wrung her hands as she watched her parents retreating. "That was exceptionally kind of you, my lady. In truth, I expected you would share in my mother's opinion."

"I can tell by Edward's face that he feared the same." The countess laughed. "For two of the most intelligent people in England, you have been remarkably stupid. Why on earth would I have invited you to my house party if I did not approve?"

"I thought it was so Cassandra could meet Lady Morsley," Elissa said.

"No, dear child. I had a full report from Harrington after the dance, you see."

Harrington waggled his eyebrows. "A *full* report."

"And praise heavens, he told me of a young lady who actually made Edward smile! A quality more important, I think, than a knack for planning parties."

"Father will not agree," Edward said quietly.

A smug smile stole across his mother's face. "Leave him to me."

"I appreciate your support, Mother. Truly, I do. But I must forewarn you that Elissa and I do not plan to be out in society in the way people might expect. She cares nothing about balls and routs and wishes to avoid the glare of the *ton's* scrutiny. We plan to take up residence at the dower house."

"An excellent idea," the countess said, "and one that will afford you some privacy in the early years of your marriage."

"We might never go to London," Edward emphasized.

"Really? I would have thought you would want to see the Greek and Roman sculptures at the British Museum, Miss St. Cyr."

Elissa looked up at Edward, her eyes filled with longing. "I… I would, but—"

"And visit the Temple of the Muses, the largest bookstore in all of England." The countess frowned as she peered across the green. "Is that Lord Barnsdale? Of all the tedious people to run into."

"I would like to visit the Temple of the Muses," Elissa said, lost in thought.

"Of course you would. Harrington, stand here so Lord Barnsdale won't see me," Lady Cheltenham said, positioning him on her left side. She turned to Elissa. "And I imagine you'd like to see a few of those classical plays you're so fond of performed in London's finest theatres."

Elissa looked torn. "As much as I would enjoy those things, if I go to London, wouldn't I also be expected to attend balls and host calling hours?"

"Calling hours—gracious no," Lady Cheltenham said, peering around Harrington. "The last thing you want is a bunch of busybodies circling you like sharks, looking for any excuse to rip you to shreds. No, what you should host is a salon. You shall invite all the finest minds in London for stimulating intellectual conversation."

Elissa's mouth fell open. "A salon? I—I didn't know I could do that."

"Of course you can. There is no reason you have to do things exactly as everyone else does. You are not like everyone else. You are a *genius*." She took a hasty step back, then made a sound of exasperation. "Oh, bother, Lord Barnsdale has spotted me. Well, there's nothing for it—I'll have to go and speak to him." She pointed her fan at Edward. "If I'm not back in three minutes, you are to contrive an excuse to fetch me away."

Elissa stared after his mother in astonishment, then shook her head. "A salon! It had never occurred to me, but… I think I could do that." She bit her lip as she glanced up at Edward. "I would even enjoy it."

Edward felt a flicker of hope. Perhaps Elissa wouldn't be miserable in his world after all. "There's no need to decide anything this afternoon. But maybe in a few months we could go to London, just for a week or two. Visit the book-shops and museums, and the theater. And you can decide what you would like to do from there."

Elissa gave him a crooked smile. "I think that is a wonderful suggestion."

Edward turned to check on his mother's progress with Lord Barnsdale, but was distracted by his brother's morose expression. "Harrington, don't look so glum. You're no worse off than you were this morning. At least you don't owe the fifteen thousand."

"You could've let me keep a thousand pounds," Harrington muttered.

"A thousand pounds is a lot to spend on drink and cards," Edward returned.

Harrington closed his eyes. "A lieutenant's commission in the Rifles goes for four hundred and fifty. I'll need a few hundred more to kit me out with uniforms, horses, and the like." He opened his eyes, his gaze steady on Edward's. "That's the bulk of it. But I do think one good night out on the town with you and Thetford and Ferguson before I ship out isn't too much to ask. Wouldn't you agree?"

"I would," Edward said quickly. "This is your choice, then? The army?"

"It is. I'm tired of feeling like such a wastrel all the time. Probably I should've done this years ago. I'd be miserable as a vicar or a lawyer, and I'm too old to join the Navy. But the army…" He squeezed his eyes shut. "I know I can do it. I even think I would be good at it." He glanced at Edward, his eyes guarded, his jaw braced. Edward realized with a pang that Harrington expected him to respond with scorn, to parrot the family's usual joke about how Harrington wasn't capable of rising before noon.

Edward's feelings about Harrington joining the army were mixed. Considering the French would be actively shooting at him, he would be in far more danger than he ever would have been in India.

But this was his brother's choice. So Edward said, "You will be an outstanding officer. I am sure of it. You have every quality the army would seek. And I don't mean merely that you're such an excellent marksman, although you will be prized for that. It is your personal qualities that make you uniquely suited to the role. You're the sort of man others naturally follow. The sort who will inspire them to give their best effort, to persevere when they would otherwise give up, so they can come out on the other side." He clasped Harrington's shoulder. "The Rifles will be lucky to have you."

Harrington's eyes were shiny. "Thank you, Edward."

"Don't give a second thought to the money. Father will cover the associated costs. I will make sure of it."

Harrington nodded, seemingly unable to speak. Edward cleared his throat. "Well, then. Shall we rescue Mother and return to the Angel?"

A hesitant voice came from over Edward's shoulder. "E-excuse me. Lord Fauconbridge?"

He turned and saw Robert Slocombe. His chin was ducked, and his hands were clasped before him. His eyes went wide as he noticed Harrington and Elissa.

Slocombe's words came out in a rush. "Oh, dear. I've

interrupted. I can see that I've interrupted. I'm terribly sorry, I'll just come back later, and, um—"

"Not at all," Edward said, waving him forward. "Elissa, may I present my friend from Cambridge, Mr. Robert Slocombe? Slocombe, this is my betrothed, Miss Elissa St. Cyr, and my brother, Mr. Harrington Astley."

Elissa kept her features placid as she dropped a curtsey and said, "Mr. Slocombe, what a pleasure. Edward has told me so much about you."

Harrington was much less discreet, his eyes agog as he jerked his gaze from Edward to Slocombe and back again.

Fortunately, Slocombe's gaze was fixed upon Elissa. "The pleasure is entirely mine, Miss St. Cyr, I assure you. I am such an admirer of your work. I enjoyed your *On the Sublime* tremendously. Just"—he waved both hands, struggling to find sufficient words—"absolutely superb. It's such an honor to meet the scholar behind such outstanding work."

Elissa's smile was fond. "Thank you, Mr. Slocombe. That means so much to me, coming from such an accomplished classicist as yourself."

"Th-thank you," Slocombe stammered, rubbing the back of his head. "I'll keep this brief, as I can see you've got other things to…" He turned to Edward. "I was wondering if I could ask a favor."

"Of course," Edward said, surprised.

"You see…" Slocombe tugged at his cravat. "Up until recently, I was working as a curate out in Stoke-by-Clare. It's a little hamlet within the gift of Baron Poslingford. The living went to one of his nephews, but he hired me to conduct the services."

"I see," Edward said. A curate was the lowest paid of clergymen. Often times, a man with good connections would be named to a number of lucrative church livings. Because no one could be in six places at once, it was common to hire someone else, a curate, to do the actual work. A curate's wage was typically the barest subsistence. For many young graduates fresh out of university, it was a temporary waypoint while they searched for a more sustainable living.

But that was for those who had connections. The son of a baker such as Robert Slocombe would no doubt struggle to find a better-paid position.

"It was going well at first," Slocombe continued. "But then my mother fell ill. I had to go back home to Holywell to take care of her."

"I'm sorry to hear that," Edward said.

"Thank you. Fortunately, she recovered, and I was able to return to my post after a few weeks. I had arranged with the vicar in the neighboring village to look after things while I was away. I didn't just abandon my parishioners. I had thought Lord Poslingford would be understanding."

"Did you lose your post?" Edward guessed.

"I did. But that's not the worst of it." He dropped his voice. "Lord Poslingford has been blackballing me. Every time I think I have a new curacy lined up, he gets wind of it, and lo and behold, it falls through."

"That's terrible," Edward said.

"That was six months ago, and I won't lie, I'm starting to get desperate." Slocombe cringed as he peered up at Edward. "Last week I heard about a vacancy in Gloucestershire. I believe it's in the gift of your neighbor, Lord Redditch."

Time seemed to slow down. "That's correct," Edward said cautiously.

Slocombe was babbling nervously. "Of course, you would know Lord Redditch. And I—I thought your families might be friends."

"Very good friends," Edward confirmed. "My sister is even married to his son and heir."

Slocombe looked positively green. "I... I know I would

never be a candidate for the *living*. But perhaps Lord Redditch could use a curate to take care of things while he searches for the right man." He swallowed audibly. "Would you consider putting in a good word for me?"

Edward froze, because the position Slocombe was referring to was his own parish, where he and his family attended services each week. And if Robert Slocombe took over the post, it wouldn't just be a matter of seeing him once a week at church. He would become an important member of the local community. Edward could expect to see him at every conceivable social occasion, from dinners to dances.

Three days ago, the notion of inviting *Robert Slocombe* to join his most intimate social circle would have seemed absurd.

And yet…

Robert Slocombe hadn't done anything wrong. He had never been anything but kind to Edward.

Why, that very afternoon, he had been the one to stand and applaud for Elissa.

In truth, Robert Slocombe was a fine fellow. He would be precisely the sort of diligent vicar Lord Redditch had been searching for these past six months.

Which meant that Edward could not in good conscience recommend Slocombe to serve as a temporary curate.

No, if he was going to do this, the right thing would be to recommend Slocombe for the living itself.

Was he truly contemplating this? *Robert Slocombe* as the priest of his own parish church? Seeing Robert Slocombe regularly *for the rest of his life?*

His shoulder gave a twitch. He glanced at Elissa, and her eyes were crinkled with concern. Harrington, meanwhile, looked openly horrified.

And there was good-hearted Robert Slocombe, looking at

him in a cringing sort of way, as if he had always known the answer would be no, but still he had to try.

Edward steeled himself, then said in a rush, "I think it a capital idea. Excepting this business about you serving as curate. You are precisely the sort of man Lord Redditch has been looking for. I intend to recommend he grant you the living."

"The—the living?" Slocombe sputtered. "I never imagined… the… the… "

Harrington's jaw was gaping open. Edward ignored his brother, keeping his focus on Slocombe. "You should ride back with us this afternoon. There's room in our carriage. You can stay the night at Harrington Hall, and I will introduce you to Lord Redditch in the morning."

Slocombe's voice was rich with emotion. "I can't thank you enough for this, Fauconbridge. I'll do a good job. I promise."

"Excellent." Edward's voice sounded a bit shrill to his own ears, but overall, he thought he was managing rather well. "We're over at the Angel Inn. Where are you staying?"

"I'm at a lodging house on Iffley Road."

Edward nodded. "We'll stop there to collect your things."

Slocombe's ears turned red. "Oh! Um… why don't I just run and fetch them? I can meet you back at the Angel in, say, a half-hour?"

Edward suspected this lodging house was not the most respectable establishment. "That will be perfect. It will take that long to have the carriage made ready," Edward reassured him.

Slocombe hurried off. Edward dug some coin out of his pocket and handed it to his brother. "Follow after him and settle his bill, won't you?"

"Have you lost your bloody mind?" Harrington hissed.

"Harrington!" Edward nodded toward Elissa. "There is a lady present."

"But that's Robert Slocombe!"

"I know. Now hurry along, and—"

Harrington tugged at his sleeve. "Look at me, will you?"

Edward turned to his brother and found nothing but concern in his eyes.

"I'm worried about you, Edward. Are—are you all right?"

He considered. "No. I'm not all right."

It was true. He still had problems. He knew he did. He was coming to realize that the way he had looked at the world and the way he had thought of himself for most of his life was fundamentally flawed.

Twenty years of thinking the wrong things couldn't be undone in a week.

But by showing a little bit of his true self to Elissa, and to Harrington, too, he was starting to see that his flaws weren't as unforgiveable as he had always assumed.

And he was stronger than he'd realized.

He had proven that to himself today.

"I'm not all right," he repeated, laying his hand upon his brother's shoulder and giving it a squeeze, then shifting his gaze to Elissa, who was on his other arm. "But for the very first time, I think I will be."

Harrington studied him for a moment, then nodded.

Edward gave him a push. "Now hurry, before Slocombe gets away."

Pocketing the coins Edward had given him, Harrington strode off.

Elissa squeezed his arm. "I'm proud of you, Edward."

"You know, I'm proud of me, too." And he was. He may not have won today, but he liked being the kind of person who was genuinely happy for Elissa when she had. And the type who did right by Robert Slocombe.

He pressed her hand. "Come. Let's go rescue my mother."

They strolled across the green. "Do you know what I have always wished?" Elissa asked. "That a pair of scholars would work together on a translation of Plato. As most of his works are in the form of dialogues, if a pair of classicists were to collaborate, each speaker could have their own unique voice."

Edward considered. It was an outstanding idea. He would love to read such a translation. "A pair of scholars, you say? 'Both of them united with an equal vigor of mind'?"

Elissa drew him to a halt. "How I wish I could kiss you right now. Not only was that the perfect thing to say. But you just quoted *Theseus*!"

He raised her hand to his lips and dropped a kiss into her palm. "And you, my darling Elissa, just recognized my quote from *Theseus*. A work that will always have a special place in my heart, as it was the one that brought us together."

Elissa leaned forward and whispered, "Perhaps someday we will read it together in a rowboat."

"I would like that very much."

Elissa's smile was wry. "And after we are done reading Plutarch in a rowboat, I think we should begin our translation."

Edward paused. He hadn't worked on a translation in years. He had honestly thought he never would again, that he had closed the book on that chapter of his life when he left Cambridge.

But the past few weeks had showed him that although cutting the classics out of his life had spared him the pain of failure, they could also be a source of joy, one that he had been denying himself.

"I'm not sure if I would feel comfortable publishing it," he said haltingly.

"That's all right," she said quickly.

"You might prefer to do something on your own. Something where there is no chance of me holding you back."

"I honestly don't mind if we never publish it. The thing I truly desire is to work on a project with you." She squeezed his arm. "We don't have to figure out the ending today. I think the important thing is just to begin."

For the past few years, beginning had been the hardest part. Edward nodded. "I think you're right."

Elissa tugged his arm, and they resumed their stroll across the green. "We could start with Plato's *Gorgias*," she suggested.

"Hmm. The *Gorgias* is good. But I think we should start with the *Symposium*. The speeches are longer, so there's not as much back and forth, but the *Symposium* is about—"

"—the nature of true love," Elissa said, completing his thought.

"Precisely. I should warn you now that I mean to make a very thorough study into Plato's theories. It is my intention to master them."

"Very good, so long as you do not imagine that your understanding shall eclipse my own."

"I have a feeling that in this particular contest, there will be no losers. Only winners."

"How right you are, my dear Edward. Very well, then, we shall start with the *Symposium*. But I want to do the *Gorgias* next."

"Certainly, my darling Elissa. We have a lifetime."

And they did.

∼

KEEP READING for a special preview of Book Four in The Astley Chronicles, *The Duke's Dark Secret*!

I HOPE you enjoyed Edward and Elissa's story! If you would be willing to take a few minutes to leave a review or rating on the site from which you purchased it, that is a great help to me as an author. And if you'd like a peek at what married life looks like for Edward and Elissa (and Caro and Henry, and Anne and Michael), be sure to subscribe to my newsletter! Newsletter subscribers receive a free second epilogue short story for each of my books, as well as other Regency fun and goodies! You can sign up via my website, https://courtneymccaskill.com/.

Secrets, Lies, and a Lock...

Ever since her father's unexpected death, Cecilia Chenoweth has felt like the heroine of a bad Gothic novel. In addition to leaving her alone and destitute, her father made a deathbed confession that it was no mere fever that took her mother's life some twenty years ago. Then he pressed a sinister key into her hands, bidding her to go forth and uncover the truth. If only she knew where to find the lock that will open to the mysterious key...

Cold, Bold, and Dangerous to Know...

There is one man who recognizes the black key bearing the emblem of a snake: Marcus Latimer, the newly minted Duke of Trevissick. Now that his abusive father is rotting in hell where he belongs, Marcus is eager for his life to stop resembling a bad Gothic novel. No one would ever have thought to pair the dangerously handsome duke with the meek little rector's daughter. But as he helps Cecilia on her quest, Marcus discovers a well of passion hiding behind her sloe eyes that may just be a match for his own.

Two Hearts on a Perilous Path...

But Cecelia's search for the truth about her mother's death unearths dark secrets from Marcus's past, secrets that will destroy the new life he has built for his beloved sister and condemn one of the few people he cares about to death. What will he do when he is forced to choose between loyalty... and love?

~

Marcus waved off the butler's offer to show him to the library. He was a frequent enough visitor to Astley House to know where it was, and where Lord Cheltenham kept the brandy.

He made his way through the crimson parlor, its walls lined with fine art.

Straight ahead, toward the back of the house, was the library.

He had just laid his hand upon the knob when the sound of a chord being struck upon the pianoforte came from the music room to his left.

Marcus froze. It was a minor chord, its very discordancy the key to its haunting beauty. But what had the hairs on the back of his neck standing on end wasn't the notes so much as the air of command with which they had been played.

A series of softer chords followed, then another accent. Without realizing his intentions, his feet drifted away from the library toward the open door to the music room. He listened to the dynamic peaks and valleys, perfectly executed and dramatic in their contrast, and recognized the piece as Beethoven's Eight Piano Sonata. He had heard it in concert not a month ago, although whoever was playing it now was far superior in their interpretation of the music.

The notes trilled into a delicate arpeggio as he reached the doorway. He stopped short, recoiling in surprise.

Because seated at the pianoforte, in profile to him, was none other than Cecilia Chenoweth.

Was this the same timid little rector's daughter who did nothing but stutter and stammer in his presence? The girl who was so meek she could not even meet his eye?

He could scarcely countenance it. Yet there she was, so absorbed in the keys that she did not mark his presence. In a way, he shouldn't be surprised. Everyone said she was a rare talent on the pianoforte. He had also heard dozens of snide remarks about how she had been forced to lower herself by offering *piano lessons* (said in such a tone you could be forgiven for assuming this must be a euphemism for selling sexual favors on the corner of Piccadilly and St. James's Street). This seemed like a callous thing to say about someone so recently orphaned even to Marcus, whose list of leading attributes did not include the word *kindhearted*.

Her right hand floated down the keyboard again in a delicate flourish. She was definitely good.

But the real test was about to come.

She paused dramatically, and then the tempo suddenly increased as she entered the technical section. She dropped down to a mezzo piano then slowly began to build, ratcheting the tension higher and higher before suddenly dropping it down again. Marcus felt rather than heard her crescendo and was startled to find that his heartrate had kicked up along with the tempo.

He held his breath as she came to a particularly challenging series of runs, but they were as clear and sparkling as a brilliant-cut diamond.

It wasn't merely her technical proficiency, although he would describe that as flawless. Cecilia Chenoweth had a visceral understanding of the piece. She knew when to back off, when to crescendo, how to wring every ounce of emotion from the keys. The passion with which she played was visible on her face, and as she threw her head back, exposing a creamy expanse of her neck, Marcus found himself gripping the doorframe with white knuckles.

She was *magnificent*. He, who had attended hundreds of professional concerts over the years, featuring the finest musicians in all of Europe, had never heard anything like it.

Who *was* this girl?

He listened, rapt, until she hammered out the final chords with a flourish, then he broke into applause.

Miss Chenoweth shrieked as she spun to face him, eyes huge, one hand flying to her heart. Her chest rose and fell as if she'd been sprinting, and he fancied it was not from her exertions at the keyboard.

He stepped into the room. "Beethoven, Miss Chenoweth? How scandalous."

She gazed up at him, her sloe eyes wide with terror. Gone was the passionate, confident performer. She was once again the shrinking little vicar's daughter, cowed by his mere presence.

He wondered if she could even manage to form an answer.

Just when he was ready to give up, she drew in a breath. "I am sorry to have offended your delicate sensibilities."

Had mousy little Cecilia Chenoweth just delivered a retort? Would wonders never cease? "I haven't a single delicate sensibility, as you surely are aware. And thank God for it. Otherwise, I would have been shocked, absolutely shocked, by the sight of you thrashing about—"

She drew herself up primly. "I was not *thrashing*."

"You were so far gone that near the end, I am fairly certain you slavered upon the keys."

She raised her chin. "I most certainly did not."

He leaned forward. "I can see a drop just there, upon the middle C."

She narrowed her eyes at him before inspecting—then wiping—the offending key. "Although I would not presume to call myself an expert on Beethoven—"

"You should, if that performance is any indication."

"—my personal opinion is that if the performer is not flailing madly and foaming at the mouth, they're not even trying."

That startled a laugh out of him. "I am inclined to agree, but still, it is shockingly unladylike."

"You prefer something ladylike, do you? Shall I play you 'The Battle of Prague'?" she offered, referring to a particularly vapid piece he was subjected to at every home musicale.

"What you should play," he said, giving her a pointed look as he flicked his coattails out of the way and seated himself upon a plush orange silk chaise longue, "is the 'Moonlight Sonata.'"

She stared at him, as still as a fawn crouched in the tall grass hiding from a wolf, as if a single blink would spell her doom.

He raised an eyebrow expectantly.

Shaking herself, she turned back to the keyboard and began to play.

Ceci was having the strangest afternoon of her life.

She was spending time with the Duke of Trevissick.

No. That wasn't quite right.

He was spending time with *her*.

Intentionally.

Considering that the expression Marcus Latimer usually

assumed whenever his gaze fell upon her could be best described with the words, *isn't that a pity*, this was a shocking turn of events.

And not only was he voluntarily remaining in her presence. Suddenly the Duke of Trevissick, the man who had always regarded her as dull and pathetic, found her impressive. Because she was certain that he did.

It was an almost incomprehensible reversal, and she wasn't sure how to feel about it. On the one hand, surely anything was better than dull and pathetic.

Yet she feared the inevitable letdown when he decided she was not so interesting as he had supposed.

She had no idea how she was going to speak to him when the music concluded. But that didn't matter at the moment, because right now she was playing 'Moonlight Sonata,' one of her very favorite pieces, and one she had been playing more oft of late. Her emotions following the death of her father had been something of a jumble. Of course she felt the things one would suspect—sorrow, loneliness, grief.

But, if she was being honest, there were times when she felt angry at her father. It was his fault that she now found herself destitute, his obsession with her mother's fate that had led him spend every last farthing on an army of investigators, none of whom had uncovered anything of value.

But her bitterness also stemmed from the fact that he had kept something so significant from her for so long. She could understand why he hadn't revealed that her mother had not really died of a fever when she had been a girl of six. But she was one-and-twenty—old enough to have been told the truth.

And mixed up with her sorrow and anger was a sad sort of confusion that was difficult to put into words. They had always been so close, and her trust in her father had been absolute.

Now, she was left wondering if she had ever known him at all.

Ceci might not have had the words to describe this mess of feelings, which fluctuated by the minute. But she did have Beethoven. And no matter how tangled and confused her emotions might be, the 'Moonlight Sonata' managed to encompass them all.

As she sank into the music, everything else fell away. She forgot about her humiliation last night at the ball. She forgot about the fact that Madeline Sherborne had failed to appear for her pianoforte lesson today, and this meant Ceci was out another shilling, a shilling she needed badly as holes were starting to form in the soles of her dancing slippers.

She even forgot that Marcus Latimer was in the room.

When you were playing Beethoven, you were allowed to wear your heart on your sleeve, to be impassioned to the point of being overwrought. You were *supposed to*. Which was, of course, why young ladies were not permitted to play certain works of Beethoven.

But here she was, playing one of those forbidden pieces. And when it came to the pianoforte, Ceci did not play anything by half-measures.

After striking the mournful final chords, she let them linger in the air. Slowly she became aware of her surroundings.

The Astleys' rosewood pianoforte.

The orange and white music room.

The Duke of Trevissick, seated nearby.

She hesitated a beat before turning to the chaise, nervous of his response.

What she saw made her recoil.

Because Marcus Latimer, the man who never had a single hair out of place, whose posture was always as upright and starchy as his meticulously arranged cravats, lay sprawled against the blood-orange cushions of the chaise.

His right foot was on the floor, but his left boot dangled in the air. He had thrown an arm across his face, which made it difficult to gauge his reaction.

He groaned and rubbed his forehead. "Incandescent," he said, sitting up. He gave a single tug at his exquisitely tailored chocolate brown coat and it settled into place without a single wrinkle. Abruptly the ordinary man who had needed a moment of repose was gone, and the immaculate duke had returned.

His gaze snapped to hers. "Why have I never heard you play before?"

The question was sharp, as if it were somehow her fault. "I honestly do not know. You are a frequent guest at Lady Cheltenham's gatherings, and she always asks me to play."

Awareness flashed in his pale blue eyes. "Ah, but Mr. Nettlethorpe-Ogilvy is inevitably in attendance as well. I am therefore forced to flee the music room, lest I be subjected to the bassoon."

Ceci bit her lip. "Mr. Nettlethorpe-Ogilvy has improved significantly in the past year, and—"

"He is atrocious," he said with a note of finality. "That still does not explain why I have not heard you play anywhere else."

Ceci gave a humorless laugh. "I am not invited to play anywhere else. The last thing a hostess wants is for her own girls to suffer in comparison to the penniless daughter of a country vicar."

"Well, you should be forewarned that I intend to request you by name at every gathering going forward."

Ceci's cheeks warmed. "That would cause gossip."

He shrugged a negligent shoulder. "Who cares?"

She felt annoyance simmering up. Spoken like a man, a

rich and titled one, who had the liberty of not giving a fig about what people were saying behind his back. "As an unmarried woman, I have to care."

"Ah, but you won't be unmarried for long. Are you not all but betrothed to Archibald Nettlethorpe-Ogilvy?"

Now her cheeks were truly burning. "You have been misinformed," she said quickly. "Mr. Nettlethorpe-Ogilvy has not made me an offer of marriage."

The duke looked baldly skeptical. "But he is courting you."

"Yes, but that does not necessarily mean a proposal will follow."

"Of course it does. I know Nettlethorpe-Ogilvy. He wouldn't have asked to court you unless he was gravely serious about marrying you."

Gravely serious. Not exactly the romantic sentiment to set a girl's heart aflutter. "I would never assume—"

"Do you mean to accept him?"

She sputtered in protest. "I do not even know how to answer that, considering he has made me no proposal."

"When he asks you—"

"Who even knows if he means to?"

He rolled his eyes. "Fine. *If* he were to ask you, what would you say?"

She swallowed. This was one of several questions that kept her awake at night, tossing and turning in her bed. Given the chance, would she marry a very good man, but one she knew with a growing certainty that she would never grow to love? Would she sacrifice the possibility of making a love match for the security she so desperately needed?

The silence stretched on as she weighed her words. Finally, she said, "I daresay that only a great fool would turn down so fine a man as Archibald Nettlethorpe-Ogilvy."

Look for *The Duke's Dark Secret* in 2023!

ACKNOWLEDGMENTS AND HISTORICAL NOTE

If you look at instances of use in Google Books, the word "perfectionism" came into widespread use in the 1830s and "perfectionist" in the 1840s. So, if you ever decide to write a book about a perfectionist character, be smarter than me and don't set it in 1803!

I hope you picked up that perfectionism is the condition Edward is struggling with, specifically, what we would call maladaptive perfectionism (or neurotic perfectionism) today. According to researchers, "both normal and neurotic perfectionists are high achievers striving for success and with a strong need for approval. However, while normal perfectionists tend to derive pleasure from the attempt to meet challenges and have flexible strategies for coping with adversities, neurotic perfectionists never feel good enough, even when they are successful and they subsequently experience high levels of fear of failure."[1] For people who have never experienced maladaptive perfectionism, it can be pretty difficult to wrap your head around. Many of us experience some degree of perfectionism, but this is the level of perfectionism where you qualify for the Olympic games, enter five events, win five gold medals, and are still convinced that you somehow failed.[2] For a true maladaptive perfectionist, it is all but impossible to enjoy your success, even when you are very, very successful, because your brain is so very good at finding flaws and convincing you that they are what matter.

This was a very personal book for me to write, because, like Edward, I was once a maladaptive perfectionist. I am so pleased to be able to use the past tense when I write that sentence. If you or someone you love is struggling with maladaptive perfectionism, there is help and effective therapy out there. I would like to thank Rebecca Newkirk, M.S.W., who specializes in helping people overcome their perfectionism, for allowing me to interview her as part of my research for writing this book. One technique recommended by many therapists is to find a trusted friend to whom you can show your real self, including the things about yourself that you hate. If a maladaptive perfectionist can bring themselves to be truly vulnerable and see that they are still loved, warts and all, this can make a tremendous difference.

This is exactly what happened for me, and I would therefore like to dedicate this book to Mike. I hope you know that you were my Elissa.

As I said, if you or someone you love is struggling with maladaptive perfectionism, there is hope out there, and resources are available. The Ask Me Anything Rebecca Newkirk did on Reddit is a great place to start. Rebecca recommends the books *Healing the Shame that Binds You* by John Bradshaw and *Daring Greatly* by Brene Brown, and there are a ton of resources online. Don't beat yourself up. It's ok to reach out and ask for help. It can get better. I am living proof of that.

❧

Whereas Edward and Elissa are classicists and can translate readily from Latin and Greek, I am not! I would therefore be remiss if I did not give credit to the actual translators of the works quoted throughout the book:

- Chapter 4: Quote from *The Life and Death of Alexander the Great, King of Macedon* by Quintus Curtius Rufus, translated by Robert Codrington (1673)
- Chapter 4: Quote from *The Odyssey* by Homer, translated by Samuel Butler (1900)
- Chapter 5: Catullus 5, translated by F.W. Cornish (1912)
- Chapter 12: *Metamorphoses* by Apuleius, translated by Charles Stuttaford (1903)
- Chapter 20: *The Direct Approach is Best* by Addaeus, translated by Dr. Stephen Bertman (2005), quoted with permission from Cognella Academic Publishing
- Chapter 26: *The Art of Love* by Ovid, translated by J.H. Mozley (1929)
- Chapter 28: Sappho 31, translated by John Addington Symonds (1883)
- Chapter 29: *Plutarch's Lives*, from the translation called Dryden's, as revised by A.H. Clough (1859)

I would like to confess to taking a few historical liberties:

- Alas, *Prometheus Bound* remains lost to history! We do know that it existed, and the general outline of its plot, because it is mentioned in surviving texts. But an extant copy is yet to be discovered. I haven't given up hope. New scrolls emerge from the sands of Egypt from time to time, and new technology is enabling scientists to uncover hidden works on palimpsests that were erased and written over again and again. And if they can ever figure out how to unroll the treasure-trove of 1,800 scrolls from the library at Herculaneum, blackened by ash but still potentially legible, who knows what lost masterpieces we might recover!

- The dance at Bourton-on-the-Water takes place at the New Inn, which still exists and is known today as the Old New Inn. Visitors will surely note that it is not of sufficient size to accommodate the number of couples I described at the dance. I hope you will excuse this artistic license, as I wished to torture Elissa to the maximum extent possible.

- King George III and Queen Charlotte really did visit Cheltenham to take the waters in 1788. They did not, of course, stay with the Astleys, but borrowed Fauconberg Hall from its owner, the Earl of Fauconberg. This was a small country house not nearly sufficient to accommodate the royal entourage, and Fanny Burney wrote in her diary about how cramped the conditions were. I therefore felt confident that, had such a grand house as Harrington Hall existed in the vicinity, the king and queen would surely have opted to stay there. During his visit, the king did indeed dress very plainly, as he enjoyed taking long rides regardless of the weather. On one occasion, he is said to have spent a quarter of an hour chatting with a farmer driving a herd of sheep. The farmer had no idea to whom he was speaking, and asked if King George had encountered… himself. The farmer noted, "our neighbor says he's a good sort of man, but dresses very plain." "Aye," His Majesty was said to have replied, "as plain as you see me now."[3] This anecdote was the inspiration behind a six-year-old Izzie having told the King that she found his waistcoat ugly, and him taking it in good grace. I also found this tale charmingly reminiscent of the incident in which an American tourist in Balmoral asked Queen Elizabeth if she had ever met the Queen, to which Her Majesty deadpanned, "Well I haven't, but Dick [gesturing to her bodyguard] here meets her regularly."[4]

- I implied that Edward was surprised to be named Senior Wrangler and found out he had won at the Senate House ceremony in which students received their degrees. In fact, the Tripos exam took place in January and the results were posted just a few days after it concluded. So Edward, and everyone else at Cambridge, would have known for months that he had won Senior Wrangler. I decided to imply that it came as a surprise for maximum impact, and because the Senior Wrangler arguing that he really isn't any good at mathematics is *peak* maladaptive perfectionist.

- A British reader alerted me to the fact that the name "Broadwater Bottom" does not sound particularly British! You can imagine my surprise, as I actually found it in an old book, *A History of the County of Gloucester: Volume 6*[5], in a list of notable places around Bourton-on-the-Water. There is little mention of Broadwater Bottom today, although it does still appear on the Ordnance Survey Map. I loved the name so much I even put it in the title, figuring I was safe using an actual historical place name. Alas, sometimes actual places and things don't sound quite right for the time or place—just ask Skyscraper, the horse that won the Derby in 1789, almost a century before the first skyscraper was built.

I would like to thank my wonderful editors Megan Records and Justine Covington, my generous and very helpful beta readers Amy and Linda, and my brilliant cover designer Bailey McGinn. Thanks again to Rebecca Newkirk, M.S.W., for allowing me to interview her regarding maladaptive perfectionism. Many thanks to Professor Stephen Bertman, Alexa Lucido and everyone at Cognella Academic Publishing for granting me permission to use a quote from Professor Bertman's excellent book *Erotic Love Poems of Greece and Rome* (which I recommend highly!). Thanks as always to the University of Texas Library, which is pretty much the only thing standing between me and bankruptcy via research books.

Last but certainly not least, I would like to thank my family: my amazing husband, my son, my parents, and my sister, as well as my many wonderful writing friends, who have made this journey better in every possible way.

NOTES

ACKNOWLEDGMENTS AND HISTORICAL NOTE

1. Parvin Kiamanesh, Gudrun Dieserud, Kari Dyregrov, and Hanne Haavind, "Maladaptive Perfectionism: Understanding the Psychological Vulnerability to Suicide in Terms of Developmental History." *Omega* 2015 Vol. 71 (2) p. 126-145.
2. *Swimmer Caeleb Dressel says his mental health suffered after Tokyo Olympics: 'I felt so lost'* by Tom Schad, USA Today, 27 April 2022
3. *Cheltenham: A Biography* by Simona Pakenham
4. https://www.yahoo.com/entertainment/american-tourists-once-met-queen-091500187.html
5. Available online at https://british-history.ac.uk/vch/glos/vol6/pp33-49#anchorn2

ABOUT THE AUTHOR

After reading Black Beauty for the 1,497th time, Courtney McCaskill was inspired to write her own stories. Reviews of her early work were mixed, with her fourth grade teacher, Ms. Compton, saying, "Please stop writing all of your assignments from the point of view of a horse."

Today, Courtney lives in Austin, Texas with the hero of her own story, who holds the distinction of being the world's most sarcastic pediatrician. She is reliably informed by her seven-year-old son that she gives THE BEST hugs, "because you're so squishy, Mommy." When she's not busy almost burning her house down while attempting to make a traditional Christmas pudding, she enjoys playing the piano, learning everything there is to know about Kodiak bears, and of course, curling up with a great book. Visit her online at https://courtneymccaskill.com/.

www.ingramcontent.com/pod-product-compliance
Lightning Source LLC
Chambersburg PA
CBHW020356110726
47899CB00006B/1741